FRIENDS
OF A L

W9-AHX-408

j
Davis, Lavinia R. 1909-1961.
Janey's fortune

Janey's Fortune

books by Lavinia R. Davis

JANEY'S FORTUNE

by

Lavinia R. Davis

DOUBLEDAY & COMPANY, INC.
GARDEN CITY, NEW YORK

JACKET DESIGNED BY ALBERT ORBAAN

COPYRIGHT © 1957 BY LAVINIA R. DAVIS
LIBRARY OF CONGRESS CATALOG CARD NUMBER 57–7280
ALL RIGHTS RESERVED
PRINTED IN THE UNITED STATES OF AMERICA
FIRST EDITION

Janey's Fortune

CO. SCHOOLS
C'749263

CHAPTER ONE

At the end of June western Connecticut wilted under a record-breaking heat wave. At Bayport on the
Sound there was a slight salt breeze, but five miles inland at
Warwick where the Baits and McGovern family lived the heavy,
humid air was suffocatingly still. At three o'clock Jane McGovern
left the kitchen, where she had been waiting for the telephone to
ring, and went out on the porch. "Hi, Janey. I brought out a piece
of watermelon specially for you." Linda Baits, Janey's eight-year-
old half sister, nodded at the plate beside her. "It's super the way
you cool off while you swallow it."

"But you don't stay cool." Peter Baits, who was Linda's twin,
tried fanning himself with a piece of rind. "Janey, d'you suppose
it's as hot as this in New Mexico?"

"Maybe, but the air's so much drier you wouldn't feel it the
same way," Janey said. "At least that's what Gramps McGovern
used to tell me."

"Too bad he never took you out there before he got dead." Pete
reached absent-mindedly for the piece of watermelon Linda had

7

saved for Janey. "But 'course he didn't know he was just going to drop d——"

"Pete! You shush!" Linda shook her head so that her short pigtails flew. "You know we both promised Mum when Hank telephoned last week that we wouldn't upset Janey and now you've gone and done it. *And* taken her watermelon. You're awful."

Peter looked stricken. "I didn't mean to," he mumbled. "Honest, Janey."

"It's O.K., Pete," she said, and picked a watermelon pit from his moist, pink cheek. "You haven't upset me a bit." She didn't add that when Mum had broken the news of Gramps's sudden death in New Mexico a week ago she hadn't felt nearly as distressed as Mum apparently believed her to be. "Now if you'd get me another slice of watermelon out of the icebox I'd love it."

Both children raced toward the kitchen, and Janey moved aimlessly toward the wide veranda railing. She looked out over the familiar overgrown flower garden and the line of tall elms that separated their roomy Victorian house from the road, not consciously focusing on anything.

When Janey's father had been killed in combat in World War II, Gramps McGovern had moved to New York to be near his daughter-in-law and two small grandchildren who were his only living relations. Gramps had been very proud of Hank, Janey's blond and capable older brother, but he had made no bones over the fact that Janey, who had inherited the McGovern coloring and temperament, was his favorite. On his visits to Warwick he had taken her part in family scraps, given her riding lessons which her mother could not afford, and done everything in his power to encourage and indulge her.

Janey couldn't remember her father, but Gramps had been the special companion of her early childhood. Everything he did and said had seemed perfect and magically arranged for her benefit. Even when he was telling stories about his youth in New Mexico she felt included. Gramps's wife, the unknown grandmother after whom Janey had been named, was invariably the heroine of his sagas, but somehow he managed to convey to the raptly listening

Janey beside him that she too was a part of everything she heard.

For years a recurring daydream in which Janey rode beside Gramps on a spirited horse across a wide golden mesa was one of the most important things in her life. She never knew how the rainbow fantasy had begun or what gave it such extraordinary vividness. Did it spring from one of Gramps's stories or his repeated promise to take Janey out West as soon as she was big enough to go and a "bonanza lode" had miraculously provided plenty of money?

Janey had stopped wondering or even caring long ago. Her intense hero worship of her grandfather had ended years ago, just before Gramps had left the East for good. He seldom wrote letters, and gradually the impact of his vital, ebullient personality had dwindled away. His sudden death last week had given his memory a meteorlike prominence to the household in Warwick, but Janey had not been deeply affected. Whenever his name had come up in the past few days she had only felt vaguely guilty, embarrassed, and more than ready to change the subject.

There's no point *pretending* to feel heartbroken, Jancy inwardly defended herself. After all I was only nine when Gramps left here, and everything he and his stories stood for belong to another world. She picked up her tennis racket and began a vigorous pantomime up and down the wide porch, unconsciously trying to shake off her thoughts by physical action. "Boy, you're peppy!" Pete looked at her admiringly as he came back to the porch. "I've been hot for so long I'm too sogged to move."

Janey smiled and took the piece of watermelon he had brought from the kitchen. "Sit here in the rocker," Linda patted the cumbersome old chair beside her. "Pete wanted to sit in it before but I said to save it for you."

"Thanks a million but you two take turns." Janey picked up a camp chair and moved it over to the kitchen door where she would be sure to hear the telephone. "I'll sit in this while you rock."

"Me first!" Pete said, but Linda moved faster and reached the rocker ahead of him. "That's no fair," he began, and an instant later changed his tack. "O.K. O.K. You can start," he said. "As long as Janey's here to be the timekeeper."

"It's five minutes past and you can switch at ten past," Janey said, and settled down to wait for Larry Saunders to telephone.

Janey pictured Larry in her mind and smiled to herself. He wasn't good-looking, but everything about him from his English clothes to his comments on people and places struck her as exceptionally sophisticated and attractive. He was several years older than most of her friends in Warwick and much more experienced and worldly wise. After meeting him the things Janey had been excited about during the winter and early spring no longer mattered to her. Even the parties and events connected with her own recent graduation from the Warwick High School, now that she looked at them from Larry's point of view, seemed small-town and provincial.

Larry's made me feel differently about everything and everybody, Janey decided. Even people I've just seen. No wonder I can't go into a decline over Gramps when I haven't laid eyes on him for ages.

"Mum said it was a blessing Hank was in New Mexico when your grandpa died," Pete said suddenly. "And I guess it was kind of lucky Gramps was there on a visit himself. Wouldn't it be awful hard to move a dead person from Oklahoma to that place outside of Albuquerque where he was bur——"

"Pete Baits, stop it." Linda started to fly at her twin, remembered the rocker just in time, and scowled at him furiously as she pushed herself back into place. The minute she was settled she turned her back on him and smiled over at Janey. "Do they have watermelons in England?" she asked in her best imitation of a grown-up-lady-at-a-party voice. "And when do you suppose Daddy'll know for sure whether he's going to be able to take us over there this summer or not?"

"I don't know about watermelons," Janey said, and struggled not to laugh. "But I'm sure we'll hear about whether we're going or not very soon."

"I'd like to go today!" Linda said. "Right away quick and get icy cool up in a plane."

Janey didn't answer. In May when her stepfather, whom she called Uncle John, had brought home the news that his firm was sending him abroad at midsummer and that if it was financially possible he hoped to take Mum, the twins, and Janey herself along she had been thrilled. But that was before Larry Saunders had come into the community and had dated her after their first meeting. It was also long before he had asked her to play with him in the Fourth of July tennis tournament. Since then her whole life had revolved on a Larry and Bayport Beach Club axis instead of around her family and friends at the Warwick High School. I don't even want to go to England, Janey thought. Not while Larry's here——

At that moment the telephone rang and she jumped to her feet.

"Mum'll answer it," Pete said. "And listen, Janey, it must be my turn for the rocker. It is, isn't it?"

Jane nodded while an unspoken fountain of superstitious hope bubbled up inside her. The telephone's for me. And it'll be Larry *if* I answer it first!

As Pete started for the rocker he dropped his plate and sent his last bit of melon flying. "Phewey!" He squatted down to retrieve what was left and unintentionally blocked Janey's path to the door.

Jane pushed wildly. "Pete. Let me out. Please! I've got to answer——" She heard another ring, footsteps, and Mum's voice answering the telephone. "Oh hello, John darling. No, of course I'm not too busy."

Janey dropped into the nearest rocker, panting with frustration. It's Pete's fault! Mother's! she told herself. If I'd gotten there first it would have been Larry for me and not Uncle John for Mum. Larry promised he'd telephone. He promised he'd arrange a practice match for the tournament. He's probably been trying to reach me all afternoon and something's gone wrong. He knows the family are stuffy about my using the car.

Mrs. Baits finished her telephone conversation and came out

onto the porch. "Was that about the trip?" Both twins jumped up to meet her.

"It was Daddy and the trip's all set." Linda's voice was shrill with excitement. "It is, isn't it?"

"You're partly right." Mrs. Baits smiled at Linda, but as she turned to Janey her dark, gentle eyes were worried. "But as a matter of fact this telephone call had more to do with Janey than——"

"Larry called up!" Janey interrupted. "He called up when I was out and you forgot to tell me until just now?"

Mrs. Baits looked confused. "Larry? Oh, you mean the boy who is working for the Gregorys? Yes, I think Linda spoke to him, but that hasn't anything to do with what——"

"Linda!" Janey turned on her half sister. "When did he call? Why didn't you tell me?"

Linda fidgeted. "You didn't ask me. And I wrote it all down. Wrote not printed. It's on the telephone pad on Mummy's desk."

Janey dashed into the living room. "Mr. Wentie called about the horse show." Linda's large letters nearly filled the page. "Larry S. called. Can't come for you today but will meet you at club at four o'clock."

Janey tore off the message and went back to the veranda. "Mum! Larry wants me to go to the club now. This afternoon. I'm sure he has a practice match for the tournament all fixed up. I've just got to go!"

"A matter of life and death?" Mrs. Baits smiled good-naturedly. "More important even than summer plans? Well, as a matter of fact it will work out very well. John's coming home early but he has a ride from the station so you can take the car over to the club and drop the twins at the Community Beach. And when you come back all five of us can have a real council of war before supper."

"And you'll tell us all about going abroad?" Linda asked as Janey hurried indoors to change her clothes. "Every single thing?"

"We'll tell you everything we know ourselves," Mrs. Baits promised. "But now if you're going swimming help me clean up these pits and get ready. Hurry, darlings."

In record time Janey and Linda were in the front seat of the family car with Pete, bathing suits, and Janey's racket in back. "Have you your glasses?" Mum called out as Janey turned on the engine.

Janey hastily grabbed in her pocket and put on her glasses. She was nearsighted, but ever since she had dented the fender when she was driving without her glasses Mum and Uncle John acted as though she were practically blind. "All set!" she called back, and they drove off toward the shore.

"Did Larry say anything about a practice match?" Janey asked Linda as they drove along. "When you took down the message?"

"He didn't say anything about tennis at all," Linda said. "But Mr. Wentie talked a lot about the horse show. He doesn't see how you can ride Sensation in the Fourth of July horse show unless you school her every day. I didn't tell him you were playing in the tournament instead."

"Good. I'll phone him tonight," Janey said. "I suppose I should have done it sooner." Old Auguste Wentie ran a riding stable near Warwick. Long after anyone had paid him for giving Janey lessons he had let her ride as often as she liked. In return she had exercised his horses when no one else wanted to ride and had occasionally exhibited for him in ladies' jumping classes in nearby horse shows. This year he was expecting her to ride a high-strung little mare called Sensation in the Fourth of July show. She had completely forgotten to tell him about the tournament.

"I think you're dopey not to ride in the show," Linda said, and Pete piped up, "Especially to play tennis with that guy Larry. Hank says he's a regular two-button pantywaist. He says most tutors are sissies."

"That's bunk!" Janey said. "Just because Hank's a great big ox who likes summer jobs out-of-doors doesn't mean that everybody else has to do the same thing."

A moment later they drove into the Bayport Club and the twins tore off to the public beach next door. Janey picked up her belongings, pocketed her glasses, and slid out of the car. As she faced the club property she noticed the trim, well-kept-up appearance of the grounds and buildings. Compared to the littered, over-populated beach next door it looked incredibly neat and cool and restful.

Janey smiled to herself as she moved forward. Her family had never been able to afford belonging to the club, and it was only because Larry Saunders had interceded with Mr. Gregory, the president, that she had been given a junior summer membership for a nominal price. I owe Larry a lot, she thought, and hurried toward the tennis courts so as not to keep him waiting.

There were only middle-aged couples playing, and Janey ran on toward the low, rambling clubhouse. The wonderful thing about Larry was that he never seemed to feel she was indebted to him. Whenever he talked about the Princeton house parties and the New York dances he was going to take her to next winter he acted as though he were the lucky one. He's giving me a whole new world, Janey thought, and her happy heart kept time to her flying feet. A beautiful, exciting, glamorous world!

The long porch which ran the length of the building was deserted except for half a dozen people of Janey's own age near the steps at the far end. The boys and girls by the steps were all part of the Bayport summer colony and were staying with their families for a few weeks after prep school and college. Janey knew that her year-round life of Warwick and the Warwick High School was as remote to most of them as China. Before the coming of Larry Saunders they had always made her feel shy, but now she was too thrilled and happy to be self-conscious. "Have any of you seen Larry Saunders?" she called out. "He wanted me to meet him at four. I guess it's to practice for the tournament."

"Here's your hat, where's your hurry?" Tubby Marr offered her the cover of his tennis racket with mock solemnity. "It's too hot to play. Only mad dogs and old fogies play in the Bayport sun."

Janey turned, trying to focus on the beach which was some distance to her left. "He's probably still down there with the Gregory kids," she said. "I'd better be moving."

"As a matter of fact he is on the beach, but I don't think he's worrying about a practice match." Maisie Taylor's charm bracelets tinkled as she turned to look at Janey. "He's with the most attractive girl I've seen in years. A niece of Mrs. Gregory's with the cutest New Orleans accent. It'll send you, Tubby. Absolutely send you."

"Who is she?" "When did she come?" "We could use new talent around here." The crowd which had barely opened to an awareness of Janey's presence recircled on itself, but Janey was unconscious of being excluded.

She hurried off and as she passed the bulletin board at the end of the clubhouse she smiled to herself. She didn't stop to look at it now but she knew that there—written down for all the world to see—was her name, coupled with Larry Saunders, on the list for the doubles tournament. He asked me the second time we met! Janey hugged herself as she hurried on. He'd known Maisie and most of the others in New York for ages but he asked me!

When Janey reached the beach she saw that the Gregory children were in the water and that Larry and a blond girl in a white bathing suit were sitting under a striped umbrella at the far end. Janey slipped on her glasses and, as Larry waved and hurried toward her, pulled them off again.

"Scots wae hae, Jeanie McG," he called out, and Janey beamed at hearing the nickname no one else used. The McGoverns had come from Ireland and Mum's family background was Dutch and English, but Janey loved Larry's name which always made her feel like the proud descendant of a noble Highland clan.

"I was afraid you didn't get my message," Larry said as he came up to her. "But I had to stay down here with the kids. Mrs. Gregory is afraid I'm neglecting her precious darlings."

Janey laughed. "Oh, I got the message. Eventually! And then I drove the twins over. They're swimming next door."

"I hope you'll understand about not playing tennis," Larry began, and Janey put in eagerly:

"Oh, it's much too hot! 'Only mad dogs and old fogies play in the Bayport sun.'"

"How right!" Larry looked relieved. "And now I want you to

meet Cynthia Ravenal. She came up to the Gregorys' expecting to cool off, and lands in this heat."

Cynthia looked cool, calm, and collected as she acknowledged the introductions. "You all don't know what heat is," she drawled. "In N'Orleans it was singeing."

" 'The female of the species is stronger than the male,' " Larry said, and looked at Janey as though he were trying to signal a secret message. "That's why Cynthia's ready to play in the tennis tournament and old man Wentie wants Janey to ride his wildest horse in the horse show. I took the little Gregs over to Wentie's this morning, and while they were plodding around the ring the old boy kept me out in the broiling sun giving me a fight talk about Jeanie McG's horsemanship. What a build-up!"

"Oh, that's silly," Janey said. "Ages ago when Gramps McGovern, my father's father, came East he took me over for riding lessons, and he and Mr. Wentie got terribly palsy-walsy."

"Don't I know it!" Larry said. "Mr. Wentie gave me a blow-by-blow account. He told me about your grandfather being a major in the Texas border campaign, and a gold miner, and I don't know what all. He said the old gentleman could ride a horse like a master, whether he was drunk or sober. I gather he was quite a character."

"Oh, he was a character all right," Janey said. "Born on the wild frontier like Davy Crockett and never got over it."

"I dote on my grandfather." Cynthia rubbed herself languidly with sun oil that was scented with apple blossoms. "I love staying with him and Grandmama in Washington."

"I guess I told you that Mrs. Gregory's father, Cynthia's grandfather, is United States Senator from Louisiana," Larry said. Janey nodded and sprang up suddenly, so uneasy she couldn't sit still.

Cynthia's grandfather could be the President himself and Janey would not have cared. It was the sudden, unescapable recollection of the last time she had seen Gramps which upset her. In the days since his death she had successfully fought off the memory, but now it was as vivid as the beach scene before her.

It had all begun with a grownups' argument during Gramps's final visit. Janey had been sent out to play under the apple trees. A little later when Hank, who was twelve then, came to find her she knew he had been crying. "It's Gramps," he blurted out. "He drinks too much and gambles and borrows money from Uncle John. He's a disgrace to the family and it's half killing Mum."

At first Janey had been angry and incredulous but finally Hank had convinced her and from then on her feeling toward Gramps had begun to change. By the end of the week when Uncle John had taken her along to see Gramps off on the train she was embarrassed and resentful in his company. When they reached the railroad station Janey had hidden in a telephone booth until the train pulled out. She had never said good-by to Gramps at all for fear the other people on the platform would guess the noisy, red-faced old man was her grandfather.

I didn't mean to be disloyal. I was just—just confused. Now, so many years later, Janey tried to justify herself. It was no use and she turned back toward the clubhouse. "I'm going to put on my bathing suit," she said out loud. "I'm parboiled."

"I'll walk over with you." Larry reached out to carry her racket. Cynthia Ravenal propped herself up on one elbow. "Don't be gone too long, Larry. I think the children should come out of the water soon. They look chilly."

"Oh, Marty and Sue could swim all day without catching cold," Larry called back. The minute they were out of Cynthia's hearing his voice changed and he took Janey's arm. "You were great," he said. "Quick as a wink at catching on about the tennis tournament. But when Wentie told me he wanted you to ride in the Fourth of July horse show I knew that was the solution."

Janey stood stock-still, staring at him. "I don't understand what you're talking about," she began, but the next instant she did and her heart turned leaden. Larry was playing in the tournament with Cynthia. It was as simple as that.

"Well, you were immense!" Larry's shrewd, rather sharp features relaxed with relief. "But I suppose Wentie was right and you'd really planned to ride his horse and forgotten it. And of course working for the Gregs and all I haven't any choice but to squire their niece around."

For a second Janey was completely tongue-tied, and then pride shot through her like a galvanizing spark. "My plans haven't anything to do with Mr. Wentie, but at that it all works out perfectly," she said quickly. "I don't think I told you, but my stepfather's firm is sending him to England on some very important work and he's insisted on taking all of us with him. I'm practically positive we'll be leaving here before the tournament anyway."

"You said you might be going abroad later on." Larry sounded surprised. "I didn't know it was all set and definite."

"Oh, I didn't know either until a little while ago." Janey struggled to make her voice as offhand and airy as possible. "But Uncle John telephoned today from New York and he's coming home early to talk over all the details. What luck that Cynthia came up here in time for the tournament. Otherwise I'd have felt terribly about letting you down at the last minute."

"That's very sweet of you," Larry said, and handed back Janey's tennis racket. "And if I don't see you again I hope you have an absolutely wizard time."

"Oh, it oughtn't to be too bad." Janey improvised a bored yawn. "Uncle John's English clients have quite interesting connections, so at least it won't be the usual touristy sort of trip."

"It sounds first-rate." Larry looked back toward the beach as he spoke. "And now, Janey, I'll have to say good-by. It's time I went back to my bear taming."

"Yes, of course. Good-by, Larry." Janey managed a beaming smile which faded the instant Larry moved off, and she started on alone up the steps toward the clubhouse. At the top step she turned to look down the beach and a sudden gust of wind blew her curly, red-brown hair over her face. She pushed her hair back in place and groped for her glasses, but long before she found them she saw Larry hurry straight back to Cynthia without going near the Gregory children.

He's fallen for her all right, Janey realized. But he can't have settled everything about the tournament before he told me about it. Maybe he was—well—exaggerating—the way I did just now about the trip or else I simply misunderstood him.

She hurried around the end of the clubhouse to the bulletin board. MIXED DOUBLES FOR MEMBERS AND GUESTS. JULY 4. Janey's eyes plummeted to the spot where Larry had written in her name and his own. Lawrence Saunders, Jr. Larry's name was still there and underneath it, printed in his own hand, was "Miss Cynthia Louise Ravenal." Janey put on her glasses and looked closer. The neat letters stood out boldly, and underneath them was a faintly rubbed place where the name of Jane C. McGovern had been erased.

CHAPTER TWO

For a long-drawn-out minute Janey stared at the bulletin board. The printed letters blurred but their meaning stayed painfully clear. Larry had not only fallen for Cynthia Ravenal but he had publicly turned down and crossed off Jane McGovern. The names on the board were both symbolic and final. As far as Larry was concerned Janey was out, not only for the tournament, but for all their vague and entrancing dates in the future.

At the far end of the porch one of the summer crowd laughed. The sound startled Janey like a slap on the face. She wheeled and saw that everyone's back was turned toward her and realized that at least no one had caught her staring at the list. But they know all about it! she thought. They've all had a chance to see the bulletin board, and Maisie probably guessed that I didn't have a hope with Larry the minute she saw Cynthia Ravenal. That's what she was hinting at when I asked where Larry was a little while ago.

Janey took another quick look back at the group by the steps to make sure they had not noticed her and then tiptoed silently around the end of the clubhouse. Once she was out of sight she began to run toward the Community Beach. I've got to get away from here, she thought, and wondered desperately how she could ever lure the twins out of the water after such a short swim. If I see Larry or Cynthia or any of Maisie's crowd right now I'll die.

She rounded the strip of hedge that separated the two beaches and to her surprise and relief saw that the twins were all dressed and running toward her across the sand.

"Goodie! You're ready!" Linda called out. "Pete and I want to get home early to hear about the trip."

"Tonight's the night!" Pete threw his wet trunks into the back of the car and jumped into the front seat. "I bet Dad'll tell us all about riding in double-decker busses and seeing the horse guards. I can hardly wait!"

"Neither can I!" Janey was aware that the defensive bluff she had used with Larry was the only possible way she could save face with him and the rest of the Bayport crowd. "I'm not going to play in the tournament after all. I'd like to fly to England tomorrow."

"You and me both!" Pete grinned up at her affectionately. "Oh, Janey, please drive just as fast as you can."

Janey drove home without any trouble, parked the car in the old barn that served as garage and tool shop, and followed the twins into the living room where Mum and Uncle John Baits were sitting.

"Now tell us. When do we leave?" Linda threw herself into her father's arms while Pete went right on asking questions.

"Is it all set? When do we go? Have you brought home our tickets?"

"I've brought home four tourist-flight tickets." Uncle John extricated himself from Linda's bear hug and moved toward Janey. "But before I show them to you I want to explain to Janey why we can't take her——"

"But I have to go!" Janey interrupted. "I can't stay here. Not this summer!"

"Janey honey, listen," John Baits began, and Mrs. Baits tried to put her arm around Janey's shoulder but Janey jerked herself free and stood facing them with her back to the living-room wall.

"I have to go, I tell you. I've told people I was going away and I've simply got to do it. It's absolutely imperative. And you promised, Uncle John. You promised you were going to move heaven and earth to take all of us to England."

"I've done my very best, Janey," he said. "I've written to the people in England and I've argued with my partners here until I'm blue in the face. Except for resigning from the firm, which is out of the question, there isn't another thing I can possibly do or say. It's finally been arranged that your mother's fare will be paid for, and since the twins can go at half price and we'd have to pay someone to stay with them if they didn't go along, we're taking them, but I haven't been able to raise enough extra money to pay for you."

"Why can't you use the money I'll need to go to college this fall?" Janey demanded. "I don't give a hoot about going to a little jerkwater school like Westerley State anyway. I know I'll loathe it."

"But, Janey, you chose Westerley yourself because so many of your friends from high school are going there!" Mrs. Baits said. "I thought when we went to see it in May you were even more impressed by it than Uncle John and I were."

"That was before——" Janey stopped short of saying that her choice had been made before she had heard Larry Saunders' scathing remarks about small and inexpensive colleges like Westerley. "That was before I knew how much I want to go to England this summer." She ended up. "I simply have to go."

"It isn't possible to use your college money," Uncle John said. "That comes from an education insurance fund your father set up when you were a baby."

"Then borrow the money!" Janey stormed. "Or if you won't I will, if I have to work for the rest of my life to pay it back. But I simply can't stay here all alone."

"But, darling, nobody ever expected you to stay here alone!" Mrs. Baits sounded shocked. "Why, only last week Mrs. Taylor,

Maisie's mother, asked if you would spend the summer with them and help look out for the younger children. Maisie's going to summer school next week."

"Stay in Bayport?" Janey's voice grew shrill. "I'd rather die. Much rather."

"But you don't have to stay in Bayport or anywhere else in Connecticut. You can go out West, Janey. To a ranch in New Mexico, just the way you always wanted to go ever since you were a little bit of a girl."

"A ranch? Jeepers, Janey, I'd rather do that than go to England anyway," Pete put in. "Don't you want to go?"

Janey shrugged. "It doesn't make any sense. I bet that staying at a dude ranch would cost as much as going to England."

"The trip West is possible because Gramps McGovern has provided it," John Baits said. "He sent on money for your ticket and arranged for you to stay with a family by the name of Baker on their ranch outside of Albuquerque. Mrs. Baker is the widowed daughter of one of Gramps's old mining partners, and she sounds very anxious to have you visit them. Your mother heard from her this morning."

Janey hardly listened to his last two sentences. "Gramps!" she said, and dropped down in the nearest chair. "But—but it isn't possible! Gramps has been dead for over a week."

"Making these plans must have been the last thing he did before he died," Uncle John said quietly, and reached for the letters on the table beside his chair. "Hank found a letter to me and a money order in Gramps's hotel room the morning after his death. Hank forwarded Gramps's letter with one of his own and they arrived at my office this morning, along with Mrs. Baker's invitation. I found out that there is a seat available on a plane flying to Albuquerque on June 28 but I didn't want to make a definite reservation until we'd had a chance to discuss the whole thing. I think before you do anything else you ought to read these letters."

"Yes, do," Mrs. Baits urged. "And, Janey darling, Hank wrote to me, too, and said that Mrs. Baker's son runs some sort of horse business during the summer to pay for his college expenses, so it can't be a fancy dude sort of place at all but a real working ranch. Hank thought you'd love every minute of it, and I know you'd be such a help with the horses it would more than pay for your board and lodging. It's just meant for you, Janey!"

Janey glanced down at the letters on her lap without really seeing them. June 28. If she flew out West on that date at least she would be gone before the tennis tournament. But she'd only be going to a New Mexico ranch that didn't sound much more glamorous than Mr. Wentie's livery stable and she had told Larry she was going to England! "When was this plan to get rid of me cooked up?" she asked out loud. "And since when has the fact that Hank is three years older than I am meant he could arrange my summers for me?"

"Janey, please don't take it that way!" Mrs. Baits pleaded. "Can't you see that you are misinterpreting everything everyone has tried to do to give you a good time?" Janey saw that her mother was almost in tears, and for a moment a twinge of guilt mixed with all the other unpleasant emotions that seemed to be stifling her. She didn't say anything but looked back at the letters and began to read what Gramps had written to Uncle John.

Bullards Hotel
Albuquerque, N.M.

Dear Baits,

You may be surprised to hear from me out here, but my heart has kicked up lately so I came on while the going was still good to make some arrangements which I hope you will approve. I've been reliving the past lately and now I know how much I want to have Janey visit her father's native state before she's settled down for life and married to some Yankee. It isn't that the East and easterners aren't fine, but for the McGoverns New Mexico is home. I know I don't have to tell you that the hardest thing I ever had to do in my life was to leave here in 1920 after my wife died, but I didn't have any choice. Janey's father was only six at the time, and when my cousins in Oklahoma offered him a home and promised me a job there was nothing I could do but pull up stakes and move.

I thought then that as soon as Dick was old enough so that he didn't need a woman to look after him he and I would go back to New Mexico to live, but somehow or other we never made it. I've never been able to face going back alone before, but now that I've taken the plunge I'm glad I did, especially if it means that Janey can be out here. Of course Albuquerque has changed out of all recognition since my day, but the New Mexico countryside is as marvelous as ever and I want her to see it just as soon as possible.

I have just cashed my pension check and bought a money order payable to you to cover the expenses of Janey's trip out here. I have one or two promising irons on the fire and I hope before long I'll be able to pay back everything I owe you with interest. In the meantime the enclosed will cover Janey's first visit to New Mexico which, to me at least, still is the Land of Enchantment.

I've only been at this hotel for an hour and haven't had time to look up any old friends but I have made a few telephone calls and I'm satisfied Janey will be received with open arms. I know people will welcome her for old times' sake, but once they've seen her they'll love her for her own!

I look forward to seeing Hank when he goes through here on his way out to the Coast. If I possibly can I'll wait out here until Janey arrives. You can guess what seeing her again would mean to me. Meanwhile I don't want you to think I have forgotten everything you have done for me and mine. Please give Eula my dear love. She is the finest daughter-in-law any man ever had, and I am glad that after my boy's death she found another man who was worthy of her.

Yours sincerely,
C. J. McGovern

Janey put down the letter and picked up the next one, which was the invitation Mum had mentioned. It was written in an old-fashioned slanting hand on paper headed RANCHO DEL FUEGO and signed Ida Randolph Marston Baker. Janey glanced at it and turned to Hank's letter to Uncle John.

As you know I arrived here the morning after Gramps died in his sleep at the hotel where he had put up for the night. I don't think any of his old friends or their families had seen him, but he had telephoned to one or two and a very fair crowd turned out for his funeral.

Since Gramps's death none of the three original partners in La Placita Mining Company is left. Mr. James Marston, who was blinded in the fire that took place just before they closed down the mine, died three years ago. Mr. Hughes died long before that, but his grandson-in-law, Herbert Weaver, who is a lawyer and a successful writer on the side, has done everything to help me. It turned out that Herb had recently been in correspondence with Gramps, which was a lifesaver, as it meant he knew all about the will and that Gramps wanted to be buried at Fortune and so on. Herb handled all the funeral arrangements and the legal details here, and as he has connections in Oklahoma he's been able to take care of that end too.

From what Herb has told me I guess Gramps didn't own much except the clothes he stood up in and that the "irons" he thought were finally going to make his fortune were just false hopes like La Placita and all of his other ventures.

I've already written Mum that I really hope you will let Janey come out here. I met Mrs. Baker and her son Rob at Herb Weaver's office and liked them both. Mrs. Baker told me she had written to Mum inviting Janey to stay with them at their ranch, which is near a little town called Lope and about ten miles from Albuquerque. Mrs. B. certainly was enthusiastic about the whole thing and kept saying how wonderful it would be for her little daughter to have an older girl from New England spend the summer with them. I didn't meet the daughter but I think she's around ten or eleven. Rob is twenty-one and just graduated from college with a *magna cum laude*. Wow! He's very quiet and his mother is very chatty but they are both obviously intelligent and respectable and I'm sure they'll give Janey a good time.

As there isn't anything more I can do here I'm going on to the Coast tomorrow and will start work with the Granada Company on Monday. It was great of you to help me line up the job and I can't thank you enough.

Janey skipped over the end of Hank's letter and reread the one from Gramps. At the bottom of the last page she saw a P.T.O. she had overlooked before and found that on the back there was a postscript addressed to herself.

Janey darling,

Now that you are eighteen and through high school I suppose I don't have to tell that all the hopeful stories I used to tell you about reopening La Placita and hitting a bonanza were just fairy tales. I made sure it was worthless before I sealed it up in 1920 after the accident in which poor Jim Marston was blinded, and everything I told you was make-believe. However, the strange part of it all is that right now I'm certain that before I'm through with it La Placita won't owe me a thing.

If I can manage to stay here until you arrive we'll borrow some horses and ride over to Fortune through the section of country I used to tell you about so often when you were small. Believe me, everything I told you about the New Mexico scenery, the people here, and especially about my darling, the grandmother after whom you were named, were not exaggerated fairy tales but miserable understatements.

Your devoted Gramps,
C. J. McGovern

As Janey reread the postscript the words "La Placita won't owe me a thing" seemed to stand out in inch-high letters and her heart beat faster. That must mean that Gramps had learned the

27

mine was a bonanza after all! And he had died before he could reach it! It was even possible that Gramps had known the mine was valuable for some time and had put off reopening it because, as he had written Uncle John, he had not wanted to go back to New Mexico alone. Or perhaps he'd been too involved with some new venture in Oklahoma to do anything about La Placita until it was too late. Either answer would be just like him.

Janey took a deep breath, and an idea came to her that was so exciting that she felt dizzy. She, Jane Conant McGovern, was going to New Mexico and she was going to find out what was in the mine. Where Gramps had failed she would succeed and put an end to all the scrimping and saving and never having quite enough money. Perhaps a year from now the cost of a trip to Europe would seem like nothing! "Where is La Placita?" she asked, and her voice shook with excitement. "Is it anywhere near Lope?"

"I think so," her mother said. "But I'm not really sure. You know I've never been to New Mexico."

"Are you thinking of gold mining?" Uncle John teased, "or have you set your heart on diamonds?"

Janey only smiled evasively, but in that instant she made up her mind not to say a word to any of the family of the thought which had just come to her. She would simply accept the trip Gramps had arranged and make her plans about the mine after she reached New Mexico.

She went through all of the letters carefully and found that Hank had written, in the part she had skipped before, that La Placita and the cemetery where Gramps was buried were both at Fortune, which was about five miles from Lope. That's no distance at all, Janey thought, and for the first time it came to her that Gramps's arranging for her to stay so near to the old mine was a sign that fate, Kismet, or whatever you wanted to call it intended her to reopen it!

Janey folded the letters neatly and handed them back to Uncle John. "I'd like to go," she said. "Do you think we ought to telephone the airline to confirm the ticket for the twenty-eighth tonight?"

"I'll do that," Uncle John said, and Mum added, "Oh, Janey darling, I hope you'll have a wonderful summer. That's all that Gramps or any of us want."

At that moment the telephone rang and Janey hurried to answer it. Larry! The hope shot through her mind, but even before she heard Auguste Wentie's voice she knew she was being silly.

"Chane, I have all day been trying to reach you!" The old Austrian was excited and his accent was more marked than usual. "Little Linda gave you the message, no, about Sensation? It is so short a time until the horse show and every day you must school her."

"But I won't be able to ride her in the show, Mr. Wentie. I'm leaving for New Mexico on the twenty-eighth."

"But, Chaney, you must be fooling. Only this afternoon the young Saunders tells me that you will be glad to ride."

"Larry Saunders doesn't know anything about me or my plans," Janey said. "I'm sorry I didn't let you know sooner about Sensation, but I didn't know when I was leaving until just a few minutes ago."

"But, Chaney, only today, this morning that Larry he says you will ride and I hear that you and he are good friends, as you say now 'going steady'."

"Then you've heard wrong!" Janey burst out. "I am not going steady with Larry Saunders and I am definitely leaving for New Mexico in four days." A few moments later as she hung up she realized with a start that what she had said to Mr. Wentie must have told the family about what had happened between herself and Larry as clearly as though she had made a public broadcast. She turned around with her cheeks burning, but no one was even looking at her. Mum, Uncle John, and the twins were sitting on the sofa, poring over English travel folders. As Janey crossed the room she passed right in front of them on the way to the stairs. Not one of the four heads even turned in her direction.

They didn't notice because they don't care, Janey decided, and suddenly her spirits sank and she felt left out and deserted. The family haven't any more idea of how I really feel about things than Larry Saunders, she thought as she started upstairs. Mum means to be nice but she simply can't understand that I'm not Linda's age and that going to a poky little ranch isn't my idea of heaven. The only thing that would make this trip worth my while would be to have La Placita pay off with millions, and that's not likely to happen. All of Gramps's financial schemes were failures, and I was a fool to be so hopeful over this one just a few minutes ago. I'm still going to go ahead with finding whatever is in the mine but only because otherwise the whole summer sounds completely flat and pointless.

Janey walked slowly into her own bedroom, and the difference between her present mood and the happy, thrilled state in which she had left it to go to the club made her feel as though she had been away for a lifetime instead of only a few hours.

I must have aged years, she thought, and looked at herself in the mirror. Her reddish hair, gray eyes, snub nose, and broad mouth looked exactly the same as they had before. She grimaced and moved off to turn on a bath. Of course my face hasn't changed, she told herself. It's my heart and soul, the real me inside of my body, that has been hurt.

She undressed and began to sing "Loch Lomond" under her breath. The haunting old tune and the sorrowing words fitted her mood perfectly. It's exactly the way I feel, she thought as she stepped into the tub. Nobody in the world understands what's happened to me today, but I'll never really get over it. The scar will stay with me always.

Janey's bath was cool and refreshing, and since she had run the first tub there was plenty of water. She lay still until she was completely cooled off and then scrubbed herself and finished off with a cold spray. The bath was definitely refreshing, and by the time Janey was dressed again in cool, clean clothes she felt almost cheerful. As she began to brush her hair her mind turned back to her childhood daydream and for the first time in years she tried to remember every detail. The ride over the Golden Mesa must have been connected with something Gramps told me about the town of Fortune, she decided, and unconsciously her brush strokes grew more and more energetic. If I can only think back far enough I'm sure to remember something that will help me find whatever is left in the mine. Even if it isn't worth much it'll only be fair to Gramps if I get to the bottom of it. After all if he hadn't arranged for me to go to New Mexico I might have had to stay in Bayport, and that would have killed me.

CHAPTER THREE

Four days later at six o'clock in the afternoon Janey was aboard a plane which was nearing the Albuquerque airport. That morning when all the family had driven down to see her off she had actually felt glad that she was going out West by herself, with her secret mission at the mine to attend to, rather than going on a family trip to England. But her adventurous mood had gradually faded and now she was more conscious of being tired and cramped from sitting in one place for so long than of anything else. She tried to stretch and, leaning forward as far as her seat belt would let her, stared out of the window. She saw a tremendous and solitary countryside that turned burning red and purple in the sunset. There were no houses or roads in sight, and the few clumps of trees were miles apart. It looks dry and deserted and lonely, Janey thought, and shivered to herself. Not a sign of human beings anywhere.

A few moments later the plane flew over a huge U which had been cut into the side of a mountain. "The University of New Mexico boys cut that out of the rocks." The elderly woman in the next seat twinkled at Janey through shiny, square-cut glasses. "Such energy."

Janey nodded but she wasn't thinking of the U cut into the rocks but of the unknown Rob Baker who had graduated *cum laude* at twenty-one from the university the letter stood for. Rob's probably just a repulsive-looking egghead or else an earnest, unsophisticated country type Hank might like but who'd bore me stiff, she thought. Oh Larry, Larry, why did you have to fall for Cynthia Ravenal when we could have had such a marvelous time together?

A few minutes later the plane landed and Janey filed out with the other passengers. As they walked into the low-ceilinged airport building she saw a tall old man in a rancher's hat swoop down on the lady who had sat beside her in the plane. "Well, Hattie," he roared. "Welcome home. I thought that convention of yours would never be over. I'm mighty glad you're back."

In that instant Janey forgot all about Larry Saunders and the unknown Rob Baker and wished with all her heart that Mum or Uncle John or even Auguste Wentie or some other old friend of the family were meeting her. She fought down the sudden unexpected wave of homesickness and forced herself to concentrate on her immediate surroundings.

The main room of the airport was decorated in a style Janey had never seen before, with heavy exposed beams of some dark wood protruding from the light tan stucco of the walls. Small groups of passengers, friends, and airport hangers-on drifted across the tile floor, while over at one corner a small boy of about Pete's age looked wistfully at a display of Indian souvenirs. If only it were Pete! Janey thought, but she knew it was dangerous to let herself dwell on anything to do with home, and hurried after her seatmate toward the baggage window. She claimed the battered suitcase which had once belonged to Mum and then looked around uncertainly, wishing that Hank had been more specific about how the Bakers looked. "Is someone calling for you, dear?" The old lady looked anxiously from Janey to her husband, who was noisily reiterating how much he wanted to get his wife home. "Can we give you a lift or are you taking the coach?"

"Oh, I'm being called for, thank you." Janey managed to sound perfectly confident as she smiled back at the old lady. The couple went off arm in arm and Janey's smile faded. She went outside and watched them drive away and a few moments later saw the airport coach roll off with most of her fellow passengers aboard. Could the Bakers have meant me to take that? Janey wondered nervously. No, when she stopped to think of it she was certain that Mrs. Baker's letter had said specifically that she would be met at the airport by car. Perhaps I missed seeing them inside, Janey thought, and went back into the main room which seemed much larger and emptier than it had even a few minutes ago. There wasn't anybody in sight that could possibly be Mrs. Baker or her son. There was a small crowd of middle-aged men in levis and cowboy boots, a tired-looking priest in dusty black, a girl who couldn't be much older than Janey herself with a baby in her arms. Janey looked at the other side of the room, and in the shadows of an archway she saw a tall dark figure in a black cowboy hat. She slipped on her glasses, and a little flicker of amusement spread over her. The man in the shadows was an Indian all right. The high cheekbones, the swarthy skin, and the way his eyes darted owlishly from side to side without his moving his neck all reminded her of Gramps's stories. If only he was dressed up in feathers and war paint I'd really have something to write the twins about, she thought. Pete would probably rather see him than a dozen London bobbies.

She made herself wait for five minutes before she went to the ticket booth to ask if there were any other planes arriving from the East within the next few minutes. There was a plane due in from California at any moment, but there was nothing scheduled from the East until two in the morning. Janey sat down on her suitcase, determined not to let herself get panicky. Uncle John, in the careful, painstaking way she had sometimes found irritating, had worked out a wire to the Bakers so there couldn't possibly be any mistake over her flight number or the change in time. Probably Rob's the absent-minded-professor type and didn't leave home early enough, she decided. If he or Mrs. Baker doesn't turn up in a few minutes I'll telephone and see what's happened.

The California plane landed, and once more a small tide of passengers flowed into the terminal and ebbed away again. This place would make a good setting for a ballet, Janey thought, with the passengers and those men in levis as the chorus and that old Indian suddenly coming to life as the central figure. She walked slowly toward him, pretending to read the advertisements on the wall behind him but actually hoping for a better look at the details of his clothes and appearance. When she was quite close she glanced up at him with elaborate casualness, and a pair of gleaming old eyes in a lined and motionless face stared back at her.

Janey hurried off, unpleasantly certain that the Indian had been watching her all along, and went straight to the telephone booth. Babbington, Bace, Bachelor, Baker—John, Baker—Joseph. She skimmed frantically through the B's until she remembered that the Bakers didn't live in Albuquerque and dialed the operator and asked for the number at the address in Lope. "It's Lope 638," the operator told her. "Will you speak to anyone who answers?"

"Yes please!" Janey felt she would be glad to talk to a village half-wit if only he could tell her the Bakers were on their way to the airport. The operator put in the call, and Janey heard the lonely, empty sound of the unanswered phone ringing at the other end. The booth grew suddenly darker, and Janey looked up and saw that the Indian was staring down at her through the glass window. At the same moment the operator came back on the line. "Lope 638 doesn't answer," she said. "Shall I call you back in twenty minutes?" C749263

"No. No thank you," Janey answered, and now her nervousness was growing into a cold, clammy fear. I'm being a fool and I've got to stop, she scolded herself, but she took as long as she could, picking up her dime and pulling back the door so that the Indian would be out of her way before she left the booth. She stopped to powder her nose and put on more lipstick and all the time she tried to convince herself that there was nothing to be upset about because the Bakers' number hadn't answered. It simply meant that the whole family, including the little girl

Hank hadn't seen, were on their way to meet her. Finally the tile floor ahead of her was clear and she left the booth, only to find that the Indian had simply moved to one side and was still watching her. She picked up her suitcase and headed for the taxi stand. The Indian was directly in her way, and as she hurried around him she sensed, without actually turning back to look, that the Indian was following close behind her.

She put down her heavy case and hurried on toward the taxi stand. It would probably cost a fortune to drive to Lope, and she had spent almost all of her birthday and Christmas money on the temporary membership in the Bayport Club. Still it couldn't hurt to ask. One of the men at the stand looked a little like Ted Giolito, who had been in Hank's class at high school and who worked for the taxi company at Warwick. At the moment when the Indian was so near her that she could hear his breathing the thought of talking to anyone even remotely like Ted Giolito was distinctly pleasant.

"How much would it cost to drive to Lope?" she asked. "To the home of Mrs. Ida Baker?"

"Is that the Baker over beyond the Sepique Arroyo where that young guy has the riding school?"

"Yes. It must be," Janey said, and saw that the Indian had moved up beside her and was listening to every word.

The taxi driver consulted a small black notebook. "I'm afraid it would cost you around ten dollars," he said pleasantly. "Sepique Arroyo's quite a poke from here. Right over on the other side of Albuquerque and you'd have to go through town."

"I think I'd better wait," Janey said, and turned back toward her suitcase. "I'm pretty certain I'm being called for but thank you anyway."

"Don't mention it," the driver said. "And there's a place through that arcade where you can sit down while you're waiting. It's dark and the seats are kinda hard, but it'd be a lot better than parkin' on your suitcase."

"Yes. I'm sure of it. Thanks again." As Janey straightened up with her suitcase in her hand she was unpleasantly aware that the Indian was right behind her again and that the sitting room beyond the arcade looked completely cut off from the rest of the terminal.

She hesitated and at that moment there was the sound of laughter, a man's deep voice, and quick, firm footsteps by the open front doors. She turned and saw a tall, broad-shouldered ensign in a summer uniform striding toward her with his hand outstretched.

"Are you Jane McGovern?" the ensign asked, and Janey nodded, feeling that Galahad mounted on white horse would be less welcome than the handsome young officer in front of her.

"Yes, I am," she said, wondering why Hank had not mentioned that Mrs. Baker's son was in the Navy. "And you must be Rob Baker."

"No indeed." The ensign laughed as he reached for Janey's suitcase. "I'm Alfred Hughes third, known as Buck, and very much at your service. My car's right outside." As Janey followed him toward the door she realized that the Indian had disappeared. "The Bakers wanted to meet you," Buck Hughes went on as he swung Janey's suitcase into a beautiful, new Thunderbird car. "But Twinks had an unexpected performance and the Lone Ranger's truck hasn't any lights so Mrs. Baker will pick you up at Sis's on her way home."

"Twinks? The Lone Ranger? Sis?" Janey said as Buck Hughes helped her into the front seat. "Who are they all? I'm lost!"

"Small wonder!" Buck Hughes said, and his cheerful, breezy voice was reassuring. "Twinks, short for Twinkle Toes, if you can believe it, is Mrs. Baker's daughter aged about eleven. She's a graceful little thing and tap dances a couple of times a week in one of our local bistros plenty much chaperoned by Momma, who plays her accompaniments and also gives piano lessons in the daytime. Mr. Baker, the father, died several years ago without leaving his family a nickel to live on, and Rob, whom I nicknamed the Lone Ranger, has taken after him in not making any sense about money. Sis is Mrs. Herbert Weaver, and my only sister. Her husband's a lawyer here in Albuquerque."

"Oh, I know about him!" Janey grasped delightedly at the first familiar name. "He was absolutely wonderful about helping my brother when Gramps died."

"Herb's a good egg, but anybody would have wanted to help out in a situation like that. Your brother Hank really had the book thrown at him."

"Well, I guess he survived," Janey said, and looked out to try and get her bearings. "But now tell me again where we are and where we're going."

"We're on the Union Drive and headed for the Weavers'. They live in my parents' old house right in town. It's on Griegos Avenue and that is the break of breaks for me, because it's on the way out to Sandia Base where I'm stationed and besides my girl, Tina Ramirez, lives practically next door."

"How, how super." Janey said what she felt was expected of her while her mind closed over the not too welcome fact that this big, beautiful, and wonderfully friendly man already had a girl. She longed to ask if they were actually engaged but decided against it and asked about Rob Baker instead. "I telephoned to Lope a little while ago and the line didn't answer," she said. "Do you suppose Rob is at his sister's performance too?"

"Not a chance. He was probably out tucking his horses into bed. He's so fussy about the way they're handled he's lost some good customers."

"What's his speciality?" Janey asked curiously. "Breeding race horses or polo ponies or what?"

"Nothing so big league!" Buck sounded amused. "It's just a small summer livery patronized mainly by old women and children because Rob won't offer moonlight rides or anything exciting that might possibly be risky for his nags. And the crazy part of it is he's always had to sell most of 'em off just before college opened when the market for saddle horses hits rock bottom."

"But what's he going to do this year?" Janey asked. "Hank wrote that he'd just graduated with a *magna cum* degree. Is he planning to branch out more with his horses?"

Buck shrugged and shot forward as the light changed. "I doubt it," he said. "He's going back to the U. for his Master's this fall, although his mother doesn't make any bones about telling people she'd rather he'd start in business. She talked Herb into wangling Rob a good job in my family's mining company and Rob wouldn't even go down for an interview. He's always been a law unto himself, which is why I call him the Long Ranger."

"I see," Janey said, and her preconceived picture of the Bakers grew gloomier than ever. Rob must be a selfish prig, and the tap dancing little sister sounded ghastly. Most depressing of all, it was now perfectly clear that they were all so hard up that they had to take in boarders. Gramps had undoubtedly paid for her visit ahead of time, and Mrs. Baker was merely saving face by not mentioning anything about money in her letter to Mum.

"It was hard luck Rob couldn't make R.O.T.C. at college," Buck went on. "But he hurt his foot a few years ago and they turned him down. He's O.K. now but I doubt if he'll ever be drafted except during a war. It's too bad because officers' training might have knocked some sense into him. He's a bright guy but pretty impractical."

A few minutes later Buck turned the car into a residential street and pulled up at the curb. "Here we are," he said, and took Janey's suitcase out of the back of the car. "And once again I'm terribly sorry you were kept waiting."

"Oh, I didn't mind," Janey said, and decided the drive with Buck Hughes more than made up for the uneasy minutes at the airport. "And thanks so much for calling for me."

"I enjoyed it!" Buck smiled as he opened the door of the Weavers' house. "I'm not wishing any of the Bakers more bad luck, but any time they have car trouble you let me know."

Janey walked in, and a tall, dark-eyed woman, who had Buck's features without any of his blond good looks, came forward to meet her. "I'm Sis Weaver and I'm perfectly delighted to see you," she said, and introduced her husband who had just followed her into the hall. "I think it's a shame you were kept waiting at the airport. Mrs. Baker checked that the plane was coming in on time before she called us. Buck, I told you that you ought to have left here earlier."

Buck, who had moved on into the living room, didn't answer, and Janey could hear him greeting someone she guessed was Tina Ramirez. Tina was dark and exotic-looking and dressed in a low-cut blouse and flowered skirt that made Janey conscious that her blue suit was wrinkled and messy-looking after her trip. Tina gave Janey a languid handshake and instantly turned to Buck and began questioning him about what he had done earlier in the week. His answers were pleasant but obviously evasive, and Janey decided they probably weren't engaged after all.

"You must be half dead." Sis Weaver smiled at Janey as she spoke. "Herb and I wanted you to spend the night here, but Mrs. Baker wouldn't hear of it. Oh, by the way, Buck, Mrs. Baker called up again while you were out and said Twinks is appearing in the second show, and I told her you'd drive Jane to Lope. Otherwise she'd have to sit up until heaven knows when."

"I'm not a bit tired," Janey began, but Buck had already turned with his arm through Tina's. "Good enough. Tina and I'll run Janey down whenever she likes, won't we, Tina?"

"Of course." Tina Ramirez' dark eyes looked up at him adoringly. "It would be fun."

"But Jane has to have something to eat first," Sis Weaver said, and motioned to Janey to sit down beside her on a low sofa covered with a striped Indian blanket. "Your brother always referred to you as Janey. Is that a family nickname or does everyone use it the way everyone I know calls me Sis?"

"No one's ever called me anything else," Janey said, and fought down the recollection of Larry's Jeanie McG. "Practically no one."

"I wish I had a name like that!" Sis Weaver said. "My mother was called Gwendolyn Alice and I was named after her so do you wonder I won't answer to anything but Sis?"

"I like Sis as a nickname," Janey said, and wished she could stay with this attractive, hospitable family all summer and never go near the Bakers. "It sounds so friendly."

Sis laughed. "Well, it isn't exactly forbidding," she said. "But

40

that's all I can say for it. Now do tell me about your trip out here. The last time Herb flew home after a business trip in Chicago it was terribly rough."

"Gruesome," Herb agreed. "I'd rather go by covered wagon."

For the next few minutes the conversation was general, until a pretty, Spanish-looking maid brought in a tray of refreshments. Herb pulled a low table in front of the sofa, which the maid loaded with fruit, honey, coffee, and some kind of square roll or pastry that was unlike anything Janey had ever seen before.

"Those are sopaipillas." Herb Weaver's smile was as friendly as his wife's as he intercepted Janey looking at the rolls. "I'm a transplanted Bostonian myself, and these were new to me when I first moved out here. You bite off one corner, pour in honey, and try to eat the whole thing without making a mess. They're strange but wonderful."

"So far everything out here strikes me as strange but wonderful," Janey said when she had finished her first sopaipilla. "These and the stucco, or is it adobe, airport and my first live Indian. If he'd been in war paint and feathers I'd have been scared silly."

Everybody laughed and Buck put another sopaipilla on Janey's plate and helped himself to a third. "These aren't half bad," he said. "Are there more outside?"

"Loads," Sis said. "Will you get them, Buck? I told Sarita she could go home. And bring back some more napkins. Herb's drowning in honey."

"I've never learned the New Mexican technique of eating sopaipillas," Herb said ruefully. "And Janey did it perfectly the first time. It must be heredity. Still I'm ready to try again."

"They're the best things I've ever tasted," Janey said as Buck went out for more. "But I simply can't understand why Gramps, that's my grandfather McGovern, never told me about sopaipillas ages ago when he used to stay with us in Connecticut. He told me enough wonderful things about New Mexico to fill a book, but he never mentioned these."

A sudden embarrassed silence followed Janey's remark. Sis Weaver started to speak, thought better of it, and ostentatiously studied her nail polish. Herb moved to the edge of his chair and rubbed at a honey stain. For an awkward moment no one spoke and then Tina turned to Janey. "I'm sure you will have sopaipillas at the Bakers'," she said, and it was clear from her voice that she was simply making conversation. "Mrs. Baker used to belong to my mother's bridge club and sometimes she brought sopaipillas to their bridge teas. Mother says Mrs. Baker has an absolute genius for pastry."

"Oh, she's a marvelous cook!" Sis gave Tina a quick, grateful look. Herb relaxed comfortably in his chair, and Janey said the first thing that popped into her head.

"Are the Bakers taking any other boarders this summer?" she asked. "Or will I be the only person outside the family at the ranch?"

"The Bakers don't take boarders," Herb said, and turned to Buck, who had just reappeared at the doorway, for confirmation. "And I don't believe they ever have, have they?"

"Good Lord, no," Buck said. "Janey, I hope you didn't get that idea from anything I told you on the drive down here?"

"N-no." Janey felt herself reddening. "I—I guess I just jumped to the conclusion from something my family told me about my grandfather's arranging the whole summer."

"Oh well, that's O.K. then." Buck beckoned to Tina as he spoke. "Tina, be an angel and give me a hand. This stove has me buffaloed."

Tina jumped up and followed Buck into the kitchen, leaving Janey alone with the Weavers. "Gramps did arrange for me to visit the Bakers, didn't he?" Janey turned directly to Herb Weaver, but he avoided looking at her. "I thought—from his letter and all—that he'd probably spoken to Mrs. Baker over the telephone the day before he died?"

Herb only shook his head and then Sis spoke. "Your grandfather tried to reach Mrs. Baker," she said gently. "He telephoned the ranch but she was out. He left his name with Twinks and said he'd call back the next day. When he didn't call, Mrs. Baker telephoned Herb's office to see if anyone there knew where he was staying and learned that Mr. McGovern had died during the night. A few days later she arranged to meet Hank in Herb's office so she and Rob could tell your brother how much they wanted you to visit them. I'm sure Mrs. Baker feels that your grandfather would have liked it, but she wants you herself, Janey. Isn't that right, Herb?"

"It certainly is!" Herb said, and he no longer seemed in the least self-conscious. "And, Janey, don't worry about anything Buck may have said. He thinks anyone who isn't driving a Thunderbird must be bankrupt. Mrs. Baker's a very good manager and doesn't do things she can't afford. She's looking forward to having you visit them more than I can tell you."

"That's terribly nice of her," Janey said, and decided it was only the mention of Gramps which had embarrassed the Weavers. "I hope it all works out well."

"It will!" Sis said, and she sounded convinced. "I thought it was a good idea from the very beginning, but now since we've met you I'm positive of it."

At that moment Buck and Tina reappeared with the second batch of sopaipillas. "These were so hot that if Tina hadn't helped take them out I'd have called up the fire company," Buck said. "I swear I think that all women are born with asbestos fingers."

Everybody laughed, and from then on the conversation was as easygoing and unrestrained as it had been when Janey had first arrived. The next hour flew by, and when Buck finally suggested that he drive Janey out to Lope she felt as though she had known him and the Weavers for years.

"We want to see you very soon again," Sis Weaver said as she and Herb walked out to see them off. "I never knew your grandmother McGovern, but my mother talked about her so much I feel as though we were some kind of cousins."

"I wish we were," Janey said as she got into the car. "And thanks again for a perfectly marvelous evening."

Buck drove off with Tina in the middle, and Janey sat on the outside, smiling to herself in the darkness. There'd been a queer minute when she had mentioned Gramps, but perhaps it was only because of his recent death. Or maybe it was Grandma they all loved, Janey thought, and for the first time in her life wondered what her grandmother, who had died in a flu epidemic nearly forty years ago, had been like. Gramps had been years younger than his two mining partners, so it wasn't surprising that Sis Weaver's mother had been a friend and contemporary of Janey's grandmother.

A few moments later Buck turned off the neon-lighted city street. As the car swept forward over an undulating country road Janey peered out of the window and forgot about ancient history.

Buck made a sharp turn, and this time there was a towering cliff on their left and a wide stretch of moonlit countryside on the right. "This is the Cordes Canyon Road," Buck said. "Lope's over there toward the mountains." As Janey looked north the moon came out, bleaching the plains and turning the shadows dramatically black.

"It's beautiful," she said. "And I do adore arriving anywhere at night. It means you wake up the next morning to a whole new world."

Buck laughed. "You'll wake up with the birds tomorrow," he said. "Robby Boy'll probably have you out grooming his horses before breakfast."

"Bucko, what time do you have to be back at the base?" Tina Ramirez spoke for the first time since they had left town. "Before midnight?"

"Doesn't matter," Buck said. "As long as I'm ready to hit the deck at six tomorrow."

"Poor Bucko, and you do so hate to get up early," Tina said, and Janey felt her move over closer to Buck.

"I'm being a perfectly awful nuisance," Janey began, when Buck suddenly slowed down the car.

"Can you tie that?" he said, and drove on again up a twisting rutted lane. "The Bakers actually left the cattle gate open for Janey. Coming from them it means a lot more than rolling down the proverbial red carpet."

Janey started to ask why, but before she could say a word Buck

44

had pulled up before a small, low-built house near the top of a treeless hill. There was no one in sight, and Janey looked curiously toward a scattering of small, dark outbuildings as Buck put her bag on the porch and knocked on the door. "Rob must be asleep," he began. "I'll just wait until he wakes up and lets you in." Just then Janey heard footsteps at the rear of the house.

"There's someone!" she said. "So you really mustn't wait." At the same moment Tina called out from the car. "Oh hurry, Bucko darling. It'll be morning before you reach Sandia."

"Do go," Janey pleaded. "I'm sure someone's coming to let me in." Buck hesitated, but when Tina called out to him again he said good night to Janey and hurried back to the car and drove off.

Janey started to walk along the ground-level porch, but there were no lights in the front of the house and she couldn't see a thing so she stopped short. She heard the footsteps again, and as a door shut on the other side of the house she decided they had tried the wrong entrance and moved out of the shadows into the moonlight. "Hello," she called. "Is anybody home?"

There was no answer. Janey listened intently, but all she could hear was the sound of Buck's car fading away in the distance. "Hel-lo," she tried again. "Yoo hoo." Her own voice was interrupted by a wild inhuman scream from somewhere in the direction from which she had just come!

She wheeled to see what it was. As she turned she saw a tall, paunchy figure cross the moonlit yard and climb into the nearest truck. The Indian! she thought, and her heart beat like a trip hammer. The one I saw in the station.

The truck motor coughed and hiccuped as the Indian stepped on the starter. At the same instant the wild screaming sound was repeated. It was nearer now and coming from the left. Janey's hand went to her throat and she stared into the shadows, fighting down a nameless and overwhelming panic. The truck rolled off unnoticed. Janey stood transfixed and lights, like round lidless eyes, moved slowly, inexorably toward her.

CHAPTER FOUR

Janey stood rooted while the lights drew nearer and nearer. Suddenly she saw the long foolish head of a donkey and realized that he carried the lamps pannier fashion on either side of his neck. The donkey opened his mouth and brayed again as he saw her, and at the same moment a tall young man loomed out of the darkness and moved stiffly toward her.

"Who left the cattle gate open?" a deep, unusually resonant voice demanded. "Was it that fool Buck Hughes?"

"No. It couldn't have been." Janey felt breathless with relief. "At least it was open when we came through. And there was someone here ahead of us! An Indian, I think, and he drove off just now in a pickup truck. But listen, is this the right place and are you Rob Baker?"

"Of course, and you're Jane McGovern." Rob took the lamps off the donkey's neck and turned him out in a corral. "You're sure the pickup truck left *after* Buck Hughes?"

"Yes. Positive." Janey went through the front door Rob had opened for her. "And I think—I'm almost positive the Indian who drove it was at the airport. He must have come over here while I was at the Weavers'. What is this all about?"

Rob Baker shrugged. "The big point is if he went after Buck the gate'll be shut. *Any* Indian *any* time would have the sense to shut a cattle gate. But not Hughes. He's as much of a fool as these darn uranium hunters. Have you any baggage?"

"Yes!" Janey was cross from fatigue, fear, and sudden relief. "It's outside the door. And if Buck Hughes is a fool at least he had the decency to meet me at the airport!"

Rob brought Janey's suitcase into the house without answering. As he turned on a bridge lamp and motioned for Janey to sit down in the chintz-covered chair beneath it she began to think her crack about being met had been unnecessarily mean. "What a pretty room," she said, and looked around her nearsightedly. "And it's such a surprise."

Still Rob didn't speak, and Janey added hurriedly, "I don't mean I'm surprised that it's so attractive. I just thought that it would be more western with Indian rugs and bowls and things like the Weavers' house."

Rob's sun-tanned face wrinkled with amusement, and Janey saw that he was both better-looking and younger-looking than she had expected. "It's a cinch you don't know Mom," he said good-naturedly. "She doesn't even think a dead Indian is a good Indian. When my dad was alive he felt the same way."

"How amazing." As Janey looked back at the neat, overfurnished room she realized there was nothing childish or precious about Rob's deep voice or his homely, soft-spoken words. "Do you know what made them feel that way?"

"My grandpa Baker was killed in one of the last Indian raids," Rob began, when they both heard the sound of a car and he turned toward the door. "Here's Mom," he said, and a moment later Mrs. Baker, followed by a little girl in a short frilly costume, hurried into the room.

"Janey McGovern. My dear girl, I am so sorry we couldn't meet you. Really, of all the absurd, fantastically confused evenings!

And with only the one car. It's so annoying that Rob can't use his truck at night."

Janey blinked as Mrs. Baker turned on a series of lights which made the living room look shabby and at the same time smaller and more overcrowded than ever. She moved forward to shake hands and found herself enveloped in short, plump arms and a cloud of violet perfume. "And this is Twinks." Mrs. Baker beckoned like the Fairy Queen in *Iolanthe* and her daughter curtsied and offered Janey a limp, cold little hand.

"And now, Twinks darling, hurry off to bed," Mrs. Baker went on. "And then tomorrow Mother will tell Janey all about the way you handled the extra performance. I want her to know just how proud I am of my little girl star."

Dear Lord! Janey wondered how her own family and especially Hank and the twins would have reacted to such saccharin. But Twinks only blew her mother a kiss and sidled out of the room as though she were leaving a stage. Rob was not in sight.

Mrs. Baker noticed his absence at the same moment. "Rob? Robbie? Robbie—Randolph?" she called. "My dear boy, where are your manners? We have a guest. A neglected guest. Bring in her bags. Show her to her room."

"Oh, he has. Truly! Thank you ever so much, Mrs. Baker." For the first time since her arrival in New Mexico, Janey felt completely sympathetic to Rob Baker. "He put the bags in there. You see, I'd only just gotten here."

"I wish this room wasn't so small." Mrs. Baker again turned on every light as she led the way into a hall bedroom. "My dear, you should have seen the guest rooms at dear old Ashburton, my mother's home in Virginia. She was a Randolph, you know, and died when I was a baby, and so I spent a good deal of my girlhood with my maternal grandmother. I really feel myself more a Virginian than a New Mexican. Still, we'll try to make up to you in warmth what we lack in splendor."

"This is a lovely room," Janey said, and the thought of actually being able to shut the door and being alone gave her voice conviction.

48

"There is a breeze." Mrs. Baker gestured to the windows on two sides. "And some people like the view. I must say I prefer the Tidewater country myself."

"I can't wait to look out in the morning," Janey said as Mrs. Baker paused for breath. "Gramps McGovern's told me so much about New Mexico I feel as though I belonged here."

For an unmistakable second Mrs. Baker stood rigid, and the expression on her faded, foolish face hardened. "You haven't seen your grandfather McGovern lately have you?" she asked. "I understood from your brother that he hadn't been East for several years. Or perhaps you and he kept in close touch with each other by letter?"

"We practically never wrote," Janey said, and looked wonderingly at her hostess. "I haven't seen him since I was a little girl, but he used to tell me the most marvelous stories about New Mexico. He loved every inch of it."

Mrs. Baker straightened the bedspread and her plump hands fluttered away non-existent dust. "I'm afraid you may be disappointed," she said, but she sounded suddenly relieved and at ease. "You know childhood impressions . . ."

"Yes indeed. Gramps warned me about that himself," Janey said, and tried to keep her own voice casual and offhand. Mrs. Baker knows something about Gramps, she thought. So did Sis Weaver and Buck. They were both embarrassed but Mrs. Baker's more than that. Whatever it is that she knows she's awfully relieved that I don't know it.

A few minutes later Janey had undressed and was lying in bed with the dry, aromatic air from outside cool and fragrant around her. All the happenings of the day faded away and her mind went back to the time when Hank, aged twelve and flushed with earnestness, had tried to explain to her about Gramps. "He's a disgrace to the family." The memory of Hank's embarrassed boyish voice rang in her memory. "When he's drunk he doesn't know what he's doing any more'n a baby."

Was that it? Was it possible that something Gramps had done when he was drunk had been behind, perhaps even the direct

49

cause of, the trouble at the mine? That might explain why he had put off returning to New Mexico, but it didn't make sense in the light of his absolute confidence that his old friends would welcome his only granddaughter. Sis Weaver and Buck, who were a younger generation and obviously friendly, might never have heard all the details and be perfectly happy to forget any scandal. But Mrs. Baker, who was years older than Mum, was something else again.

Janey remembered the look on Mrs. Baker's face, and instantly her mind rejected the possibility of Gramps's guilt. Mrs. Baker had looked guilty herself. And shrewd. And so hard that her aging kitten's face had suddenly looked hawklike. There's something she knows or wants and she's afraid of my being in on it, Janey thought, and the idea that had come to her when she had first read Gramps's postscript grew more vivid than ever.

Buck or the Weavers would take me to the mine, Janey decided, but at that idea her thoughts tripped over Rob Baker as though he had been an actual rock at her feet. He can't stop me, she thought. He may not even want to stop me.

I think Rob's just a cipher—Janey breathed more slowly and her nerves relaxed—he's bored and embarrassed by his mother and probably only cares about his horses, the way Buck said. Janey's eyes closed in the soft darkness, but the recollection of Rob Baker —a wiry figure in worn blue jeans and boots—stayed with her until she slept.

The next morning Janey woke up to the sound of music. She didn't know where it came from but it was distinct and emphatic. The beat of the rhythm—oom pa pa—oom pa pa—oomp—was as inescapable as the glaring sunlight that filled her room. She looked out of the window as she dressed, and then hurried through the empty living room into the kitchen, following the sound.

Mrs. Baker jumped away from the stove as though she had been caught doing something naughty. "Oh, my dear, has Twinks's practicing disturbed you?" She whipped off an apron so quickly Janey was not sure she had seen it on. "I am planning to have

50

her studio sound conditioned but we have had to put it off. Labor's so difficult, you know. I do hope you slept well?"

"Like a top." Janey looked at the kitchen clock, which said nearly ten. "I'm ashamed I'm so late."

"But you mustn't feel that way!" Mrs. Baker's high-pitched voice went off into a wail of protest. "I was going to bring you in a little tray. But if you're sure you don't mind eating on the porch we'll do that this once, because I have to drive downtown for an eleven-thirty appointment. Oh, it is so inconvenient, being so far from the center of things."

Janey started to insist on getting her own breakfast but she was defeated before she began and it ended with her walking around the house in the sunlight while Mrs. Baker scrambled eggs.

On her left Janey saw a broad stretch of bare, tawny-colored land going on for miles before it reached up into the mountains. It's endless, she thought, but plainer, tanner, more the same than I expected from what Gramps said. She moved on and looked over at the cluster of adobe ranch buildings and the corral she had seen the night before. Several nondescript cow ponies and the burro were tied to a fence. A car, probably belonging to one of Rob's customers, was parked beside a battered pickup truck with broken headlights. It all looked shabby and poor in the bright, unrelenting sunlight and Janey decided the high-sounding name Rancho del Fuego was not very appropriate.

The burro brayed as she passed and she grinned, remembering how the sound had startled her last night. Rob was infuriating, Janey thought. She had realized at the time that Rob was not in the least surprised by the Indian's turning up at the ranch, but between the excitement of her arrival and the growing mystery surrounding Gramps she had forgotten to ask who the man was and why he had shadowed her out at the airport. I'll find out all about the Indian today, Janey decided, and went back to the door just as Mrs. Baker came out carrying a tray of delicious-looking food.

"I thought you might like to eat in the sunshine," Mrs. Baker said. "It's nice now but later on in the day you'll miss the shade. Sometimes on Sundays we take a picnic over to Cinder Cone Canyon because of the trees, but I find it makes Robbie terribly nostalgic for the old home."

"Canyon? Homesick?" Janey's face was a question mark as she looked down the hill in the direction in which her hostess was facing. Had Robbie, too, spent time at "dear old Ashburton"?

"Homesick for my father's old ranch," Mrs. Baker said, and it dawned on Janey that the fluttery, pretentious little lady beside her was anything but a fool. "We all lived there until my father's death in 1951. It's over there beyond those cottonwoods."

"Oh, I see." Janey looked where Mrs. Baker had pointed, but she still had no idea whether the canyon was miles away or next door.

A moment later Mrs. Baker went in to change and Janey settled down to scrambled eggs, coffee, and crisp, light corn bread. Mrs. Baker was an excellent cook, and as Janey carried the dishes into the immaculate kitchen it was apparent that despite her flutters, apologies, and constant conversation she was an efficient housekeeper. She came in, dressed in the clothes she had worn the night before, and started to take the dishes that Janey was washing away from her. This can't go on, Janey thought, and stood her ground by the sink, or we'll both die of politeness.

"You really must let me do something!" she said, looking over her shoulder. "I'm used to it at home, and, besides, Hank definitely understood that I could be useful. I know he thought I could help Rob with the horses, but he must have meant in the house too. Mum would have a fit if I didn't."

For the second time since Janey had known Mrs. Baker she was momentarily speechless. Her expression changed, too, but instead of hardening she smiled and her blue eyes softened. "Why, Janey, my dear child. With the sun on your hair and your chin up I declare you're the living image of Major McGovern. It's really amazing. Your family must have told you about it."

Janey nodded, too amazed to speak. For years she had vaguely resented being likened to Gramps, but now she was so surprised by Mrs. Baker's reaction that she didn't even think of that. Before she could say a word Mrs. Baker straightened up, dabbed at her eyes, and hurried out to her car. When she was in the front seat she called back, "Oh Janey, I wonder if you'd mind checking up on Twinks? She's supposed to stay at her practicing until half-past ten."

"Why, yes. I'll be glad——" Janey began, but before she could ask exactly what she was expected to do Mrs. Baker waved and drove off.

Janey turned around and as the music was still playing she decided to go back to her own room before she followed the sound to "check up."

Somehow in the moments they had been apart Mrs. Baker had made Janey's bed and tidied up. Just as well I held out on washing the dishes, Janey decided, and as she thought over what had happened she was more curious than ever about the effect of Gramps's name on his old friends. This time nobody even mentioned Gramps, she realized. It was just that I reminded Mrs. Baker of him. And she didn't look scared or hard but dripping with sentiment. I don't understand it.

She sat down by the window and started a letter to Hank. She covered her safe arrival in one sentence and wrote on asking him if he knew anything more about Gramps's life in New Mexico. She was so absorbed that she didn't hear a slight scrabbling noise behind her.

"Are you writing a letter to your lover?" a voice asked.

Janey jumped and saw Twinks, in a faded sunsuit, standing by the door. "No, to my brother! But aren't you supposed to be practicing? Your mother said you were to stay at it until half-past ten."

"Oh, are you on her side?" All of Twinks's staginess of the night before had gone with her costume. She stood with her hands on her hips, looking up at Janey through a mop of straight, mouse-colored hair. "I hoped you'd be with old Juan and Rob and me. We think tap dancing stinks."

53

"Who's Juan?" Janey asked, and tried not to laugh. "Is he an old friend of your family's?"

"He was a friend of Grandfather's," Twinks said. "But listen, are you sure you go for tap dancing? Miss 'Nita Murphy, that's another grown-up friend of mine, doesn't like it at all. She's definitely on my side."

"I don't know enough about it to take sides," Janey said. "But I promised your mother I'd see you went on practicing, so why don't you show me how you do it before I go out to find Rob?"

"O.K." Twinks led the way into a shed that was attached to the kitchen. Except for two kitchen chairs, an upright piano, and an old-fashioned record player it was unfurnished, but it was clearly what Mrs. Baker referred to as the studio. "I don't really mind dancing," Twinks went on. "It's all the practicing in here and resting before a performance and staying in bed late after one that I hate. Mother says those are the sacrifices I have to make to my art. Phewey!"

Once more Janey tried not to laugh. Twinks was a character and so, in an older, stranger way, was her mother. I wonder about Rob, she thought, and suddenly she was eager to see what he was like on a second and more revealing meeting.

Twinks turned on the record player and began to dance. Janey knew nothing about the fine points of tap dancing, but it was clear that Twinks was exceptionally, miraculously graceful and that she had an ear for time. "Bravo. You're good. That was super." Janey clapped enthusiastically when she had finished. "I don't blame your mother for making you stick at it. Why, pretty soon you'll be good enough to be in a musical comedy."

"For Hollywood, you mean." Twinks's narrow little face looked old and wrinkled as she spoke. "Thar's gold in them thar hills."

Janey said nothing, but when she went outside she realized uncomfortably that the need for money was behind most of the difficulties and apparent contradictions that had happened to her since she had arrived—was it only last night?—to stay with the Bakers.

A car filled with a woman and a family of three girls left the

54

corral as she came up. When she reached Rob he was unsaddling one of the ponies they had ridden, and he nodded without speaking.

"Can I help?" Janey moved toward a big gray gelding at the edge of the string of horses. "What do you do, just sponge 'em down now and groom later?"

"I clean before breakfast," Rob said, and unsaddled, unbridled, and turned out a chestnut mare in what seemed like one fluid, continuous motion. "There isn't time later on."

"I see," Janey said, and frowned at the unfamiliar combination of metal loops and rings under the saddle flap. "How do you undo this? I don't know much about a western saddle."

Rob showed her, but his hands moved so quickly she could hardly follow him. "Have you ridden in a Mexican saddle?" he asked. "I don't own any eastern ones."

"That's O.K.," Janey said, and refrained from saying that she was quite certain she could handle any of the horses before her bareback. "I'm anxious to try your kind. To hear my grandfather talk you'd think anything but a Mexican saddle was an insult to both horse and rider."

"He might be right at that!" Rob smiled, and she saw his teeth were very white and his eyes sparklingly blue against his ruddy tan. He's more attractive than I thought, Janey decided as he walked over to the stable. Not handsome like Buck or sophisticated like Larry, but there's something about him that's more than just clean-cut Joe College. I wonder why I didn't notice more about him last night? She remembered what had happened and laughed out loud. He wheeled around with his back to the dilapidated shed. "What's so funny?" he asked. "My horses, or the saddles, or this stable?"

"Neither." Janey laughed harder than ever at his stern expression. "It's you *and* me. The way I landed here last night, and the burro, and everything else that happened. We've hardly even seen each other before. The living room was nearly dark until your mother came home, and then you disappeared."

"I guess I did." Rob relaxed visibly and leaned against the ramshackle door. "And now you're probably ready to ride. Your brother said you were the original horse-crazy female."

"I like to ride. Period!" Janey said. "But by horse-crazy I mean little kids who've practically never seen a stable, or old fox-hunting fogies who've ridden so much they look like horses."

"I think I'll see how you make out with Chesty." Rob apparently had not been listening. "He's the horse I usually give to beginners."

I'm not a beginner. The words came to Janey's lips but she held them back, suddenly sure that Rob Baker could only be impressed by action. "I have ridden a few western ponies," she said blandly. "But only with an eastern saddle."

Rob said nothing but led a sleepy-eyed chestnut from the stable and saddled him expertly. "Better put on your glasses," he said when Janey mounted. "Gopher holes are hard to see and we've got plenty of 'em."

Janey was annoyed, but she put on her glasses without saying a word. She knew she had had them on last night after Buck had left and in the excitement that had followed hadn't taken them off, and Rob had noticed it. "You're very observant," she said as Rob adjusted her stirrup leathers. "I'm surprised you didn't guess the length of my stirrups just from seeing me standing around."

"Oh, I could have." Rob either missed her sarcasm or purposely ignored it. "I thought maybe you'd want 'em up around your neck like some of the eastern jockeys I get out here. Their big idea seems to be get on and race."

"On this horse?" Janey asked, and stared ostentatiously at the chestnut's front feet which were heavy with ringbone. "You surprise me."

Rob saddled a lightly built bay gelding for himself and swung into the saddle. "Which ride do you want to take?" he asked. "You name it."

"How should I know?" Janey tried not to be irritated at his manner. "Your mother said something about Cinder Cone Canyon and sometime I'd like to go to Fortune where the mine was, but those are the only two names I've ever even heard of."

"They're both too far," Rob said. "I guess we'd better try Frijoles Ridge. I haven't too much time to spare."

"Lead on, Macduff." Janey followed him along the trail leading away from the corral. They rode for perhaps ten minutes when Rob swerved so suddenly that it was all Janey could do to keep her horse from colliding with his.

As she straightened up she saw that the truck with the Indian she had seen last night was parked at a fork directly ahead of her. She turned to tell Rob, but he was galloping off through the sagebrush and cactus on her left!

CHAPTER FIVE

The old chestnut struggled to follow Rob's horse,
but Janey managed to keep him on the wagon-rutted
trail. Chesty seemed sure-footed, but until she was certain of it
she had no intention of dashing off over the open range.

She passed the Indian, but although it was perfectly clear that
he saw her he gave no sign of recognition. The Original Cigar-
Store Brave, Janey thought, but the idea was cold comfort since
she couldn't share it with anyone. As soon as she was on the left-
hand fork, which was in the general direction that Rob had disappeared, she urged Chesty into a canter. He was ready to go, and
she realized that despite his ringbone his gaits were excellent.

At the top of a small sandy hill Rob rejoined her and pulled
his horse down to a decorous walk. "And what was that all about?"
Janey demanded. "Was your horse scared of the truck or didn't he
like the Indian?"

"Neither." Rob said, pointing to where a wide cement road lay
white and glaring against the tan plains below them. "Lope's in
that direction. Would you like to ride down there?"

"On a horse with ringbone? Are you kidding or just trying me out?" Janey asked. "Riding along that hard-surface road would make Chesty lame for a week, and you know it."

"I know most dudes feel they aren't out West unless they ride hell for leather into a little old cow town," Rob said. "In the livery business I see plenty of people who've just moved to New Mexico and I aim to be hospitable."

"I'm surprised that last night you didn't get out a pair of Colt 44's and shoot off both barrels to welcome me," Janey said. "That would have been a good way to give a Yankee dude a spine-tingling thrill."

"Old Tote, the burro, braying in the dark seemed to do the trick," Rob said, but his smile was disarming and Janey smiled back as she relaxed in the huge, unexpectedly comfortable saddle.

"All right. You win!" she said. "But who is that Indian? I thought last night you knew him."

"Juan Martinez?" Rob looked surprised. "Known him all my life. He worked for my grandfather Marston, and we lived at Grandpa's ranch until just a few years ago."

The Indian was the Juan whom Twinks had mentioned, Janey realized, and as she saw an answer to why he seemed to have trailed her the night before she turned to Rob. "Do you suppose your mother asked him to meet me last night and somehow or other the message was mixed up?"

"No!" Rob said. "One reason why Mom has such a scunner on all Indians is because Grandpa preferred Juan to any of her high riding Virginia friends and relations and said so. Ever since I can remember, Grandpa was blind and completely dependent on Juan and Mom had to put up with him, but she never liked him. She used to call him The Useful Evil Eye."

"That's very descriptive!" Janey remembered the impression Juan's cold, unrevealing stare had made on her the night before. "If he made your mother nervous all those years I don't blame her for not liking him. It must be mostly his fault."

"Maybe." Rob's voice grew gruff and he shifted uneasily in his saddle. "But what really hog-tied it all was Grandpa's leaving Juan his truck and enough money to keep it going. Mom didn't know about Grandpa's will ahead of time and she thought every penny of the little he had ought to come to us."

"Oh, I see," Janey said, and went on more quickly, determined to steer clear of the Bakers' money troubles. "Is Juan a full-blooded Indian? Juan Martinez sounds so Spanish. Has he an Indian name?"

"Yes. It means Slow-to-Kindle in English," Rob said. "He was born at the Isleta pueblo the other side of Albuquerque, and both his parents were Indians. As far as I know the family's closest tie to any white man was through Grandpa Marston. When Grandpa was eighteen he saved Juan's father from drowning, and after that they considered Grandpa an adopted brother and member of the pueblo."

"How exciting!" Janey put in. "When you were a little kid didn't it make you as proud as Punch?"

"I reckon it would have if I'd known about it," Rob said. "But Grandpa never talked about his past, and I suppose Mom never mentioned it because she probably felt recognizing even an adopted relationship would just make Juan more uppity. The first I heard about it was when Juan told me soon after Grandpa died."

"I think it's amazing Juan didn't tell you sooner," Janey said. "Don't you think that's queer?"

"Not a bit." Rob looked amused. "Most Indians naturally clam up with any white man. The only odd thing about Juan is that he has always kept in touch with his pueblo but never gone back to the blanket—even now when he doesn't have to work. From everything I've read and from what Dr. Bliss, who's the top man on contemporary Indians at the university, has told me, that is unusual."

"But why did Juan trail me last night?" Janey asked. "I don't see how he knew I was coming or even who I was."

"He knew your grandfather McGovern, and Mom says you favor him," Rob said. "Besides, ever since my grandpa died Juan's made a fetish of keeping an eye on all of us. He's canny as a coyote about keeping clear of Mom, but he always knows exactly what's going on at the ranch and what we're all doing. I know it's his way of showing his loyalty to Grandpa, but sometimes it drives me loco."

Janey only nodded as Gramps's stories about Indian tribal loyalty filtered back into her mind. "I can understand Juan's caring about you and Twinks," she said finally. "But I don't understand why he's interested in me and I certainly don't understand why people act so queer, in front of me anyway, the minute Gramps McGovern's name is mentioned. Do they think there's still gold in La Placita and that Gramps was holding out on it for my benefit?"

"Wouldn't do you much good if he had," Rob said dryly. "Between taxes, labor prices, and the country's being off the gold standard nowadays it doesn't pay to work a mine that's ten times richer than La Placita ever was. You can ask any miner and he'd tell you the same thing."

"Oh, I believe you." Janey nodded as her hopeful vision of a bonanza lode disappeared forever. Rob's deep, intelligent-sounding voice and the direct, simple way in which he put things were entirely convincing, but at the moment she was too curious about Gramps himself to feel any regret. "Then why is everyone so sort of embarrassed and odd over Gramps as a person?" she asked. "I know he used to drink too much but I can't imagine his doing anything very terrible even when he was drunk. I can't even believe that he was ever clever enough or powerful enough to be dangerous. And yet last night your mother acted—I don't know—almost afraid of him and this morning she made me feel she'd been terribly fond of him."

"I don't know a thing about it"—Rob looked straight over his horse's head as he spoke—"and it's nearly time I went back to the ranch, so how about a gallop?"

"Yes, but listen," Janey began, but Rob had already galloped off, and it was clear that as far as he was concerned the conversation was over. I wish I'd just mentioned the Weavers and Gramps, Janey thought as she hurried after him. The minute his mother comes into anything he gets on the defensive.

After a few minutes Rob fanned off from the trail, guiding his horse expertly around clumps of yucca, cactus, and sage. "Chesty's perfectly safe!" he called back. "In spite of his ringbone."

Janey nodded, and gave herself up to the pleasure of galloping off the trail into the open and unfenced countryside. Old Chesty was obviously enjoying himself, and as Rob went faster and faster Janey kept at an even distance behind him, glorying in their speed. It's like following a good skier, she thought. Rob's broken the trail and all Chesty and I have to do is to follow.

When they came to the top of a ridge they stopped to let their horses rest, and Rob pointed out the back of the Bakers' house far down below them. "Golly, but it's all high and—and—big!" Janey struggled for the right words. "I feel as though I'd come from a country of ant heaps and molehills."

"This isn't anything," Rob said, but he sounded pleased. "Someday we'll go over to Fortune by way of Cinder Cone Canyon. Then you'll see some real views."

"And we'll find La Placita!" Janey said eagerly. "And go in and look at it for ourselves."

"No." The single clipped syllable carried more weight than a dozen sentences. "Not a chance."

"But—but why not?" Even as Janey spoke she guessed Rob wouldn't answer, so she concentrated on following him down a sudden slope and keeping a careful distance behind his horse's sliding hoofs.

Rob turned eastward as the grade leveled off, and once more they were able to walk their horses two abreast. "Does Twinks like riding?" Janey asked. "Linda and Pete, my kid brother and sister, would just go hog-wild out here, they'd love it so. And I should think Twinks would be a natural because she's so graceful."

"Twinks isn't bad for her age, but she isn't horse-crazy, either your kind or mine," Rob said, and it was clear that he had listened to Janey before they left the stable. "Right now while I'm running the livery stable I guess it's just as well, because I don't know how I'd manage to find time to teach her decently. I count on using any spare time I can get away from the horses, reading and taking notes for a paper I want to write."

"What about——" Janey began, but before she could finish Rob pointed across a valley to the left.

"Janey! Look quick!" he said. "There's a mule deer standing by that old hogan."

Janey turned and saw the animal quietly grazing beside the ruins of a round adobe building. "He's beautiful," she said as the deer moved off out of sight. "And he seemed so at home. As though he knew the Indian who built the hogan liked his being there."

"He probably would at that," Rob said. "The old-time Indians only hunted for food when they were hungry. They felt that all animals and the hills and streams, too, had an individual personality or soul, like a human being, and they acted accordingly."

"That hogan looks it," Janey said, her eyes still on the small building across the valley. "It's very crude but it's built *with* the countryside instead of just plunked down on it, if you know what I mean."

Rob only nodded, but from then on he rode more slowly and began pointing out the different kinds of desert plants and animals and telling Janey their Indian names.

"That's a desert tortoise," he said once. "Some Indians call him The-One-Who-Makes-Haste-Slowly. You don't have that kind in the East, do you?"

Janey shook her head and grimaced as an ugly-looking lizard slithered away to her left and ducked out of sight behind a clump of reddish rock beyond the turtle. "And we don't have big lizards like that either," she said, "or poisonous snakes, around where I live anyway."

"You're as bad as Twinks." Rob grinned down at her. "But you needn't worry. We're too high up for snakes most of the time around here."

"Three loud cheers," Janey said. "And now can we canter again or won't that give us a chance to cool off the horses before we get home?"

"It'll be O.K." Rob moved off in such perfect time with his

horse that Auguste Wentie's old adage about a good rider being a modern centaur came into Janey's mind and she smiled to herself. Rob's and Wentie's style of riding's different, she thought, noticing Rob's upturned rein hand and his long-stirruped seat, but they're both part of the horse.

Five minutes later they came to a narrow plateau and saw a pickup truck on the road below them. "First car we've seen," Janey said, and added excitedly, "Rob, look! It's Juan, the Indian who worked for your grandfather. Why do you suppose he parked down there?"

"To see us. The minute I rode east and you took the left fork when we saw him this morning he'd have been sure we'd come back this way."

"I don't see how he did it," Janey said as the truck drove off toward the main road. "The country we've been over all looks alike and we haven't stuck to any regular trail. I don't see how he could tell."

"Juan knows this countryside inside out," Rob said. "And besides, he's probably been able to keep an eye on us almost all the time we were out. This isn't exactly ambush territory. It's wide open."

"I love the openness!" Janey looked around her delightedly. "I'm nearsighted, but out here everything's so clear and brilliant I feel like a hawk. But why did Juan care about us? He doesn't keep tabs on every horse and rider you take out, does he?"

Rob shook his head. "Nope. But you're staying here, so he wants to know how well you can ride. You can bet he noticed it when you didn't let Chesty follow me but waited until you knew what you were doing."

"And so did you!" Janey said. "This whole ride's been a test run as far as you're concerned, hasn't it?"

"Sure thing," Rob said, "and when you see some of the riders I get you'll know why I did it." Janey itched to fish a compliment out of him, but before she could think up an approach he dismounted and walked beside his horse. "You stay where you are," he said when Janey would have followed suit. "I'm just giving

Beau a breather. He's been out before today and Chesty hasn't."

They moved along slowly, the horses shoulder to shoulder, until they reached the gate, when Rob handed Janey his reins and limped ahead to open it. Why, he's lame, Janey realized, remembering what Buck Hughes had told her about an accident. He's simply dragging that left foot, but he didn't do it this morning. It must get worse when he's tired, unless he's just hurt himself. At that moment Rob turned to let Janey pass through the gate and saw her staring at his foot. "Did you twist your ankle just now?" Janey asked. "It looks as though it hurt."

Rob shook his head, his cheeks brick colored, and Janey went on nervously. "Buck told me about your accident and its keeping you out of the R.O.T.C.," she said. "I think that's absolutely rotten luck. Are you sure it's all right your walking all this way?" Even before the sound of Janey's words faded away she knew she had made a mistake, but the damage was done. Rob only nodded as he took back Beau's reins, turned, and led the way on foot toward the corral in antagonistic silence.

As Janey followed on Chesty she saw Rob's shoulder blades stiffen and set as he forced himself to walk on without favoring his left leg. She bit her lip, annoyed at having made a break, and then compassion, as overwhelming and direct as though Rob had been Pete's age, swept away her self-consciousness and she thought only of the tense, painfully erect figure before her. Rob's terrified of pity or condescension, Janey realized. That's why he shies away from talking about his mother, or money, or anything even vaguely personal where an outsider might undermine his pride.

"Here we are." Rob spoke without turning around. "Sorry I can't offer you a mounting block or an English groom to help you off."

"Oh, I'll live without 'em." Janey decided to act as though nothing unpleasant had happened. "Do you know that was one of the best rides I ever had in my life? You can't imagine what a kick it is to feel you have a whole glorious state to ride over when you've been used to nothing but a ring or a few miles of fenced-in, woody trails. It was a completely new experience."

Rob, his face hidden behind his saddle flap, made no answer, and as Janey started unsaddling she tried again. "I've decided I like a western saddle," she said. "If I can get on to the cinching and un-cinching I think I'd like it better than an English one. Golly, I can hardly wait to ride again."

Rob said nothing but his hackles seemed to have lowered, and a few minutes later they walked toward the house in a silence which, if not companionable, was at least unhostile.

Mrs. Baker was home again and had lunch all ready and waiting. "This isn't much of a meal," she apologized, "but I had a business appointment in town after giving a lesson and I didn't get back in time to fix anything decent."

"So you did go to see Keith after all?" Rob looked inquiringly at his mother. "I hoped you wouldn't."

Mrs. Baker frowned at Rob and ignored his question. "Twinks, drink your soup while it's hot," she said. "And take your elbows off the table. Janey's going to think this is a poor white-trash household."

"My, this is good pea soup," Janey said, and took another of the sandwiches Mrs. Baker passed to her. "And the homemade bread is absolutely out of this world. I wish I knew how to make it."

"It's really very easy," Mrs. Baker said, and she looked pleased for the first time since they had sat down at table. "Some morning when we both have time I'd love to show you how to do it."

"If I go home knowing how to make bread my family will be impressed!" Janey said. "Right now Linda, my eight-year-old sister, is a better cook than I am."

"I can make corn pone, and Navajo stew, and I know how to jerk venison—well, sort of," Twinks put in. "Could Linda do that?"

"I doubt if she'd want to." Mrs. Baker spoke before Janey could answer. "In the East little girls don't try to do everything Indian-fashion."

66

"Linda's only real speciality is fudge." Janey smiled at Twinks as Mrs. Baker turned away to pick up a yellow pad lying beside the telephone. "I was joking about her being a good cook."

"Rob, I don't see how you'll manage everybody this afternoon," Mrs. Baker said, and handed him the pad. "Mrs. Sydney telephoned just before you came home and she wants to bring all three of the children over to ride today. You already have the Stokes boys coming, and the Bylers, and Mrs. Appleton and her daughter, and Juanita Murphy, but of course you can put Juanita off for another time."

"No need of putting anyone off." Rob glanced at the pad. "I'm going to take the little shavers who come early out in the ring, and later on the others can have a trail ride. The horses are fresh enough."

"I still think you ought to cancel 'Nita Murphy." Mrs. Baker sounded cross, and Janey decided that Twinks's 'grown-up friend' was not a favorite with her mother. "Any flighty young widow who wastes the time 'Nita does taking snapshots of Indians shouldn't object to having her hours changed. And it isn't as though she paid for her rides."

"Miss 'Nita paid with the pictures she has taken for me," Rob said quietly. "And she'll go out at three with the Appletons. Janey will be in charge on Chesty and take them over Frijoles Ridge while I ride herd on the Bylers and Stokeses. It's all settled."

Miss 'Nita Murphy? A widow? Janey was too intrigued over the paradox to notice that Rob had paid her an indirect compliment. She started to ask whether it was Miss or Mrs. when Twinks slumped back in her chair in a noisy imitation of someone fainting.

"Zowie! I'm knocked out. Shock crazy." Twinks peered out at Janey from under the hand she held pressed to her forehead. "Or did someone else hear Robert Randolph Baker really say that Janey was going to ride his precious Chesty, in charge of one of his superprecious classes! And with his super-duper-precious Miss Murphy! I can't believe it."

"Twinks. Twinkle Toes! Really," Mrs. Baker said. "What do

you suppose Janey will think of us? I can't understand why you have to be so silly and Rob so stubborn all of a sudden." Twinks only grinned imperturbably, Rob finished his lunch, and Mrs. Baker went right on talking. "Seriously, Rob, I do think you should put off Juanita and the Appletons, too, until you can take them out yourself or Janey's had a chance to get acclimated. This dry air and the altitude can be very trying until you get used to them. You feel exhilarated at first, do too much, and end up exhausted. It happened to me over and over again when I spent part of the year in Virginia and came out here on visits to Father."

"Thank you, Mrs. Baker. But I'd honestly like to ride this afternoon!" Janey felt as though she were physically pushing her words through the cascade of her hostess's conversation. "Truly."

At that moment the telephone rang and Twinks answered it. "For you, Mom," she said. "Mrs. Bulkley wants to know if you can change Susie's lesson."

"Please ask her to hold on a moment." Mrs. Baker sprang up as she spoke. "My calendar's in the other room and I'll take the call in there." As she hurried toward the door she glanced at Janey. "By all means ride this afternoon if you want to," she said. "But don't let anyone force you into it if you're tired. Rob's better than most, but consideration isn't a strong point in New Mexican men or women."

"That was a crack at Miss 'Nita!" Twinks said as her mother shut the living-room door. "Ever since last summer when Miss 'Nita took me down to the Indian ceremonials Mom's had it in for her."

"In a way you can't blame her." Rob stood with his hand on the back door and smiled at Twinks. "Mom works like a slave to give us both a good time, and then Miss 'Nita comes along, whose speciality is Indians, which is the one thing Mom can't stand, and we both fall hard for her and her work. We've both foamed at the mouth about Miss 'Nita until Mom's tired of it."

Rob went off to the stable, and as Janey began to wash the dishes Twinks made a face. "Rob never foamed about anything but I guess I did," she admitted. "But jeepers, Janey, that trip down to the ceremonials in Gallop really was simply super. Wait until you see the pictures Miss 'Nita took of it."

"Is she Miss or Mrs.?" Janey asked. "Have you and Rob known her long?"

"She's Mrs. Hugh Talbot but she's always called Miss, I guess because she wasn't married long enough to get used to the Mrs.," Twinks said. "Rob met her winter before last at an exhibition at the U. and later on he took me down to her new-old house in Lope to see some of her pictures. Miss 'Nita'll do anything to get what she wants and Mom thinks it's all nutty but I don't. I just bet you'll like her."

Janey nodded assent, but as an image of a young woman as exotically beautiful as Tina Ramirez only more assured, experienced, and ruthless flashed through her mind she began to wonder. "Is Miss Murphy about Rob's age?" she asked out loud. "Did she just move to Lope two years ago?"

Twinks stared at Janey and began to giggle. "Miss 'Nita's ancient! And she's lived in Lope for ages except for the six months she was married before Mr. Talbot was killed in a train smash. Are you goony?"

"Your mother said she was a young widow." Janey defended herself but Twinks looked more amused than ever.

"Oh sure," she said. "That's because Miss 'Nita's a year younger than Mom is herself. They've known each other to say 'hi' to for ages, and Rob and I'd seen her, but we weren't real friends until after Rob fixed it up."

"I'm glad I'm going to meet her," Janey said as she dried the last of the dishes. "She sounds fascinating."

"She isn't pretty," Twinks warned. "She's little and old and sort of crippledy. That's why Rob needed you to go out riding with her this afternoon. That Betsy Appleton's too dumb to help anybody."

Twinks turned on the radio to a brass-band concert, and as Mrs. Baker came back into the kitchen and began talking over the music the sound was deafening. Janey slipped off to the bedroom and shut the door, grateful for even a partial silence.

She looked out of the window next to the door and tried to figure out just where she and Rob had ridden to that morning. We didn't pass those cottonwoods until we were coming home, she remembered, and moved to the window she had looked through before breakfast to see the trail they had started out on. I turned left after we met the Indian and then we both kept going uphill and I guess toward the east.

As Janey's eyes traveled on to the uplands she forgot all about directions, suddenly captivated by the way the view in front of her had changed since morning. The sparsely covered earth which had been a monotonous tan before was a rich brown turning to purple in the distance. Not far from the window a tall branching cactus, which Janey had not even noticed earlier, stood out like an artist's symbol of the Southwest, while further away the contours of the bare hills and the distant mountains had a new boldness and majesty. As the sunlight shifts the same view changes completely, Janey realized, and felt as exhilarated as though she had just made a dramatic discovery. Gramps was always talking about the magic New Mexican light but I never knew what he meant until now.

At that moment Janey heard a car horn honk by the stable, and tore herself away from the window. As she hurried out of doors she looked around curiously, not at all sure of what she was expected to do next. There were several cars parked in the rutted driveway, and a number of women and children in blue jeans and sombreros moved around the corral fence where the horses were tied. Rob was saddling Beau as Janey reached him, and made introductions without looking up from his work. Janey shook hands with a blond, thin Mrs. Appleton and her blond, fat daughter Betsy, who appeared to be about twelve or an overgrown eleven.

"And here's Miss Murphy." Rob stopped saddling long enough to gesture to Janey to look behind her. "Miss 'Nita, this is Janey McGovern."

Janey turned and found herself looking down at a little bit of a woman in faded green riders and an orange shirt. Why, she's almost a dwarf! The thought flashed through Janey's mind, but as Miss Murphy smiled up at her she forgot everything but the deep, luminous eyes which gave warmth and almost beauty to Miss Murphy's weather-beaten face.

"I'm delighted to see you've arrived safe and sound," Miss Murphy said, and her voice was as unexpectedly beautiful as her eyes. "I brought over my camera to take Rob's horses, but I'd much rather do his assistant." They talked for a moment or two, and then Rob led over a piebald pony and helped Miss Murphy to mount.

"Good old Spot." Miss Murphy patted the pony's plump neck. "If you grow any bigger I'm going to need a derrick or an extension ladder. Which way do you want us to go, Rob?"

"You know all the trails and how long they take," Rob said, and seemed to be everywhere at once, checking the bridles, tightening a cinch, and hoisting the Appleton girl up into her saddle. "But I thought the Frijoles would be about right. It'll give you time to take the pictures when you come back."

"I don't li——" Betsy Appleton began, but as her horse started forward she hunched over her pommel, suddenly silenced.

Janey mounted Chesty, and as she left the corral Rob reached up to her, his face so close to hers that she could see where the short hair below his Stetson hat was sun-bleached to a light gold. "Keep an eye on Betsy Appleton," he whispered. "She's O.K. starting off, but as she gets more confidence she's likely to rile up her horse or go rampagin' off on a longer ride than Miss 'Nita ought to take. I thought you could keep her on the home range without actually bulldozing."

"I'll try." Janey rode off after Betsy Appleton's sacklike figure, smiling to herself over Rob's choice of words. At the top of the first long rise she turned and saw Rob leading Beau toward the ring where four small boys were eagerly waiting. He saw her, too, and lifted his big hat in greeting. Janey waved back and as she faced forward again saw Miss Murphy rein Spot in beside Chesty.

"Rob's a marvel with small fry!" Miss Murphy said, and gestured toward the ring. "And a fantastically hard worker. I'm so glad that you're willing to help him. Since old Mr. Marston died Rob hasn't had a soul he could count on as an ally. That old Indian Juan Martinez worships Rob, but for some reason I don't understand he does more harm than good."

"Juan gives me the creeps." Janey saw that Betsy Appleton was still plodding along ahead of her and settled back to talk. "But I haven't any idea how Rob really feels about him. Rob and I talked quite a lot out riding this morning and most of the time it was good fun, but every once in a while Rob made it clear that I was butting in where I wasn't wanted. I mentioned his accident and it couldn't have been a worse break. I'm sure he'd rather die than accept pity."

"That's why he needs an ally," Miss Murphy said quietly. "I'm confident Rob'll come out of his shell eventually, but right now the pride he's used as an armor against the world and especially his own family can be devastating. His mother would do anything for him and he's devoted to her, but their ideals and values are such poles apart that for the time being they are at complete cross purposes."

"What about Mr. Baker?" Janey asked. "Is Rob like him?"

"In looks, and perhaps in his knack with animals and small children, but I imagine that's all. As I remember, Tom Baker was just a simple, easygoing cowboy without any intellectual drive or ambition in his make-up. He died when Twinks was a baby, and Ida Baker has had to cope with everything since and it can't have been easy. She was brought up with every luxury, and when she was still a very young woman the family was financially ruined in a mine disaster in which her father was blinded."

"You mean La Placita?" Janey put in eagerly. "My grandfather was one of the partners. Do you know anything about the mine or did you ever meet Gramps? He lived here until 1920 when the mine closed."

"I only moved here from Santa Fe in 1930," Miss Murphy said. "So I'm sorry to say I never met your grandfather and I don't know the first thing about the mine. Is there anything special to know?"

"Yes, I think so." Janey told Miss Murphy about Gramps's letter, his plans for her trip, and her own hopes of striking a rich lode. "Rob convinced me the gold idea was hopeless," she said. "But what I can't understand is the way people out here react to any mention of Gramps or the mine. If he'd hidden stolen millions in it they couldn't be much queerer."

"I'd love to hear more about it if you feel like telling me," Miss Murphy said. "The Appletons seem contented, so we still have time to talk."

Janey outlined the part Gramps had played in her childhood until his return to Oklahoma, and then gave Miss Murphy a more detailed description of everything connected with him that had come up in the past few days. "It's all so strange," she finished. "I almost forgot Gramps for all those years and now I can't escape thinking about him and remembering things he said practically all the time."

"I wouldn't try," Miss Murphy said. "From what you've said he sounds like a delightful person to think about."

"In some ways," Janey said, and for the first time all afternoon she felt vaguely uncomfortable. "Of course he was hopelessly impractical about La Placita and everything else, but I imagine he had something definite in mind he'd want me to find out here as long as he didn't live to do it himself. Don't you think so?"

"I feel quite sure of it," Miss Murphy said. "But you may need a great deal of patience before you succeed. This is an old inscrutable countryside and it gives up its secrets slowly."

At that moment Betsy Appleton turned in her saddle. "This is an awful dull poky ride," she shouted. "I'm going to take the left fork up ahead and go home by way of Lope. It's more fun and Mom doesn't mind."

"I'm afraid I do." Miss Murphy spoke so that only Janey could hear. "I hate being a spoilsport, but going by Lope is a great deal longer and I honestly can't ride that far. D'you suppose if you explained——?"

"I'll fix it!" Janey trotted off before Miss Murphy had finished speaking. "Do you mind if we stay on this trail?" she asked Mrs.

Appleton. "Miss Murphy is getting tired and Rob thought this ride was just the right distance."

"You two go straight ahead." Betsy spoke before her mother could answer, and began kicking at her old horse's sides. "Mom and I'll go by way of Lope and race you home."

"I'm afraid we can't do that. Rob told me we were all to stay together," Janey said. As Betsy shook her head stubbornly and started to curl the end of her reins into a lash Janey hurried on, improvising as she went along. "You see, Miss Murphy's going to take pictures as soon as we get back. I guess Rob wants all the horses, and maybe the riders, too, back at the same time, looking fine and dandy, ready to be photographed."

"Why didn't he say so?" Betsy said, but she stopped ominously twisting her reins and turned to her mother. "Say Mom, let's get some pictures for Daddy's birthday. If he saw a photo of me on a really decent horse he might buy it."

"You two girls ride on ahead while I go talk to Miss Murphy." Mrs. Appleton sounded excited. "I know she never accepts orders for portrait sittings, but perhaps this once if she's taking pictures anyway she might consent to taking a few informal poses."

Mrs. Appleton turned her horse around, and Janey and Betsy rode on straight ahead. "Boy, oh boy, but Miss Murphy's horse pictures are terrific!" Betsy bounced exuberantly up and down in her saddle. "Have you ever seen 'em?"

"No. But Betsy, go easy. Your horse must hate being bumped up and down on like that."

"Old Pigeon's too dumb to notice," Betsy said, and gave him a resounding slap with the palm of her hand. "I wish Rob would let me ride a decent horse. Pigeon's peppery for the first mile, and then he practically goes to sleep."

Just as well for him, Janey thought, but she managed to keep from saying so and suggested a canter instead. "But we won't race and we'll walk the horses to cool 'em off before we reach the stable," she added. "I always do that at home."

"Do you own your own horse or just rent?" Betsy said, and struggled ineffectively to make Pigeon go faster.

74

"Neither. I exercise horses for the man who owns the stable near where I live, so he lets me ride free."

"Sounds like fun," Betsy said. "But I'd rather own a good horse of my own than anything. Will you get going, Pigeon?"

"Stop pulling on your reins and let him stay with Chesty," Janey said, and eased her own horse into a slow canter, "and keep your hands down!"

"Boy, it worked!" Betsy got out as the two horses finally moved along side by side. "When I get my own horse I'll let you ride him. And I'm going to get one mighty soon. That's for sure."

"I hope you do," Janey said, remembering how years ago she had counted on Gramps's unfulfilled promises. "And I'd love to ride it."

Betsy went on chatting about her dream horse, and Janey thought of her recent talk with Miss Murphy about Gramps. The obvious place to begin looking is at La Placita, she decided. Herb Weaver probably knows exactly where it's located, and if I call up and say I'd like to see it Buck Hughes will take me over to Fortune. Last night just before we saw the Weavers and Tina Ramirez, Buck as good as said he'd be glad to drive me any place any time.

CHAPTER SIX

The idea of driving with Buck again and exploring for unknown treasure was so pleasant that Janey continued speculating about it until they reached the corral and Miss Murphy began photographing. From then on there was so much going on that Janey didn't think of the mine again until she and the Bakers were finishing their supper. "How far is it to Fortune from Albuquerque?" she asked out loud. "Hank thought it was about five miles from here."

"Oh, I'm afraid he was mistaken," Mrs. Baker said. "It must be easily ten miles from here on horseback over a very rough trail, and fifteen miles on the motor road. And from Albuquerque it must be twenty miles."

"That isn't bad in a good car," Janey said, and smiled to herself at the thought of Buck's Thunderbird.

"Right now you couldn't get there in any kind of car," Rob said curtly. "Flash flood last week tore up the motor road, and it hasn't been fixed."

"Mr. Blitz, the rural mail carrier, says so few people use the road they may never fix it," Twinks put in. "He told me this afternoon that the only person who's gone into Fortune since the flood was some goony prospector who went over this morning, and he had to walk the last mile. I don't get it. I wouldn't walk a step to see that dump."

"I want to go over because Gramps——" Janey began, when Mrs. Baker interrupted her.

"Of course, my dear, you want to go over to see your grandfather's grave. I think that's only natural and fitting and I'll take you over myself just as soon as the road's repaired. I'm sure Mr. Blitz doesn't know what he's talking about."

As she finished Rob pushed his chair back, muttered an excuse, and stalked out of the room. Something Mrs. Baker said upset him, Janey realized, but it can't have anything to do with my going to Fortune. He talked about riding over there this morning.

A little while later she and Twinks went outside to look at the sunset. Rob was backing his pickup truck onto a small incline beyond the stable. "Are you going to Lope?" Twinks ran toward him. "Can we go with you?"

"Tomorrow," he said, and slid out of the battered cab. "When the feed store's open. I just wanted to be sure I could get it started. Battery needs charging."

"But can we go? Janey and me both?" Twinks had the same little-girl persistence as Linda. "Please, Rob."

"Sure. Miss 'Nita said she'd try to have the pictures ready, and there's one of you and Tote that ought to be a honey."

"And Janey? She's never been to Lope. Can she come?"

"Of course," Rob said. "*If* she'll ride in the truck."

"Oh, I'd like it," Janey said, but Rob had already disappeared into the stable.

"Rob's just not car-minded," Twinks said, and skipped off toward the back of the house. "As long as he can get down to the U. and back that's all he cares. Come with me, Janey, if you want to see something."

Janey followed her and forgot both Rob, the truck, and everything else as she looked at the violent and dramatic beauty of a desert sunset. The fiery spectacle was over surprisingly quickly, and as Janey went indoors her mind turned back to ways and means of reaching Fortune. I'll have to ride over, she decided. It'd be more fun than driving, anyway. The mental picture of riding alone into the little ghost town was decidedly pleasant, and Janey was still thinking about it when she undressed for bed.

The next morning Janey went down to the corral right after breakfast and helped Rob saddle and bridle the horses. "I have four librarians from New Jersey coming over," he said. "I bet none of them have ridden before so I'll need Chesty. You can ride Spot."

"Do you think you trust me?" Janey teased. "After all, you never told me whether I passed yesterday's test in elementary horsemanship."

"You could have flunked and still be safe on Spot." Rob's voice was dead-pan but his eyes looked amused. "Especially on the Sepique trail. It's as easy as riding in the ring and a lot prettier."

An hour later as Janey followed Rob and his party she realized he had not exaggerated. Spot was as gentle as a rocking horse and the trail was exceptional. Shortly after they left the ranch Rob turned sharply and led the way down a wide shelf-like path that hugged the high red walls of Fuego Mesa.

"This is spectacular." The librarian nearest Janey looked around her eagerly. "Breath-taking."

Rob rode Beau steadily forward onto an old wagon road from which they could look down on Sepique Arroyo, twisting and strange in a great serpentine pattern below them. "Indescribable!" the librarian breathed. "Oh, if only I'd brought my camera."

If only mine wasn't sold! Janey thought regretfully of the day only two weeks ago when she had traded her camera at the War-wick exchange for money to buy new tennis shoes for the tournament in which she had never played.

She had worn the shoes a few times before she had learned she was going out West, and so it had been too late to take them back to the store. At the moment they lay unused in Janey's closet at home, while she rode along wishing she had enough

78

money so that buying cameras and tennis shoes could never be a problem.

A few minutes later, as Rob led them away from the arroyo, the road spread out onto unfenced range land. Rob pulled Beau back to the left flank of his party and motioned Janey to take up the same position on the right. "From here on we can move faster," he told the librarians. "No point in you people going home without having ridden a cow pony at anything but a walk."

"You're the expert."

"I don't want to miss a thing."

"I'll try anything once." The four women were inexperienced but game, and with Beau and Spot acting as guidons their horses cantered without any trouble. Five minutes later Rob called out "whoa" and brought Beau to an instant standstill. Janey held Spot back, and the laughing excited women joggled or bumped to a stop between them.

"That was wonderful," one of the women said. "But now I'm lost. I don't even know in which direction we're headed."

"We're nearly home," Rob said, and pointed out the shabby cluster of adobe buildings of the Rancho del Fuego. "We'll cool off going down."

Janey looked around her and was surprised to see that the windmill, which she had been told yesterday was on the ranch of some people named Murez, was on her left when she had expected it to be straight ahead. I'm all mixed up too, she realized. It's going to take me ages to get my bearings, unless the rides we've taken so far are exceptionally confusing.

An hour later when she and Rob and Twinks rattled onto the main road to Lope in the truck she asked them about the trails.

"But they're all cinchy!" Twinks looked shocked. "I could find my way around Sepique and Frijoles Ridge blindfolded, and yesterday morning you and Rob only went around the little hills nearest the house. I couldn't get mixed up if I tried."

"I reckon you could in Connecticut," Rob said. "Or any other place you hadn't been before. You keep forgetting that everything out here is brand-new to Janey."

"But it doesn't always seem new." Janey nodded to the tin porch roof that connected the feed store and a half a dozen other shops that were the center of Lope. "This looks like a town in a western movie. And so do those men in Stetson hats and boots outside that bar. It's the country itself that throws me. I keep thinking I've been there before or know the way and then I am lost!"

"We'll take Frijoles Ridge again this afternoon," Rob said as he led the way into the feed store. "That and Sepique are easy to learn because they're mostly through open country. The country west of the ranch's more closed in and besides the trail washes out pretty often. After a heavy rain you have to pick out decent footing and keep your bearings at the same time, and that can be tricky even for someone who was raised here."

"It sounds impossible!" Janey said, and inwardly rejected her idea of riding to Fortune by herself. "Unless you'll get me a horse with built-in radar!"

"Yes, ma'am." Rob grinned as he moved over to the counter. "I reckon it wouldn't be much harder to find than the horse Betsy Appleton's looking for."

"Betsy wants a horse that's fast, snappy-looking, *and* gentle as a cow, all in one," Twinks explained, and took a deep breath of the sweet, malty air. "Boy, this place smells good."

Rob bought a sack of oats and a quarter ton of baled hay, which a young Indian helped him to carry out to the street. "Let's go, Janey," Twinks urged as they began loading the truck. "'Nita lives right around the corner from the drugstore."

Janey shook her head, too intrigued by a group of Indians, three men in big undented black sombreros and two small boys, who had gathered around the truck, to move. Rob greeted them by name, they answered in guttural monosyllabic Spanish and went on watching him load in stolid, unembarrassed silence. As the young man from the store handed up the last bale a few strands tore loose and dropped beneath the truck. The smallest Indian boy picked it up, said something in Spanish, and gave it to one of the men. He dusted it off against his trousers and put it

80

on the truck with a comment in Spanish that made Rob laugh out loud.

"The joker was Tom Little Finger," he told Janey a few moments later as they drove off. "He said if we didn't get rain soon my horses probably wouldn't thank him for dusting off that hay. If it's a real drought he said to bring 'em down and they could lick off his breeches."

Twinks giggled and Janey looked up at Rob. "I'm surprised. I thought watching them just stand there without even offering to help they looked more wooden than human."

"Don't you believe it," Rob said. "They didn't help because Pedro, the chap from the feed store, and I hadn't asked them to, and so according to their lights it would have been rude—almost insulting—if they had. But they didn't miss anything and you can bet that Tom isn't the only one who was amused. Indians have a mighty keen sense of humor but they don't go in for showing it off any more than they like to show pain or fear."

"How about Juan?" Janey asked. "D'you mean to say he's capable of seeing that things are absurd and being amused by them?"

"Juan can be awful funny when he wants to be!" Twinks spoke up before Rob could answer. "Much funnier than that Tom."

Rob shrugged. "Perhaps Twinks is right," he said. "But for the last few years Juan and I haven't been amused by the same things. Anyway I don't see enough of him any more to judge." He pulled up near a small adobe house as he spoke, and Twinks jumped out before he had turned off his engine. "There's Miss 'Nita," she shouted. "Hi. Hi! Miss 'Nita, have you the pictures ready?"

"The ones that were worth printing are ready," Miss Murphy said as she shook hands with Janey and Rob. "You can look at them now and then we'll go to the drugstore for a soda. Unless you'd rather have a Coke here. I'm so thoroughly packed to go off tomorrow I can't offer you anything else."

"Soda for me." Twinks skipped down the hall apparently completely at home. "I wish you weren't going away. I hate it when you're off picture taking."

81

"Oh, I won't be long." Miss Murphy led the way into a cool whitewashed room that looked out on a tiled patio beyond. "This is my combination studio and all-purpose living room," she told Janey, and spread out the pictures on the dark, polished surface of a big table. "My darkroom's in what was built as a kitchen by a Spaniard who didn't pamper his wife or cook with excess windows."

"Janey, look at these!" Twinks was already pawing over the photographs. "This is the first picture we've ever had of Tote that makes him look as cute and bright as he really is! Miss 'Nita really sees things!"

As Janey looked over the clear, revealing prints she realized that Twinks's comment held for the rest of Miss Murphy's work as well as the photograph of the donkey. "I was right there when you took these," she told Miss Murphy, and held up a study of Betsy Appleton, "but I feel as though I must have had on blinders. This picture of Betsy really looks like her and yet it's positively handsome."

"That's because most of her is hidden behind the corral fence," Twinks said, "so you only see her face and don't know the rest of her looks like the fat woman in a circus."

"No, it's because her features and her character, which are good, will last," Miss Murphy said. "And the puppy fat won't. But these are my successes and I didn't print the fiascoes."

"I've never seen photographs like them," Janey said when Miss Murphy handed her half a dozen small reprints.

"These are for you," Miss Murphy said, "and the top one is for you to send to your mother. I hope she likes it."

"Thank you! But you really shouldn't," Janey began, and as she saw the picture of herself holding Blue Belle, a horse she had not ridden as yet, she looked up in amazement. "Why, I didn't even know you were taking this!"

"That's why it's good." Twinks craned her neck to see better. "Posed pictures are mostly awful stiff and dopey."

"Not all of them," Miss Murphy said, and handed Rob a big manila envelope. "These are the ones you wanted, Rob. If you need more let me know. I haven't begun to pay you back for all the rides I had last spring."

"You've paid and then some!" Rob said, but when he began to open the big envelope Miss Murphy put out her hand and stopped him. "Wait and open it up when you get home," she said. "You've seen all the prints already, and it's time we went and had our soda."

Both Rob and Janey tried thanking her again, but she cut them short and picked up an album that looked almost as large as she was. "We'll take this along to look at in the drugstore," she said. "I want to prove to Twinks that some posed pictures are worth printing."

She led the way the half block to the drugstore. There was no one at the counter but she marched past it into a back room where three round tables and a collection of wire-backed chairs stood in front of the shelves of druggist jars and bottles. "This used to be an ice-cream parlor," she said as they sat down. "In the days when the U.S. cavalry wives first tried to make Lope respectable. Now Bill Grieves saves it as a retreat for a few specially lucky and favored customers."

The small wispy proprietor beamed at her. "You're special for sure, Miss 'Nita," he said. "You and any of your friends."

"Thanks, Bill," she said, and after they had given their orders spread out the album where everyone could see it. There were portraits of Indians in full war dress and in ordinary clothes like the ones Janey had just seen. There were white people, too, Spaniards and Yankees, and toward the back of the book pictures of Lope itself and the country immediately around it.

"I've tried to take a composite portrait of a town," Miss 'Nita said once, and pointed to a picture of a wrinkled old man in an antiquated uniform. "Do you remember him, Rob? Sergeant Sam Gallaghar?"

Rob nodded enthusiastically. "Don't I, though! He could throw a quarter up in the air and wing it with a rifle when he was nearly eighty. I saw him do it myself."

From then on as Miss Murphy turned the pages she drew Rob

out into giving them snatches of local history or short, pithy descriptions of the people in some of the photographs. "That's old Jack Farquar," Rob said once, and pointed to the man's high-heeled cowboy boots in the picture. "He used to make his own boots and he told me that years ago he could tell what every man in Albuquerque did just by looking at his feet. Cowhand, prospector, salesman, or anything else. I guess you could still do it in a small place."

Near the end of the book there was a portrait study of a tall, dark man towering above the table Janey had just seen at Miss Murphy's house. "That's Hugh, my husband," Miss Murphy said. "He loved that old Spanish table because it was high enough for his long legs."

"My, he was tall!" Janey said, and, feeling she had made a break, added, "and very good-looking."

"Yes," Miss Murphy said, "and he needed me—that was the miraculous thing—almost as much as I needed him." Janey stirred and Miss Murphy looked up, her dark eyes glowing with remembered happiness. "Need may not sound very romantic but it's an essential part of love, of the lasting kind anyway."

She turned to the last pictures, and as she spoke about them she sounded as natural and unself-conscious as when she had begun. "That's the lot," she said, and jumped up, looking gnomelike and diminutive next to Rob. "And if Twinks isn't convinced that posed pictures don't need to be stuffy or if Janey's bored stiff it's all your fault, Rob Baker, for letting them fall into my clutches. You know I never know when to stop."

"I wouldn't have missed it for anything." Janey struggled to find words which could express what the last hour had meant to her. "I can't possibly thank you enough."

A few minutes later they said good-by and drove back to the ranch. "That was fun," Twinks said as Rob backed the truck to the crumbling adobe stable. "I haven't had a chocolate soda for ages."

"Miss Murphy's unique." Once more Janey tried to communicate what she had felt, but Twinks wasn't listening and Rob had already begun to unload.

"This hay isn't too good," he said, and lugged a bale forward. "But I had to buy it."

"Where are you going to put it?" Janey peered up at a small, square window. "Up there in the hay loft?"

"No, I'm not!" Rob said, and Twinks giggled noisily. He turned to her, frowning, and Janey saw his face and neck grow crimson. "You two go along and tell Mom, I'm coming," he went on, and pushed a bale irritably with his foot. "I'll handle storing this sawdust alone."

The girls walked up to the house, and Janey went into her own room to tidy up for luncheon. Rob was really put out, she thought as she brushed her hair. Was it Twinks's giggling, the hay, or something I said? I wish Miss Murphy wasn't leaving so soon. She's the only person who can tell me what is and what isn't a boner in this family.

Fortunately that afternoon and the next few days went off very smoothly. By Saturday, Janey felt that she really understood the invisible tides that controlled the Baker household. Mrs. Baker's music lessons, always given away from home, and Twinks's Tuesday and Friday evening performances in Albuquerque created as definite a time schedule as Uncle John Baits's commuting trains. The time of Rob's work which dealt with customers necessarily varied, but he cleaned and groomed his horses as regularly as though he were punching a time clock.

He was always up and out before anyone else in the household, and usually worked out-of-doors as long as there was light. She never saw him go through the door to the room next to Mrs. Baker's, which she assumed must be his, but he often disappeared in the direction of the stable right after supper.

A few evenings after her arrival Janey wandered down to the stable and reached the corral in time to see Rob canter away from it, mounted on Beau, with all the other horses herded riderless in front of him. She looked after him curiously, her ears ringing with the thud of the horses' hoofs on the hard-packed clay. "He's taking them to graze." Twinks came up beside her. "There's a place beyond the gate where they can get a decent feed, if he doesn't use it too often and nobody else gets there first. And now come on up to the house and play cards with me. Please, Janey."

"O.K." Janey followed her toward the house, but her mind was still on Rob driving his little herd of horses through the twilight. No wonder he had been upset at the thought of the gate being left open the night she had arrived. The Bakers were better off than most of their neighbors as to water, but, even so, feed was a constant problem and grass that Mr. Wentie would have scorned was well worth protecting from stray cattle.

"I'm afraid the evenings are going to be terribly dull for you." Mrs. Baker turned off the radio as they came into the house. "We're so far from any other young people."

"Lucky for me." Janey struggled unsuccessfully to hide a yawn. "The air and being out-of-doors all day makes me feel simply marvelous, but as soon as it gets dark I'm practically asleep."

It was perfectly true. As one dry invigorating day followed another Janey was out-of-doors and riding for hours. In the evening she was so healthily sleepy it was hard to write letters or put down anything in the diary, which had been Mum's going-away present, and almost impossible to think constructively about new ways and means of locating Gramps's treasure.

Usually if there was anyone riding who knew the countryside Janey went out with a small party the way she had with Miss Murphy, but once or twice Rob asked her to help him in the ring with the younger children. Rob was often very quiet or gruffly outspoken with his family, but Janey was amazed at his patience and skill in handling the energetic children who made up a big part of his business.

"How do you stand it?" she asked one Friday afternoon when two especially obstreperous small boys had finally been called for. "I thought when those kids began snatching at the horses' bits and trying to fire off those toy cap pistols I'd wring their necks."

"It's all part of the job," Rob said, "and I'm lucky in liking little kids." He started toward the corral and turned suddenly. "Listen, it's early yet. How would you like it if we saddled up and went below Sepique to see if there's any grazing over there? I'll take Beau and you can ride Blue Belle. You haven't tried her yet."

"I'd love it!" Janey said. "But are you sure it's O.K.? You don't use Blue Belle much, and if I do something wrong you'll be upset and I'll feel guilty!"

"I'll chance it," Rob said, and a few moments later they rode off toward the west, where the fading light made the Sandia Mountains mysterious and beautiful.

"Belle's a treat," Janey said, when they settled down after their first canter. "You could ride her with a silk thread and she has gaits that are out of this world. How old is she?"

"Four," Rob said. "I traded in a pretty good Chevvie for the truck I have now to get the money to buy her. She was dirt cheap because if anyone yanks at her mouth she's too hot to handle and she's no good at range work. I'd like to keep her for Twinks to grow up to, but I won't be able to afford it. Best thing would be if I could find someone who can ride her the way you do and sell her to a good home."

"That sounds exactly like Auguste Wentie and a mare called Sensation!" Janey said. "He's an old Austrian who runs a livery stable at home. I was supposed to ride Sensation in the ladies' jumping class at the Fourth of July horse show to help him find a buyer, but first I gave it up for a tennis tournament and then I came out here before the Fourth anyway."

"How come?" Rob asked. "Are you a champion tennis player or didn't you like the mare?"

"Neither," Janey said, and before she realized what she was doing she told Rob the whole story, not only about her long-standing friendship with Auguste Wentie, but even about Larry Saunders and the miserable afternoon when she had found her name erased from the bulletin board.

When Janey had finished Rob said nothing. As they rode on the creak of saddle leather seemed as accusing as mean laughter, and Janey reddened uncomfortably. I'm a fool! The words pumped through her mind. I shouldn't have told him about Larry. From now on he'll think I'm just out for what I can get. "It somehow sounds so small and disgusting out here," she said finally, and nodded at the tremendous, constantly shifting landscape ahead of her. "But the world and the people Larry kept talking about sounded terribly exciting compared to Warwick and the Warwick High. I—I'm not usually a gold digger."

"I wasn't thinking about you," Rob said. "I was thinking about that tutor—Larry what's his name. Do you mean to say that maverick is going to be a teacher?"

"No." Janey looked up surprised at Rob's vehemence. "Larry's going to law school and then I think he wants to go into the foreign service and eventually politics. That's why the Gregorys and Ravenals were so important."

"Thank God!" Rob said, and grinned over at her. "And don't look so startled. I'm interested because I care a lot—too much probably—about kids and teaching."

"And you're going to teach yourself? Have you always wanted to?"

Rob nodded. "Yes," he said. "Ever since I was a little kid at Los Alamos School. That's the place that shut up overnight when the atom project was set up. A friend of the family's gave me a scholarship there during that last year."

"But you must have been awfully young," Janey said. "Really small fry."

"I was but I knew then and I know now that someday, somehow, I'm going to run a school like that myself. I've even got the site picked out—Cinder Cone Canyon, our old ranch. And now go ahead and laugh. Mom and her friends think I'm cracked. Cuckoo. Lunatic."

"I don't!" Janey found herself hating Mrs. Baker for what she had done to her only son. There was nothing she could say about that, and she came out with the next thought that entered her mind. "Was it at Los Alamos that you first were excited about

Indian archaeology? I envy you stumbling on an interest that's stayed with you while you were in grade school."

"In a way that's how it happened. At least Los Alamos was the first place that I saw intelligent grownups who were as fascinated as I was. Janey, look, the first day I can get off when Mom doesn't need the car we'll drive to Chaco. The prehistoric pueblos up there are really worth seeing. And before that, when we have a small party of people who can ride decently, we'll go over to see the ruins of a kiva east of Lope. I didn't realize Indians were a special interest of yours or I'd have tried to figure out some side trips for you to take before now."

"Well, you pointed out that hogan the first ride we took." Janey smiled at Rob's enthusiasm. "Only I don't really know anything about Indians, living in Connecticut all my life."

"But there's the collection at the Natural History Museum in New York and the Heye Foundation. And right in your own state there's the Peabody Museum. The U. subscribes to their journals and periodicals, and some of the field work they've done out here is magnificent."

Janey frowned at Blue Belle's neck, momentarily silenced. Even when she was a very small girl and had listened spellbound to Gramps's stories of the West, including his tales of Indians, she had been bored stiff by school trips and reading about the same subject. It would be tactless to say that to Rob, so she tried a different approach. "I'm an absolute ignoramus," she said, and thinking of Maisie's and Cynthia's clinging-vine technique, she let her voice grow drawling and arch. "An Indian ignoramus. But if you drove me off on trips perhaps I could learn not to be. Why don't you all start off by showing me your own collection?"

The eagerness faded from Rob's face. "How'd you find out I'd ever made one?" he asked. "Twinks been blathering? You surely didn't guess just because I pointed out that hogan."

"No. And Twinks hasn't said a word. It was Buck, I think. Yes, I'm sure of it. Buck Hughes when he drove me out here."

"He told you the Lone Ranger was all wound up in pot hunting and his gee-gees," Rob said bitterly. "I can hear him."

"But, Rob, why do you care so much?" Janey was too interested to stick to her clinging-vine pose. "Why does anything that Buck Hughes says matter to you? Your paths don't cross much, do they?"

"No." Rob swatted a non-existent fly on Beau's neck, and the light slap was a full stop and period to the conversation. They rode on for another half mile when Rob turned his horse toward home. "Not enough grass here to make it worth bringing the horses over," he said. "We'll have to find grazing nearer home or I'll have to buy more feed."

"And I'll bet it's expensive," Janey said, and brought Blue Belle up beside Beau. "I know at home Mr. Wentie's overhead's really wicked."

"I'm doing better than I expected," Rob said. "I get a dollar an hour for straight rides and extra for a guide and double when there's instruction. Since you've been out here to help, things have been going great guns. If it keeps up I'll have all I need for next winter and be able to help out a little at home."

"You mean Hank was right and I'm earning my keep?" Janey's natural candor completely replaced the archness she had attempted a few minutes earlier. "I thought that was sort of nice Nellying to my pride from the way Mum built it up."

"I thought it was going to be worse than that." Rob grinned at her as he spoke. "When Hank mentioned that you liked horses and Mom said what a help you'd be I didn't see it. I thought I'd be riding herd on you all summer, instead of which you've really helped. You earn your keep for sure."

"Good." Janey was too pleased and surprised at his compliment to say more, and they rode on for a little while in a companionable silence until Rob broke it by talking about Blue Belle.

"I think if you like her it'd make sense if you rode her regularly from now on," he said. "The dudes can't manage her and she really needs someone to handle her who won't get impatient or tough with her. She'd be a honey if you worked on her for the next few weeks."

"I'd love it." Janey patted the mare's gleaming neck as she spoke.

"And if she turns out well it'd make me feel better about letting down old Mr. Wentie about Sensation."

They rode home the rest of the way talking easily about the horses, the need of rain, and their plans for the next day. Rob's not bad company when he's sure of himself, Janey thought as they neared the corral. It's only when he's unconfident that he goes all stiff and secretive and prickly. At that moment they both heard Twinks shouting to them. "Hurry up, you two," she called out. "There's fried chicken, southern style, and sopaipillas for supper and I'm practically starved."

"My favorite foods!" Janey said. She turned out Belle and followed Rob into the stable. Neither of the stalls was used, but she knew he always swept up the hard-packed earthen square of floor before he left and so she looked around for the broom. It stood against the ladder to the loft. As she moved toward it Rob blocked her way and Twinks cried out, "Oh, Janey, don't! Please don't."

"Why ever not? Cleaning up a stable floor isn't going to kill me."

Rob stood rigid and Twinks smiled with self-conscious sweetness. "I don't think Mother would like it," she said, and it was clear that was the first excuse that had come into her head. "I don't think she'd approve of a young lady doing stable work."

"Silly!" Janey said. "She's never objected to my cleaning tack or rubbing down the horses."

"That's, well, that's different." Twinks pulled at Janey's arm as she spoke. "Come on, Janey."

"I will." Janey struggled not to get irritated with Twinks's mosquitolike insistence. "Just as soon as we've finished. Rob, do you want me to go up to the loft for grain?"

"No! Not now!" Twinks answered for him and pulled Janey harder than ever. She turned and saw that Rob was still standing by the ladder, looking as tense and alert as an Irish terrier. "You two go ahead," he said, and his eyes avoided Janey's. "Tell Mom I'll be up in just a couple of minutes."

Janey hesitated, wondering if she had imagined the feeling of trust, almost of partnership, which he had conveyed to her while they were out riding. "I don't understand," she began, but Mrs. Baker's high, carrying voice calling from the kitchen porch interrupted her. "Janey, Twinks, Robert. Do hurry. The chicken won't be fit to eat."

"We're coming!" Twinks answered, and, latching her arm through Janey's, jerked her forward toward the house.

CHAPTER SEVEN

Nothing more was said about the stable or the stable loft that evening. The next morning as Janey walked down to the corral after breakfast the whole episode seemed much less significant than it had the day before. The loft's probably Twinks's secret hiding place, Janey decided, and she's made Rob promise not to let anyone else up there.

As Janey came up to the line of groomed and saddled horses she realized that Rob must have been working since daybreak and remembered that he had told her Saturday was always his busiest day. He had a small party of office workers from Albuquerque all ready to go off, but when he saw Janey he left them and hurried toward her. "The Appletons are booked for ten," he said. "Can you take them over the Frijoles Ridge trail without getting lost?"

"It's the only ride I'm fairly sure of," Janey said. "What horses shall we take?"

"Same as the last time you went out with them." Rob swung into his saddle as he spoke. "And don't let Betsy swap horses midway no matter what happens. You can take Blue Belle out this afternoon."

"O.K. Thanks." Janey expected Rob to canter off after his party. He hesitated, looking down at her, and suddenly his face lit with one of his rare, amused smiles.

"If you need any help ask old Juan," he cracked. "He'll turn up sure as shooting as soon as Mom leaves. Oh, Lord! Look at those dames!"

He cantered off after the giggling, shouting girls, and Janey watched him until he was out of sight. A few moments later Mrs. Baker drove off, but there was no sign of either the Appletons or Juan's pickup truck, and after a few minutes Janey went back to the house to get her watch.

When she went outside again the Appletons' car was not in sight. The cement road looked emptier and uglier than ever. Janey grimaced at the litter of beer cans and rubbish that glittered on both sides of it as far as she could see. It takes longer for things to disintegrate out here, she realized, as she walked on. It's too dry for weeds and grass to grow over everything, and there aren't any trees so trash shows up more than it does at home.

She was already accustomed to the tawny color of the adobe walls, and no longer missed the familiar white and green of the houses at home. Still it continued to strike her as strange to walk off the ground-level porch straight into open country without any intermediary of steps, or path, or enclosed lawn.

If I lived out here I'd have to have a garden, she thought, and looked with disfavor at the line of wilting zinnias someone had planted a little way from the back door. Not just a few dried-up flowers, but bushes and shade trees. She was thinking of the overgrown garden at home with the old-fashioned swing and the green, bushy hiding places the twins adored, when she heard a thin, reedy little voice singing somewhere behind her.

It's Twinks, Janey realized, and after one more look down the road she moved up over a small dunelike hill to find her. At the top she stopped short, staring in fascinated wonder at the sight directly below her.

Twinks was naked to the waist, dressed in a short kiltlike garment of perfectly matched white feathers. Her bare feet padded in time to her own wordless singing, and as she lifted her arms a white and purple feather stole rose and fell in a perfect image of wings. The child wove forward and backward, bowing toward the sunlight and then dancing again, utterly unconscious of an audience.

It's beautiful. And it all has a form, a meaning, Janey realized. It's some kind of a ritual dance she has been taught. She looked around instinctively expecting to see Twinks's teacher, but the great sweeping countryside was perfectly empty except for the small solitary figure below her. Janey held her breath for fear of breaking the spell, while Twinks danced on as tirelessly as though all of the unseen energy of the sun-baked hills funneled up inside of her.

The child bowed to the west, then to the north and the south. As she turned to bow to the east she faced Janey and stopped short. She did not speak, and in the sudden silence the feathers on her wings settled with a murmur that was like a sigh.

"Don't stop. Please." Janey was so certain she had intruded on something secret and precious that she fumbled for words. "I'm so terribly sorry I interrupted you. I didn't mean to spy. I—just—happened to be out here."

"And you won't tell Mother? Not ever, ever, ever?"

"No. I won't. But, Twinks, wouldn't she like that dance you've just done? I think it's the most perfect thing I've ever seen."

Twinks swore, letting out a blast of experienced obscenity that was an appalling contrast to everything else about her. "Mom'd hate it," she said, "because it's Indian and because doing it makes me just despise tap dancing more than ever. That's why Mom almost didn't let me go to the ceremonials with Miss 'Nita last year and it's why she thinks Miss 'Nita's a bad influence. You bet Mom knows Miss 'Nita thinks this is real dancing and tapping is just bunk."

"Did Miss Murphy give you the feathers?" Janey asked. "They're perfectly beautiful."

"Nope. Old Juan gave 'em to me," Twinks said, and took a step forward so that once more her costume spread out in a perfect winglike pattern. "But Mom wouldn't let me do an Indian dance in public even if it paid like anything. I tell you she's so against anything to do with Indians it's nuts."

"When did Juan give you all this?" Janey asked, and touched the cleverly contrived stole with wonder. "Rob said he'd be up here this morning but I thought that was a joke."

"Are you kidding?" Twinks put her hands on her hips, and once more her feathers dropped around her. "Juan only comes to see me when he knows for sure I'm alone. He gave me these almost a year ago."

How did you ever keep it a secret? Janey wondered. Mrs. Baker cleans every inch of the house almost every day. Suddenly she thought she understood, and smiled down at Twinks. "Does Rob keep them for you?" she asked. "Is that why the door to his room beyond your mother's is always locked?"

Twinks looked puzzled, and then her face cleared and she giggled. "That's just a closet and you're in Rob's room!" she said. "He sleeps over the stable and he only got the space fixed up the day before you came and Mom had been after him and after him. We thought you were trying to go look at it last night."

"And you keep your feathers up there?" Janey said. "Is that why you didn't want me to go up yesterday?"

Twinks made a delicate little tracery with the toe of one foot. "Well not 'xactly," she said. "I did all last winter, but now that it's a bedroom and Mom goes there once in a while to clean when Rob isn't around to stop her, I don't."

Janey swallowed, as a whole series of incidents from Rob's cold welcome on became unpleasantly clear. "I get it, or I begin to," she said, but Twinks didn't notice her discomfort.

"Rob and Juan aren't special friends any more," she said. "Not since the summer after Grandpa Marston died, when Rob hurt his foot."

"But—but surely Juan didn't have anything to do with Rob's accident?"

"'Course not!" Twinks said. "Rob hurt himself in an old mine shaft, and Juan had been warning him not to go into it. But when Rob was in the hospital Juan practically camped out down there, and I guess what he said made Rob fidgety."

"I don't blame Rob!" Janey said. "I think if Juan or anybody else kept saying 'I told you so' to me I'd hate him."

Twinks grinned. "Me too," she said. "But Rob isn't like that. He doesn't see Juan any more'n he can help, but when Juan was sick last winter Rob felt awful. I guess Rob doesn't really hate anybody 'cept maybe Buck Hughes. And even that isn't what I'd call hating."

Janey took a step toward Twinks. "I know Rob doesn't like Buck," she said. "But I can't understand why. Do you know?"

Twinks looked amused. "Oh, sure," she said. "Mom keeps saying how perfect Buck is but she really doesn't know much about him. Chuck Hemsted, Rob's best friend, had a girl—name of Dolores—and Buck snitched her. Chuck had never had a girl before and he was just sick over losing Dolores. And Rob felt awful badly for Chuck. They've been buddies for ages."

"What about this Dolores?" Janey put in. "Does she live near here?"

"Not any more. She married a guy named Scott and moved to Texas. But Janey, come and look. I've got something special to show you." Twinks took Janey's hand and led her toward a clump of barrel cactus further away from the house. "See that," she said, and pointed to a wooden box half buried in the dry clay behind the cactus. "That's my own private hiding place and I didn't even have to dig the hole. It was there all the time, but I never saw it until a couple of months ago when Juan and I found it together."

Janey looked around her and realized that the hole was probably a minute branch of what had once been a small river bed. "Is the hole as dry as this all year around?" she asked, and Twinks nodded enthusiastically.

"Sure thing, because if it rains the water runs off into the deep part of the arroyo. And see, the feathers are just perfect. Juan

97

says if we trust to Earth to take care of our treasure for us she'll always guard them." Janey nodded, thinking of what Miss Murphy had said about the countryside being slow to relinquish its secrets. Even the surface of the earth around here is mysterious and inscrutable, Janey thought. In spite of all the open space and bright sunlight.

Twinks turned and peered up at Janey's face. "You promise you won't tell?" she demanded, and it was clear Janey's silence had made her apprehensive. "You must swear by the four seasons and the four sacred crops you won't tell. Or are you like Mom and don't believe in any Indian things, even the very old magic ones?"

"I don't know anything about them," Janey confessed. "But I swear honor bright I won't tell anyone about your secret."

"O.K. I guess that'll do," Twinks said, and took off her feathered costume and slipped into the faded sunsuit. "But I wish someone around here besides me really liked Indians and Indian things."

"How about Rob?" Janey began, but Twinks interrupted her.

"Oh, I don't mean studying and brainy work. I mean having fun and being favorite friends like Juan and me. Rob's stuff's pretty dull, and it just makes Mom hate Indians worse'n ever. You see Rob doesn't make any money out of it and, besides, he hurt his foot when he was looking for Zuni pots. Mom wasn't a bit sorry when Rob had to get rid of most of his collection this spring."

"Could you tell me more about that?" Janey asked, when a horn sounded on the road below them and she realized it must be the Appletons. "Twinks, I'll have to go," she said. "But thank you for showing me everything, and I promise again I won't tell a soul."

Janey hurried off, but at the top of the rise of ground she looked back. Twinks had already hidden her treasure and was scuttling away down the arroyo with a speed that reminded Janey of the lizard that had disappeared from under Chesty's nose the first day she and Rob had gone out riding.

CHAPTER EIGHT

As Janey neared the stable Betsy Appleton jumped out of the car and ran toward the corral. Mrs. Appleton was in a cotton dress and was obviously not intending to ride. "I'm going to ride Sponge!" Betsy shouted. As she rushed toward the sorrel horse he put his ears back and shifted his feet ominously.

"Look out or he'll kick!" Janey reached for Sponge's head.

"Oh, Sponge is very gentle," Mrs. Appleton called out from her car. "And I haven't time to ride today, so I thought Betsy could ride him instead of me. Obviously Rob wasn't planning to use him for anyone else."

"No, of course not." Janey struggled to be tactful and firm at the same time. "And Sponge is fine. He just doesn't like anything fast or unexpected happening."

"Well, I'm going to ride him," Betsy said. "And I want to go to Elbow Crest. I'm sick of that old Bean Ridge Frijoles ride."

"I'm afraid I'd get lost going to Elbow Crest," Janey said, and turned toward Mrs. Appleton. "Rob was expecting us to go over Frijoles. It takes just an hour."

"Oh, Betsy's been to Elbow Crest," Mrs. Appleton said. "And it's good with me if you take her off for a long ride. I can't possibly call for her in an hour."

She drove off and Betsy hauled herself up on Sponge's back. "Everything's all set," she said, and grinned smugly at Janey. "We're going to have a swell time."

Janey said nothing as she turned Pigeon into the corral and unhitched Chesty. She had an uneasy feeling that Rob would disapprove of Betsy's new plan, but now that Mrs. Appleton had driven off she didn't see what she could do but give in. Rob should have stayed around until we left, Janey told herself. After all, he's the one who's responsible.

She mounted Chesty and rode off beside Betsy at a slow walk. At the first fork in the road Betsy went to the left and Janey hitched around in her saddle looking for a landmark. "Look, Betsy," she said, "shouldn't we keep that windmill to the right?"

"Nope," Betsy said. "And don't start fussing. I never forget roads and I don't get lost either. I could go to Elbow Crest blindfolded."

"Well, I couldn't," Janey said. "And I'm not at all sure Rob wants us to take such a long ride. He's probably counting on using Sponge again this afternoon."

"He can use Pigeon. And Mummy's going to pay for the long ride we're taking, so he isn't losing out."

Janey said nothing, and Betsy reined in and looked up at her curiously. "Why don't you want to go to Elbow Crest?" she demanded. "Are you scared of Rob? Or just smoochy about him the way people are in the movies?"

"Neither!" Janey snapped. "It's—it's only that you're on a strange horse and I'm not at all sure——"

"Don't worry!" Betsy interrupted. "You stay here and watch how I can make Sponge canter off by himself. It's only that dopey old Pidge that's the trouble. Just look at this!"

"Be careful!" Janey warned as Betsy cantered awkwardly forward. "Stay where I can see you."

"Oh sure!" Betsy called back, and at the same moment Janey

heard a man's deep voice at her right-hand side. She looked over her shoulder and saw Juan walking toward her, motioning for her to stop. "*Un momentito, por favor,*" Juan said. "*Me da susto este de irse sola la señorita a la Fortuna. Seguramente, no lo permita el señor Roberto.*"

He reached for Chesty's bridle as he spoke, his hand so close that Janey could see the pink of his finger tips startlingly light against his dark hand. She recoiled instinctively and pulled Chesty off to one side. Juan made a forlorn gesture and did not attempt to follow her. "*Perdóneme la señorita . . .*" he said gently, and it was clear from his voice and the expression on his face that he was trying to be helpful. "*Tengo que decirle que para ella no es sin peligro un paseo a Fortuna. No lo quisiera el señor McGovern su abuelo.*"

Janey looked around her, hoping against hope that Rob or someone else who could explain what Juan was trying to tell her might be within sight. There was nothing but the bare, range land nearby, and she looked further up the trail just in time to see Betsy Appleton disappearing around a curve.

"I can't wait!" Janey burst out and forced Chesty forward. "I don't understand a word you're saying and I've got to catch up with that girl!"

Juan stepped aside as she galloped off. A moment later she glanced back and saw him shuffling off to his truck with his head down and shoulders sagging—a perfect profile of disconsolation.

I can't help it, Janey thought, and shouted to Betsy to stop. Betsy slowed down and within a matter of moments Janey drew up beside her. "You shouldn't have done that!" she scolded. "I told you to stay where I could see you."

"I thought you could. And I don't see why you have to get all hot and bothered. Rob always lets me canter along here."

"It isn't that," Janey said breathlessly. "It's just that Juan, an old Indian who used to work for Rob's grandfather, stopped me and began jabbering at me in Spanish. I'm almost positive he was warning me about the trail to Fortune. And Rob says that the trails around here do wash out overnight."

"Sure they do," Betsy said. "But we're not going as far as Fortune, and I know the trail to Elbow Crest is O.K. I've been over it since the last flash flood. Jeepers, you really must be goofy about Rob."

"Don't be absurd!" Janey said, but for the first time all morning she was determined to take the Elbow Crest ride if it was her last act. "I think Juan made me nervous because I don't understand a word of Spanish."

"Neither do I," Betsy said soothingly. "And next year I'll have to start taking it at school and I know I'll just hate it. I never would have had to learn a word of it if we hadn't moved out here from Winnetka."

Betsy chattered on and on, and Janey rode beside her trying to figure out exactly what Juan had said. It was clearly about Rob and the trail to Fortune, and Gramps McGovern's name entered into it. What more there had been or why Juan had looked so concerned she had no way of knowing.

Finally Betsy stopped talking and there was no sound except the soft thud of the horses' hoofs, the creak of saddle leather, and the light tinkle of the bits. "I like riding noises," Betsy said once. "Don't you, Janey?"

Janey nodded, but as they moved on and on over the unfamiliar trail the muted, horsy sounds grated more and more unpleasantly on her tense nerves. I'm being a fool, she told herself. We're not going nearly as far as Fortune, and Mrs. Appleton knows exactly what we're doing. No matter what Juan was trying to say this ride can't be really dangerous.

Still, Janey's apprehensive mood increased, and when the trail narrowed so they had to go single file she suggested they turn back and take the Frijoles Ridge ride after all. "Nix!" Even Betsy's plump back looked stubborn. "Mum wants us to go to Elbow Crest. I told you she's paying for it."

Janey couldn't think of anything more to say so she followed Betsy in anxious silence. As the hill steepened, the soft, sandy footing of the open trail across the range gave way to a rocky slit of a path that twisted and turned between huge boulders and stunted precariously rooted pines. At last they went up an abrupt rise which was so narrow the dark mica-studded earth formed trenchlike walls on either side of them. This is a nightmare, Janey thought. We'll never get home alive. A moment later they came out onto a wooded ridge and Betsy shouted: "There's the Elbow!" She pointed to a shaft of red rock that appeared above the treetops beyond them. "I told you I knew the way! And now let's change horses. Sponge was hanging his head and sort of buck walking coming up, and you're lighter'n I am. Sponge almost made me dizzy."

"We're not changing horses!" Janey said. "Every horse goes up a steep incline that way. Now we ought to get off and let the horses rest and then go right back the way we came."

"Not a chance!" Betsy rode straight ahead. "There's a much better trail down over here and I'm going to take it. You can go back the old way if you're scared. But Rob wouldn't like it. He told me always to take the trail just north of the Elbow going down."

I wish Rob were here to make sure you know how to find it, Janey thought as she followed Betsy along the ridge. And even more I wish he'd never sent me out with you in the first place!

After a few moments they came to an opening where there was a view northward which seemed to stretch out to the very edges of the world. "That isn't bad, is it?" Betsy said, and went on before Janey could answer. "And now let's swap horses. I hate the way Sponge went up that last hill."

"Chesty did it exactly the same way." Janey patted his hot neck as she spoke. "It's the only way a horse has of climbing."

"Well, maybe." Betsy didn't sound very convinced. "But I bet Rob's Beau or that little mare Blue Belle would be different. Sponge is just an old plug. Almost as bad as Pigeon."

"You asked to ride Sponge," Janey pointed out, but Betsy didn't answer and only shrugged and veered off in what seemed to Janey a totally wrong direction. "Look, Betsy, are you sure this is the right way? I'll have to admit I'm lost."

"Well, I'm not!" Betsy said, and wheeled so sharply that Sponge missed colliding with Chesty by inches. "The good trail's right below us."

As far as Janey could see the mountainside below them was completely impassable and she called out: "Please, Betsy, let's go back the way we came. I'd much rather. Honestly."

"Oh, no, you wouldn't!" Betsy wobbled dangerously as she turned in the saddle to grin at Janey. "This is the trail Rob Baker always uses going home."

The next second Betsy and Sponge disappeared around the base of Elbow Rock and Janey hurried Chesty after them. I've got to stay close to her! Janey realized, and now her mouth felt dry with a kind of fear she had never known before. If Betsy falls off up here she'll be badly hurt!

Janey rode around the tall storm-pitted column of red rock and a moment later saw the trail for herself. It had been hidden before by trees and boulders, but now she could see a good, zigzag path slanting diagonally directly below her.

"Come on, Janey, it's super!" Betsy called back. "Easy as going down in an elevator. The horses just love it."

"Good," Janey got out, but she felt so lightheaded with relief that she didn't trust herself to look back until they had reached the tableland below the mountain. Then she turned in her saddle and caught sight of the top of the Elbow, but the trail itself was once more completely hidden. "I hand it to you," she said out loud. "I couldn't find that trail, from either end, in a million years."

"I told you I knew the way!" Betsy exulted. "And I told you I could ride old Spongy. It's a cinch." She clapped her heels into his sides as she spoke and the old horse reared with surprise. She jabbed at his mouth with her reins and the next moment he bolted!

For a nightmare instant Betsy jounced in her saddle. As Janey raced after her the child regained her balance and the two horses rushed forward together. "Give and take on your reins!" Janey ordered. "Now!"

Betsy did her best, and as Janey pulled Chesty down to a trot Sponge settled down beside him. "Jeepers!" Betsy panted when they finally had both horses standing still. "Sponge was awful!"

"I don't blame him." Janey pulled off her belt and looped it through Sponge's headstall to use as a lead line. "The way you kicked him and jerked him it's a wonder he didn't buck you off."

"I almost did fall off," Betsy wailed. "And Sponge was racing so I might have been killed. And that would have been Rob's fault. He told Mummy he had *safe* horses."

"He has!" Janey flamed up. "And you know it. You and your mother asked for Sponge when Rob knew you couldn't manage anything but Pigeon, and then when something goes wrong you start making excuses. Blaming Rob's the most perfectly disgusting thing I've ever heard and you'll be lucky if you ever ride any of his horses again."

Betsy burst into noisy tears. "I didn't mean it," she blubbered. "But please, please don't tell Mummy what happened."

"I won't," Janey said. "As long as after this you promise to ride the horse Rob has picked out for you over the trail he's decided on. And now let's get going."

They walked and trotted and walked again over the long sandy plain without any further trouble. As they came within sight of the corral Janey took back her belt. "Go ahead," she said, and nodded at Betsy. "And from now on if you ride Pigeon decently we won't say anything at all about what happened today."

"You mean you won't even tell Rob?" Betsy's voice fell to an awed whisper. "Not ever?"

"Not ever," Janey promised, and a little later they saw Rob hurrying toward them across the corral. Rob had his hat pulled way down over his forehead and he moved with such purposeful strides that he reminded Janey of a young and American version of Mr. Auguste Wentie. "Hi there, Rob," she called out. "You look like the riding master in Warwick when he's all ready to tell somebody just exactly how they did things in the old Imperial Cavalry."

Rob didn't answer or even glance at Janey until he had inspected both of the horses thoroughly. "They're both pretty well tuckered and Sponge has a loose shoe," he said finally. "So would you please tell me what this was all about? I thought you understood that Betsy was to ride Pigeon over Frijoles Ridge. When Mrs. Appleton drove in just a minute ago and said you'd gone to Elbow Crest I could hardly believe it. You told me yourself Frijoles is the only ride you know around here."

"Oh, Betsy was the pathfinder," Janey said airily, and slid out of her saddle. "She has a marvelous bump of direction."

Betsy gave Janey a look of slavish gratitude and scuttled toward her mother's car. When she reached it she called back, "Thanks for a swell ride, Janey. And Rob, next time I'm going to ride Pigeon. I'd really rather."

Janey waved good-by, and as she turned back saw that Rob was still looking at her with a stern, unsmiling face. "I'm waiting," he said, "to hear why you let Betsy ride Sponge to Elbow Crest."

"Because Mrs. Appleton said she could." Janey struggled for self-control as she spoke. "You weren't there, and if I'd been firm I had the feeling they'd have been so annoyed you might have lost two of your regular customers."

"I'd rather lose ten than take a chance on a bad accident. If Betsy had lost her head or been silly in any way near the top of Elbow she might have been badly hurt."

"I thought of that one myself!" Janey burst out, and told Rob just what she had gone through at the top of the mountain. "It's the most miserable experience I've ever had in my life," she finished. "Being scared for oneself is bad enough, but being scared and responsible for someone else is absolutely horrible."

"I know," Rob said. "It's the worst fear there is, and I'm sorry that in a way I let you in for it." Janey stared back at him, too amazed by his sudden understanding to speak, and he went on: "You know, I've been trying to figure out how to handle Betsy for months and from the way she asked to ride Pigeon just now I guess you've found it. What's the secret?"

Before Janey could answer, Twinks tore toward them. "Janey! Telephone for you. Beat it. In the kitchen."

"Go ahead," Rob said. "I'll put away the horses and come right along."

Janey hurried off to the house and picked up the receiver. "Hello," she said, and heard Buck Hughes's voice at the other end.

"You sound winded," he said. "Have the Bakers been running you ragged? I'm calling from Sis's, and she and Herb and I want to know if you all could come down here for supper tonight and practice some square sets? Herb's a pretty good caller."

"It sounds like fun. Would you hold on while I find out if Rob can use the car tonight? I think he's just coming up from the stable."

"I'd like to drive out and pick you up," Buck said. "So if Rob can't get the car or doesn't want to go, tell him there are plenty of guys out at the base who'd jump at coming. My friend Tom Pierce is driving in to town as soon as he's off duty so he can give anybody extra a lift. My cousin Mary Alice Hughes is staying here with the Weavers, and we've lined up a married couple and a neighbor of ours by the name of Elsie Kohler but we really need you for the fourth lady."

"How about Tina Ramirez? Isn't she going?" The words popped out of Janey's mouth before she could stop them, and she heard Buck's laugh rumble over the telephone wire.

"Oh, Tina and I are all washed up," he said, "so I'm back in the lonely hearts club. But if you'll come the eight will be all set. I'll just get another navy pal and we'll let Rob keep on playing cowboy."

"No." Janey felt suddenly protective. "Hold the wire. Rob and Twinks have just come in." She turned and spoke with her hand over the mouthpiece. "Rob, Buck Hughes and the Weavers want us for supper and afterwards to practice some square sets. Do you want to go and will your mother need the car tonight?"

"No. She never uses it on Saturdays, but listen I'm not sure if you'd like——"

"Buck, we'd both love to come!" Janey spoke into the telephone before Rob finished his sentence. "Mrs. Baker doesn't need the car so we'll drive down to the Weavers' around seven. Thanks a million."

She turned to see Rob walk through the kitchen, his shoulders thrown back and his wiry body tensed as he forced himself not to limp. I'm a fool, Janey thought, and her hand flew to her mouth. It probably kills him to dance on that bad foot. I wonder if I ought to call Buck right back?

"What's bitten you?" Twinks asked curiously. "First you look all thrilled and girly girly and now you look scared sick."

"It's Rob. His foot. I should have thought about it sooner. Won't it kill him to dance on it?"

"Nope. Do him good," Twinks said. "He's supposed to exercise it and not just hold it stiff in a stirrup all day. If he keeps doing his exercises the doctor says he'll be perfectly O.K. in a year. He was just being stuffy about going to Buck's and the Weavers'. Don't let him get away with it."

"I won't!" Janey laughed at Twinks's firmness. "I think we'll have fun."

"Sure you will," Twinks said. "Rob's good at square sets. But how you do it all beats me."

"Do what?" Janey was so pleased and relieved she wanted to hug the small, quizzical girl in front of her. "Do what, Twinks?"

"Everything!" Twinks said, and for once her pale, too old little face looked as open and wondering as Linda's or Pete's. "Get Rob to go to Buck's, get that fat Betsy Appleton so she *asks* to ride Pigeon, and get me to tell you about my you-know-what. How do you do it, Janey?"

"Luck!" Janey pirouetted across the kitchen floor as she spoke. "What my Gramps used to call the 'wild Irish McGovern luck.'"

"Mr. McGovern didn't sound lucky himself," Twinks said. "I answered the telephone when he called up to speak to Mom the day before he died, and he didn't sound wild, or Irish, or a bit lucky."

"What did he say?" Janey stopped in the middle of a dance step to look at Twinks. "Exactly what did Gramps McGovern say to you?"

"Oh, nothin' much," Twinks shrugged. "Just asked for Mom and when I told him she was out he said he'd call her back."

"Did he say anything more?" Janey asked, suddenly sure that here was a clue to both the Weavers' and Mrs. Baker's strange reaction. "Have you told me every single thing he said?"

"He just said he was looking forward to meeting Rob and me and seeing Mom again," Twinks said, and once more a shrewd, wary look came into her eyes. "I only told you he didn't *sound* lucky. His voice was very low, and quavery, and sort of sad. Maybe he was tired or felt awful but he didn't say anything that I haven't told you about."

"I see," Janey said, just as Mrs. Baker hurried into the house and called out that lunch would be ready in five minutes.

CHAPTER NINE

An hour later, when they had finished lunch, Twinks brought in the mail from the R.F.D. box near the road. "Lots of postcards for you, Janey, from your folks," she said. "And a letter with a California postmark. Is that your boy friend or your brother?"

"My brother," Janey said, and took her mail into her own room. She opened Hank's letter first and skimmed over the beginning which was about his job and the work camp where he was living. When he mentioned Gramps, Janey sat down and began to read intently, poring over every word.

"My guess is that the only mystery about Gramps or the mine is in your imagination," Hank wrote. "Maybe it's because Gramps was such a wonderful storyteller and what he told you when you were a little kid is all mixed up with the facts. At any rate I guess Herb Weaver could tell you as much as anyone because he's handling Gramps's estate—what there is of it! I didn't meet anyone when I was in Albuquerque except Mrs. Baker who was old enough to remember Gramps in his mining days and you say she isn't any help, so if I were you I'd skip the whole thing. The rest of your summer sounds terrific, so why don't you stop imagining things and have fun? Ages ago when we were both kids you used to get so steamed up over something Gramps had told you that you didn't know what was real and what was a fairy tale, and my guess is this is the same kind of deal."

Hank ended his letter with a paragraph of more general but definitely patronizing advice. Janey had written to him about Buck's meeting her in the Thunderbird, and now Hank wrote back that as far as he was concerned Rob Baker was worth ten of Buck Hughes. Janey read his final admonitions and dropped the letter on her bureau with a little snort of disgust.

I didn't write to Hank to ask for a sermon, she fumed. But because he didn't know anything useful about Gramps he fills in with a lot of Big Brother warnings. It's infuriating.

She read the postcards from her mother and the twins and then decided to spend the next hour or so getting ready for the party at the Weavers'. She shampooed her hair and pressed the clothes she was going to wear that night. She was just thinking of changing out of her blue jeans when she saw Rob's customers drive off and went out to ask him what time he was planning to leave for the Weavers'. As she left the porch she saw Rob mount Beau and guessed he was about to take the horses out to graze. She waved but he didn't see her and she ran down the hill, suddenly certain he had forgotten or given up the party. "When are we leaving for the Weavers'?" she called out as she reached the corral. "Or does this mean you're ducking the whole thing?"

"Of course not." Rob dismounted and came toward her. "We're leaving at quarter of seven. But it isn't five yet, and so I've time to take the horses down beyond the cattle gate to graze."

"Oh, I see." Janey felt herself grow red and turned away from the corral. "I'm sorry I bothered you."

"But you didn't." Rob's voice was eager. "I'm glad you came down. I've just had a great break and I wanted to tell you about it. The people who left a few minutes ago want me to start a class for cub scouts three mornings a week. They even paid a deposit ahead of time."

Janey hesitated. She had been at the ranch long enough to know that balancing the slack and rush times was one of Rob's hardest problems. "Sounds good," she said. "Especially if they'll come early in the morning when nobody else rents the horses."

"That's it!" Rob said, and she turned slowly around to face him again. "About eight kids at nine o'clock sharp every Monday, Wednesday, and Friday. Oh Janey, will you help?"

"Yes." Janey saw his eyes were sky blue and his cheeks glowing. His enthusiasm was catching, and her own spirits spiraled upward. "Of course I'll help. I'd love it."

Rob did a neat little heel-and-toe jig step in the soft dirt, and she moved after him laughing. "And now can I take Belle out grazing? It doesn't do her any good to be herded off with the others, and besides I'm beginning to feel gypped if I don't have two rides a day."

"Why not?" Rob moved off and saddled Belle with the effortless ease Janey still found amazing. "We can do this a lot faster if there are two of us."

A few minutes later they rode off with the other horses and Tote, the burro, cantering ahead of them.

"This is it!" Janey shouted to make herself heard above the racket of hoofbeats. "My idea of the wild and woolly West!"

Rob grinned and pointed to Tote who led the way up a sandy rise ahead of them. "Look at your welcoming committee!" he called out. "Idea of food turns him into a race horse."

"Enter him in the Derby!" Janey called back. "He's terrific."

At that instant Tote stopped so short that the other horses nickered and squealed as they broke around him and tore on over the hill. Tote lifted his head and brayed loudly. It was the same wild, trumpeting sound he had made the night of Janey's arrival.

She held Blue Belle back and looked down at the burro. "What's the matter? Lost your appetite?"

Rob passed her at dead gallop. "Trouble!" he shouted. "Tote's no fool."

Janey urged Blue Belle to the top of the rise and looked down. She saw the horses and a small herd of strange cattle. The gate!

Left open! She looked to the right and saw that the gate swung wide. Beyond it on the road was Juan's truck. Directly below her Rob and the Indian struggled to separate the horses from the scrawny, half-starved-looking cattle.

"Janey! Stay there!" Rob ordered. "Right where you are." Janey tightened her reins and gripped hard with her knees. If the cattle passed her they would be headed straight for the stable and Rob's precious feed! I've got to block them, she realized. If only Blue Belle doesn't panic!

In the hollow below her Rob flashed in and out among the animals like mounted lightning. Juan stood at one side, ducking and weaving and waving the cattle forward with his hat. The horses'll get out too! Janey's heart beat faster at the thought. They'll run all the way to Albuquerque.

At that instant a red and white steer threw up his head and bellowed. Then as Juan came behind him he charged clumsily toward the gate. A second later the others galumphed off in his wake. "Shut it!" Rob roared as he blocked the horses. "Now."

Janey tried to urge Blue Belle forward. The mare reared, plunged, and then stood trembling with fear. For a fraction of a second Janey wanted to jump off and run for the gate on foot. The next instant she knew it would be fatal to leave Blue Belle even for a moment.

"Easy, girl," she soothed, and used her legs, reins, and voice to coax the frightened mare forward. Blue Belle reared again, shivered, and stepped out sideways. "Easy, girl. Easy." Janey's voice was calm but firm as she forced Blue Belle to do what she was told.

She reached the gate just as Juan managed to shut it behind the cattle.

"Good work." Rob made sure his horses were safe, and galloped over to the gate himself. "Juan, you were great!" He dropped out of the saddle the instant Beau came to a standstill. "What was it? Uranium hunters?"

Juan nodded and gestured toward his truck as he answered in Spanish. "Juan saw three guys in a new Buick driving out of here as he came up," Rob translated. "Then he saw the cattle. He was trying to round them up by himself when Tote brayed and we came along."

"Did he get the men's license? Can't you sue them for trespassing?"

Rob shrugged as he remounted. "You'd have to sue half the state. Practically everybody owns a Geiger counter. And this is government land free to anyone except for the grazing rights. The only thing the men did wrong was to leave the gate open. But you'd lose your shirt trying to prove or collect on that."

"Oh." As Janey's excitement leaked away she realized that she was tired and breathless after her tussle with Blue Belle. She looked down and saw Juan move to the mare's head and stroke her sweaty neck. "*La señorita va a caballo como van los angeles mismos. Claro, es natural, siendo ella la nieta de un cabellero tan valiente como era el señor comandante McGovern, su abuelo.*" The Indian spoke to Rob in Spanish and then, looking up at Janey, spoke in English for the first time. "Hot! Ver' hot!"

"I agree!" Rob said. "And thanks again for your help, Juan."

"*De nada!*" Juan nodded to Rob and Janey and walked off to his truck without looking back.

Rob moved after the horses and Janey stayed where she was, glowering down at Blue Belle's neck. "We might as well go," Rob called back. "There isn't enough grass left to feed a gopher."

"I couldn't care less," Janey said. "Here I've turned inside out to do what you said *and* to make Blue Belle behave and the only thanks I get is for that Indian to say she's too hot and for you to agree with him."

Rob put back his head and roared with laughter. "You—you idiot," he got out when he could speak at all. "Juan meant your horsemanship. What he said in Spanish is literally 'She rides like an angel. Better even than the major, her grandfather.' And thinking you'd understand the compliment in American slang, he translated with the two words 'very hot' and you thought he meant Blue Belle. Oh, brother."

Janey looked down the road at the disappearing truck and back at Rob and suddenly she, too, began to laugh until the tears came to her eyes. "Rob! Of course that's it. And he knows I don't know a word of Spanish because this morning when he talked to me I just shouted I didn't understand and beat it after Betsy. Do you suppose he was trying to tell me that the trail to Elbow Crest was hard to find? All I could get was something about Fortune."

"Elbow Crest's on the way to Fortune," Rob said thoughtfully, "and Juan's always been dead set against going near there. He probably came over this afternoon to make sure you got home safely."

"But why does he care?" Janey asked. "It isn't as though he'd known me always, the way he's known you and Twinks."

"I don't understand him myself," Rob said. He started to herd the horses back to the corral so that it was impossible to talk above the sound of hoofbeats, but Janey went on wondering about the old Indian's strange behavior. A little while later, when Rob was carefully dividing what was left of his oats, she thought she saw an explanation.

"Rob," she began, "do you suppose Juan saw Gramps out here the night before Gramps died? Do you think Gramps asked Juan to watch out for me? Gramps might have, you know. I was nine when he left Connecticut, and he probably always thought of me as staying the same age."

"It's possible," Rob said. "But you'll never find out about it from Juan. Compared to the way an Indian can clam up a stone wall is a chatterbox."

"I'm sure of it," Janey said, and told Rob about Hank's letter. "Hank told me to skip the whole thing, but I thought I'd ask Sis Weaver and Buck Hughes. Hank really was infuriating. He practically told me to settle down and play with my dolls."

"I doubt if either Sis or Buck knows anything," Rob said, and frowned down at his boots. "Their grandfather sold out his share in La Placita before the accident. Your grandfather and mine paid him a terrific price and a little while later the mine proved to be worthless. That's one more reason why the Hughes family owns practically everything in Albuquerque."

And why you can't stand Buck, Janey thought, but she managed not to say so and began cleaning the saddle she had just used. A few moments later Rob came over to help her and rubbed at the stained leather with a worn sponge. "Blue Belle sure did get hot!" Janey said, and they both started to laugh all over again.

"A laugh like that's worth losing some grass and being indebted to old Juan," Rob said as they started toward the house. "I haven't felt so grateful to him since he gave me Tote about ten years ago."

"Juan gave me the creeps the first time I saw him," Janey said, and thinking of Twinks's stole, she added; "but I guess he is generous and terribly loyal."

"Oh sure. But in those days you could buy a burro for a couple of dollars and, besides, Grandfather probably paid for it. It was that kind of thing that made Mom so furious. Juan was Grandfather's Man Friday for years but in a way he called the tune. What Mom wanted was a regular pre-Civil War black-slave attitude, and you'd never find that in an Indian. They're the proudest people on earth."

Except for you, Janey thought, as she hurried off to get dressed. Except for Robert Randolph Baker.

She put on a low-cut cotton blouse, and a bright red, blue, and yellow circular skirt Mum had made for her last Christmas, and red ballet shoes. The feel of the light feminine clothes after a diet of levis was distinctly agreeable, and Janey began to hum to herself as she dressed. She put on her lipstick with care, tucked her glasses back into her top bureau drawer, and went out into the living room in a decidedly partyish mood.

All three of the Bakers were waiting for her, and for once Twinks spoke before her mother. "Janey looks sharp," she said, and walked around looking at every detail of Janey's clothes. "And the same rig will be all right later on for the exhibition. They want the dames looking snazzy but girlish. It's good corn for the tourists."

"Twinks. Your language!" Mrs. Baker put in. "Really, my darling, I simply don't know where you pick up such things."

"Exhibition?" Janey blinked nearsightedly at Twinks. "What

do you mean?" Rob moved forward, a trim, wiry figure in clean levis, polished boots, and a bright blue shirt.

"It's why I hesitated about going," he began. "I didn't think you understood and I don't think it's fair. I know——"

He was interrupted by an explosion of protestations and advice from Mrs. Baker. At the same moment Twinks threw her arms around his neck and pulled his head down to the level of her mouth and began whispering into his ear.

"I'm sorry. I still don't understand." Janey said. "I thought we were just having supper at the Weavers' and doing some square dancing afterwards."

"Sure, that's it. Nothing to it!" Twinks hurried over to Janey. "Rob's just being stuffy again."

"Twinks, I'll handle this," Mrs. Baker said, and turned to Janey. "My dear girl, Rob really was making a mountain out of a molehill. It's simply that if your eight goes well tonight the Weavers may want to practice it again and then some Saturday evening later on have you all do it at La Tavernita. La Tavernita's the very nicest restaurant in town or I wouldn't let Twinks perform there. And in August they sometimes have an amateur eight of square dancers and it's really most attractive."

"I hope I'll be good enough." For the first time since Janey had been in New Mexico she felt insecure and unsure of herself, the way she had felt at the Bayport Club. "I've done a few figures like 'Birdie in the Cage' and 'Pop Goes the Weasel' but I'm no expert."

"You'll be great." Twinks never took her eyes from Rob as she spoke. "Super."

"Of course, you'll do splendidly." Mrs. Baker began shooing Rob and Janey toward the door. "And now you really should leave. And I know, Janey dear, that you'll have a perfectly lovely evening. Buck Hughes is so good-looking and with such delightful manners. He has a real sense of social responsibility toward his family and guests. I almost wish, Robbie dear, that you were a little more like him."

Now she's ripped it, Janey thought as she followed Rob's suddenly rigid back to the car. Really fixed things! They rode in silence down the rutted driveway. When Rob climbed back in after opening and shutting the gate Janey reminded him of Juan and Blue Belle. "We had our fun out of that," Rob said austerely, "but it's over."

"Parents can be absolutely maddening." Janey tried a more direct approach. "I know Mum and my stepfather made me furious the way they arranged my trip out here as though I were Twinks's age. I'd really been counting on going to England this summer."

"Too bad you got stuck out here with the hicks," Rob said. "A pity."

"That's not what I meant and you know it!" Janey began, but Rob seemed as remote as though they had been on different planets and she gave up trying to reach him.

Neither of them spoke again until Rob parked his car near the Weavers'. "Have you got your glasses?" he asked gruffly. "You may need them square dancing, even if you don't like the way they look."

"I left them home on purpose." Janey struggled not to be cross. "Along with my seeing-eye dog."

"Too bad." Rob looked over her head as though he were speaking to a spot somewhere above the Weavers' door. "It may make things hard for your partner."

"Well, that won't be you!" Janey swept into the house on a quick wave of temper. "So you don't have to brood over it."

CHAPTER TEN

A moment later the Weavers' maid opened the door and Janey walked in with Rob behind her.

"Janey! It's good to see you."

"Glad you could come, Rob. We haven't seen you for ages."

The two Weavers, who stood with Buck in the front hall, were as friendly and hospitable as before. As Buck took Janey's wrap and Sis led her into the mellow, softly lit living room she felt as though she were returning to old friends. She saw Rob disappear into another room with Herb Weaver and heard something about Herb's showing him an old Navajo blanket he had bought a few days earlier. A moment or two later when they came back Herb nodded at Rob and said that he was a real connoisseur of Indian crafts. Rob said nothing but grinned back at Herb, apparently as pleased by the compliment as though he were Pete's age.

So Herb cheered him up again, Janey thought, and her own flash of temper vanished as she glanced at Rob with a comfortable feeling of superiority. *He's as easy to distract as a babe in arms.*

"Janey, I'd like to have you meet our cousin, Mary Alice

Hughes," Sis began, and Janey turned as Sis went on introducing the other guests. There was a young married couple by the name of Hoguet, a tall navy lieutenant called Pierce, and a neighbor—Elsie Kohler—whom Janey couldn't help noticing was as sandy-haired and plain-looking as Tina Ramirez had been dark and exotic.

None of the men were in uniform but were in clothes much like Rob's. Buck had on a wine-colored shirt and dark, close-fitting trousers that were even more becoming than his uniform. He's fantastically good-looking, Janey thought, and noticed that when Tom Pierce, who was the same general build and complexion, stood next to him Tom looked like a gray heron next to a bird of paradise.

They ate in the living room from bright pottery plates that Herb Weaver and Buck piled high with ham, Spanish rice, salad, and sopaipillas from a table in one corner. "Janey, have another sopaipilla," Sis urged. "I ordered them especially for you."

"They're my dish!" Janey said, and meant the whole evening as well as the light delicious rolls. "Just perfect."

She looked around, enjoying every detail of the big informal room and the gaily dressed people. The soft candlelight was a relief after Mrs. Baker's fetish for electricity, and Sis's easygoing hospitality was equally welcome after Mrs. Baker's delicious but obviously labored-over meals. Best of all it was wonderful to feel popular and wanted in the midst of this amazingly welcoming crowd.

Tom Pierce had gone to Harvard and in his senior year he had lived at Adams House, which Hank was entering next fall.

"Can you tie it? Great!" Tom Pierce settled down beside Janey as though the faint coincidence made them long lost friends. Before Janey could answer, Martin Hoguet came over to say that he had done graduate work at Yale and had often motored through Warwick. He started to sit down at Janey's other side when Buck moved him away. "Not a chance, Hoguet," he said. "I've worked hard for this privilege."

He smiled down at Janey, and as she smiled back she was more than ever certain that this evening was especially festive and star-spangled. It isn't just that Buck's so good-looking, Janey thought, and tried to forget everything that Twinks had said. He really enjoys life and he makes other people enjoy it too.

After dessert Sis Weaver turned on the electric light and sat down at the piano while the men pulled back the rugs. "Time for a round dance," Herb Weaver called out. "And then we'll start practicing 'Butterfly Whirl.'"

Tom Pierce held his hand out to Janey, but Buck was too quick for him. "Janey's dancing with me," he said, and led her onto the floor.

Buck was an accomplished dancer, and as they swept smoothly around the room Janey felt that she herself was more expert and graceful than she had ever been before in her life.

It seemed only a matter of moments before Herb went to the piano and spoke in Sis's ear. "Time's nearly up, folks," he called out. "We'll have to start practicing." He dimmed the lights as he spoke and Sis finished off the tune with a series of flourishes. For one electric instant Buck pressed Janey close to him. The contact was momentary but Janey was as aware of his strong overwhelmingly male presence as though he had kissed her on the lips. She blinked as Herb turned the lights on again, and her whole body tingled.

"All set for 'Butterfly Whirl.'" Herb began lining up the partners. "Ladies on this side. Men over there."

Janey moved to where Herb pointed, feeling as though she had stepped from one world to another and back again in a matter of seconds. "Ready, everybody?" Herb called out. "Rob and Janey, Elsie and Buck, you Hoguets together, and Tom and Mary Alice. Ready, Sis? Let's go! Honor your partner one and all, ladies fair and menfolk tall."

Janey curtsied to Rob, and as he bowed back he seemed so boyish and familiar after the elemental force of Buck's personality that she beamed up at him in unconscious relief. "So you got stuck with me after all," she whispered. "Even if I won't wear my specs."

"Stuck nothing!" Rob spoke right in her ear. "Twirl to the left now, Janey. That's the girl."

The set was a new one to Janey, but the separate steps were familiar and with a little discreet coaching from Rob she had no trouble in following the directions.

When Herb Weaver finally called a stop they were all glowing, breathless, and pleased with themselves.

"We're good." Tom Pierce grinned over at Janey. "Absolutely tops, all of us."

"Could you come back next week, same place, same station?" Herb asked. "And after one more practice we'll be plenty good enough to do it at La Tavernita on the third of August."

"Yes."

"You bet. We'd love it."

Janey looked inquiringly at Rob. "Fine, Herb. Thanks a lot. Janey and I'll be here," he said, and she wondered all over again at the seesaw quality of his moods.

The Weavers brought out tall drinks in greeny blue Mexican glasses. Several of the guests clustered around the television set, and Janey found herself on the sofa alone with Herb Weaver. He looked very relaxed, and she decided this was the time to ask him about Gramps and the location of the mine, even if he did get embarrassed.

"I didn't even know the mine was located in Fortune until you mentioned it just now," Herb said when Janey had finished. "But may I ask if Rob knows about your interest in all of this?"

She fought down an impulse to say "What business is it of Rob's?" and smiled instead. "Rob knows I'm interested in the mystery about Gramps," she went on. "But actually it was my brother Hank who suggested I talk to you."

"Mystery?" Herb put on his glasses and looked down at her as he spoke. "Your brother didn't indicate to me that he was concerned about anything out of the way or, as you say, mysterious."

"Oh, Hank wasn't—isn't." Janey found herself floundering for the right words. "It's just me. Ever since I've been out here, every time Gramps's name has been mentioned it seems to me that people act—well—queer."

"Perhaps you have exaggerated it in your own mind." Herb Weaver crossed his legs with meticulous care. "Or it may be simply that out here the older people who remember your grandmother were so devoted to her that their recollections of your grandfather paled in comparison."

"But I haven't seen any older people, except Mrs. Baker! And Gramps simply wasn't a person you could forget. He was a very colorful character."

"So I've been told." Herb actually smiled, and Janey plunged in to press home her advantage. "He was a regular old rip-roaring westerner and proud of it," she said. "But what I don't understand besides the—well—queerness is what he meant when he wrote me just before he died that he was sure before he was through La Placita wouldn't owe him anything."

"I have no idea what Mr. McGovern had in mind," Herb Weaver said, and Janey realized that the genial host in Herb had disappeared and the cautious lawyer had taken over. "But perhaps you are not aware that the claim to that mine ran out years ago and that there were no other claims or even mining stocks in his estate."

"I don't care about that!" Janey said. "I guess Hank and the rest of my family were relieved to know he didn't leave any tremendous debts."

"Not at all." Herb's voice was more judicial than ever. "The decedent was apparently well aware of the condition of his own health and made careful and very sensible provisions a few months ago." Janey's hands twisted in her lap but she didn't dare interrupt. "A savings account will take care of his funeral expenses and so forth, and he directed that his clothes should be given to a fellow boarder of his in the boardinghouse where he lived for the past few years in Oklahoma. He left his books and his watch to your brother and his saddle and his—er—diary and papers to you."

"Did Gramps leave me the saddle?" Janey asked, and as Herb

nodded she almost forgot he was sitting beside her. How often Gramps had described that saddle! Even as a child Janey had understood that it was not simply his most cherished possession but a symbol of something so precious that he found it hard even to loan it to a friend. If only I'd said good-by to him decently, she thought, and written to him, real letters, not just the Christmas cards Mum made me send.

Herb Weaver cleared his throat, and Janey was vaguely aware that the group around the television was breaking up. "As a matter of fact McCollum, the lawyer in Oklahoma, has just informed me that those small bequests might be distributed very shortly," Herb said. "Your brother indicated that he would like his things sent to Warwick."

"Could mine be sent here?" Janey looked up just as Rob came over to her and said it was time to leave. "Rob's sold me on a Western saddle and I think Gramps would like to have me use it in New Mexico."

"No reason why that couldn't be arranged," Herb said, and Janey had the feeling he was mentally taking notes for his secretary. "I'll see to it on Monday."

A few minutes later the whole party drifted out into the hall, picking up wraps and making plans for the next square dance. "Janey, how about you driving down to El Moro with me tomorrow?" Buck suggested. "You ought to see more than just the local sights."

"Thanks a lot but I can't," Janey said regretfully. "Sunday's one of the busiest days of the week at the ranch."

Buck shrugged and spoke to Janey while he looked inquiringly at Rob. "Would your boss let you off on Monday afternoon to go for a swim at the officers' club?" he asked. "I'm on early duty so I could pick you up at the ranch at three if the boss can spare you."

"It's up to Janey," Rob said stiffly, and walked off to Herb's study. "She's a free agent."

"I'd love to go for a swim," Janey said, and Buck reached toward her and then drew back as Elsie and the Hoguets came into the hall.

"Three o'clock, then," he said, and spoke so low that only Janey could hear. "We'll swim and plan our strategy for future fun and games. I'm counting on seeing a lot of you this summer, so consider yourself duly warned in advance."

"I'll do that!" Janey said, just as Rob reappeared. "And thank you." There were further good nights, and a few minutes later Rob and Janey started back to the ranch.

Rob drove in silence for the first mile, but Janey was too elated to wonder what sort of mood he was in. She sat quietly beside him, inwardly purring over her triumphant evening. Buck's fallen for me, she realized. He's the most attractive man I've ever met and he went out of his way to say he was going to date me as often as he possibly can. She smiled to herself and on a sudden impulse to make everyone else as happy as she was looked over at Rob just as he turned onto the canyon road. "That party was fun," she said. "And I think you were terribly nice to take me when you didn't want to go in the first place. I loved every minute of it."

"I had a good time, too, and thanks for going with me," Rob said, and it was clear that despite his momentary brusqueness in the Weavers' hall he was in excellent spirits. "I think we needed to step out after all our dude wrangling. And the worst is yet to come. Some of the people who have signed up for tomorrow have never even seen a four-legged horse before."

"We'll teach 'em!" Janey said. "Even if we have to start out with demonstration lessons on Tote. After going over Elbow Crest with Betsy Appleton anything sounds easy."

They talked about the horses and plans for the coming week during the rest of the drive home. It wasn't until they were having milk and cookies in the Bakers' kitchen that Janey remembered her talk with Herb Weaver and told Rob about it. "Perhaps I made a mistake mentioning it at a party," she ended up. "But Herb certainly went out of his way to sound off like a legal eagle. My, he was standoffish."

"Herb Weaver's a prince," Rob protested. "And a good friend of mine."

"Oh, I didn't mean that!" Janey shrugged. "I think he's fine, too, but it's simply that the more people try to put me off about Gramps and La Placita the more I simply itch to learn what all the mystery's about."

Rob moved away from the kitchen table, and Janey went on thinking out loud. "It's all so strange," she said. "But I'm getting more and more convinced that Gramps had something definite he wanted me to do out here, and I wouldn't be a bit surprised if it was connected with the mine."

"I don't believe it!" Rob rapped out, and faced back toward the table. "Leave it alone, Janey. Please."

"But why?" Janey asked. "*Why?*" He didn't answer, and she stood up trying to read his expression. He looked down at her, through her, she felt, and she went on more quickly. "Why shouldn't I do anything I like to clear up a mystery that seems to surround my own grandfather? I don't see why you or anyone else should want to stop me."

Still Rob said nothing, but his blue eyes, dark now and somber-looking, never left her face. For a seemingly endless moment they stood and stared at one another. Janey was the first to look away. I wish you'd say something—anything—she thought, and stirred uneasily. No matter what you said about Gramps or about me it would be better than this.

Rob stood as motionless as though he were bewitched. Finally Janey couldn't stand the silence any longer. "It can't be all that important," she burst out. "I'm sure Gramps didn't do anything frightfully bad or—or wonderfully good. He wasn't that kind of man. And Rob, about my going over to Fortune, surely there isn't anything so awfully queer about my wanting to do that. After all Gramps is buried there and your own mother thought I ought to go."

She touched Rob's arm. He pulled away but she sensed the spell was broken. A moment later he took a deep breath and began to tidy up their glasses as though nothing had happened. "I'll take you to Fortune," he said, and his deep voice was perfectly matter-of-fact. "It's a beautiful ride over and we'd both enjoy it.

But I won't be able to show you La Placita because I don't know where it is."

"Then we'll just have to find it!" Janey said jauntily. "An old mine can't be all that difficult to locate."

"This one is." Rob walked toward the kitchen door. "I spent most of the summer the year after my grandfather died going through deserted mines in Fortune and I never found it."

"You were looking for La Placita the time you hurt your foot?" Janey wanted to take back the words the minute they were spoken but it was too late.

"Yes," Rob said, and his face had a pinched, frozen look to it. "An old mine shaft or tunnel is supposed to be a good place to find Indian artifacts. But perhaps I'm not lucky. Juan warned me that I wouldn't be. Good night, Janey."

Janey nodded, too startled to speak. Rob went out without another word, and as Janey looked after him she was so aware of the sudden pain she had seen in his eyes that she stopped thinking about herself. Poor Rob, she thought, he looked like a mute who's suffering torture but couldn't ask for help.

She put the milk bottle into the refrigerator and the small everyday act brought her back to herself again. I didn't have anything to do with making Rob look so unhappy, she decided, and as she walked to her own room she went on justifying what had just occurred. After all if Rob is still so tied up over an accident that happened three years ago that it kills him simply to have it mentioned it isn't anyone's fault but his own. I certainly didn't mean any harm.

She undressed, and for the first time in years remembered what Gramps had told her when she had unintentionally broken Hank's kite during a childish tantrum. "Not meaning harm isn't enough, Janey," Gramps had said. "We McGoverns are so quick on the trigger that we have to be specially sure of the safety catch. Otherwise we can cause a lot of trouble. For other people *and* ourselves."

The thought was unpleasant and Janey tried to get rid of it

by vigorously brushing her hair but it was no use. Gramps's words rang on in her memory so that she could almost hear the sadness in his usually cheerful voice. . . . We can cause a lot of trouble. . . . For other people *and* ourselves.

CHAPTER ELEVEN

It took Janey a long time to go to sleep. She was
overstimulated by the party, and the scene with
Rob, and more than ever confused by the evasiveness that hung
like a cold, veiling mist about Gramps and La Placita.

"Leave it alone, Janey!" Rob's voice had held overtones she had
never heard before, and yet a few minutes later he had actually
offered to take her over to Fortune. It's the mine that changes
everybody, she thought, remembering Mrs. Baker the night of her
arrival and Herb Weaver only a few hours ago. She wriggled down
further under the cool sheets, trying to find an answer. Perhaps
Buck could help me, she thought. And even if he can't he won't
brood over it or sound off like a stuffed owl.

She lay very still, and the recollection of Buck holding her
close swept over her with such vivid intensity that she blushed
in the darkness. It wasn't anything to be ashamed of! Janey's
thoughts were as defensive as though she were arguing with
Hank. I like Buck. He makes people feel gay and happy and
glad they are alive. You and Rob and probably every other man
Buck meets are jealous without knowing it. Tina Ramirez? The

129

girl Twinks told me about? They probably rushed him so he had to cut loose. But I won't do that. I don't even want to. I can take care of myself.

She rolled over, stretched out more comfortably, and closed her eyes. As her body relaxed, unrelated images passed slowly and more slowly through her mind. She saw Buck in his uniform. Twinks dancing in the sunlight. Juan in the shadows of that airport waiting room. At last, far off, she saw Rob. He stood beside Beau, the reins hooked over his arm, looking away from her across a vast treeless mesa. As she seemed to float toward him he turned, and his sensitive mobile face which had been so stern and forbidding in the kitchen was radiant with welcome. Janey fell fast asleep.

The next day was as busy as Janey had expected. There were several small parties of inexperienced riders in the morning. While Janey took three schoolteachers over the Sepique trail Rob worked with a group of children in the ring and left with another party for Frijoles Ridge before she returned.

When she saw him at lunch he seemed cheerful and at ease, but with his family around it was hard to tell. We'll really talk later on, Janey thought, and then I'll know why he was so hurt and touchy last night. It certainly wasn't my fault. She hurried down to the corral as soon as she had helped with the dishes, but it was plain there was not going to be any chance for a private conversation. Mrs. Appleton and Betsy had already arrived, and Rob had Belle saddled for Janey to ride when she went off with them. "Won't this start a riot?" Janey managed to speak directly into Rob's ear. "If Betsy sees me riding Belle she's sure to want to swap."

"I'm not worried," Rob said. "I think you really turned the trick last time. And I need Chesty for my next dudes."

"Keep your fingers crossed!" Janey mounted Belle and started after the Appletons. Betsy waited until her mother was well in the lead and then she pulled up close beside Janey. "You didn't tell on me?" she whispered. "Please, Janey, say you didn't?"

"Of course not. I promised I wouldn't."

Betsy gave a noisy sigh of relief. "Boy, I feel better. I'll ride Pigeon forever if you ask me to."

"You won't have to," Janey said. "If you make sense with him for a few weeks I know Rob will let you try Mike and Chesty and perhaps Belle. He wants you and the other kids to ride as many different horses as possible but he's got to be sure it's going to be safe before he does it."

"I'd rather be able to ride Belle than eat!" Betsy breathed. "But I don't believe it's very likely to happen. Rob doesn't let practically anybody ride her and even if he did let me I'd be scared stiff. She looks awful frisky."

"Belle's not hard to handle," Janey said. "And if you prove that you can really ride Pigeon perfectly it'll be the first step toward riding her. Suppose you start off by making Pidge canter without counting on his going along with Chesty. If you keep your hands down and don't jerk at him I know you can do it."

"I'll sure enough try!" Betsy said, and leaned forward earnestly. "I'll do it just the way you say."

From then on they had a pleasantly uneventful ride and headed back toward the stable at a little after five o'clock. Rob had all of the horses in use and except for Tote, the donkey, and Twinks, who was perched up on a fence post, the corral was deserted. Janey and her charges dismounted and a few moments later the Appletons drove off.

"You sure get your own way, Janey McGovern!" Twinks grinned down at her like a small and lively gargoyle. "It beats the Dutch."

"You mean because Betsy rode Pigeon on the right trail?" Janey looked after the Appletons' car as she spoke. "I'd have died of fright if she'd tried another ride like the one to Elbow Crest."

"Oh, I don't mean just that." Twinks dropped to the ground as nimbly as a cat. "I mean that Rob came into the house between customers this morning and telephoned Chuck Hemsted to come out here and stay all day Tuesday so that Rob can ride with you to Fortune. Rob's going to pay Chuck five bucks for dude wrangling here while you two go off."

"But that's crazy. Rob shouldn't waste the money. We could go over some afternoon in his truck when the road's fixed."

"Not a chance. That truck isn't any use except to haul feed. No wonder Mom nearly popped when Rob traded in his Chevvie and used the extra money for Blue Belle."

"But he bought her for a song. And with a little work she'll be worth plenty. People in the East would pay a fortune for her."

"Rob would have to get her there first," Twinks said sagely, and turned as her mother called down from the house. "Oh, Twinks. It's time you did your practicing. You forgot all about it this morning."

Twinks made a face as she moved reluctantly homeward. "You talk about the luck of the McGoverns," she said as she passed Janey. "That's just what I ain't got."

Janey waited at the corral for Rob to return. She busied herself grooming Blue Belle and the horses the Appletons had used, but there was no sign of Rob or his party. Just before supper Twinks, finally freed from rehearsing, came out to get her. "Rob'll be starved," Janey said. "And absolutely dead tired. Couldn't you and I wait for him and eat when he comes?"

"Nope. Mother'll keep supper for him but she has to have Sunday supper on time. It matters to her."

Getting a good meal with some company when he's been wrangling dudes all day might matter to Rob, Janey thought, but she didn't say anything, and it was a surprise when Twinks stopped and peered up at her. "You don't understand," she said. "Mom isn't trying to be mean and she'll keep plenty of super food hot for Rob. It's just that when she's working all week she can't keep the house going the way she wants to have it, so Sunday she always uses her best dishes and stuff and gets all slicked up herself and likes to eat on time and listen to a concert on the radio. She works all day cooking and cleaning, but Sunday evening she sort of pretends she's going to a party in her own house. Do you get it?"

"Yes," Janey said, astonished at Twinks's perception. "And thank you for telling me. I didn't understand before."

"Okey dokey." Twinks skipped along once more apparently as unconcerned as Linda or Pete. "After supper let's play cards. But I want to listen to the bagpipe show first."

They had all finished supper and it was nearly dark when Rob came into the kitchen. "Some workout," he said. "I thought they were going to ride until the horses folded. And now Beau has a loose shoe!"

"Take your time washing up, dear." Mrs. Baker stirred, re-heated, and poured as she spoke. "You can eat in here and maybe Janey wouldn't mind keeping you company. I'd really like to listen to the Cluff Hour. Sure you have everything you need?"

"Yes. Thanks." Rob seated himself at the kitchen table and Mrs. Baker crossed toward the door. As she reached it she turned on another light switch, and in the sudden glare her face looked wrinkled and infinitely tired.

Mrs. Baker's exhausted, Janey realized, and felt ashamed of her own unspoken criticisms. And what really matters to her isn't herself but her family.

"Thanks for cleaning the tack and the horses." Rob interrupted Janey's thoughts. "That was a great help. Tomorrow morning we'll be all set for the cub scouts. I'll fix Beau's shoe right after they leave or after lunch."

"Thanks for arranging the ride to Fortune," Janey said. "Twinks told me you'd gotten someone to take over here on Tuesday."

"That's our lightest day," Rob said. "And besides I want you to see Cinder Cone Canyon where someday I'm going to have my school. We'll pass it on the way back. It's just right for a school, Janey. Water, woods, and good range land. A kid would learn natural history, just by living there."

Teaching is what really matters to Rob, Janey thought, and for an instant she felt as deserted and left out as when the family had first told her they were going to England without her.

"It must be a beautiful ride to Fortune," she said aloud. "Gramps talked about it so much that when I was a little kid I rode the wooden horse he gave me on what he and I called the Golden Ride to Fortune."

"Hope you like it," Rob said, and carried his dishes over to the kitchen sink. "But I think Fortune is hideous. Like every other abandoned mining town."

"That's what Gramps always said too. It's the country leading up to it that he was crazy about." As Janey rattled on she entirely forgot what had happened in the kitchen after the party when they had talked about Fortune. "I'm aching to see the place. Gramps hoped he'd be able to stay out here long enough so that we could rent horses and ride over there together. It was only after Gramps died that I started thinking perhaps he wanted me to go to La Placita too."

Rob didn't answer, and Janey hurried over to the sink wondering if he was upset again. "Let me help wash up," she said. "I've been gabbing like a Chinese chatterbox."

"All done," Rob said, "and I think we're squared away for tomorrow. If you'll help me in the morning I can handle the afternoon easily when you go swimming with Buck."

"What's the officers' club like?" Janey decided to stay away from the subject of the mine until they were actually in Fortune. "Have you ever been there?"

"Once," Rob said, and grinned to himself at the memory. "It's very lush and super super country clubbish. I felt like a prairie dog at a kennel-club show, if you know what I mean."

"Don't I!" Janey said. "I always felt like that at Bayport. What Mum calls feeling like a cat in a strange garret. Gruesome!" At that moment Twinks came into the kitchen, determined to get her card game, and their talk was over.

The next morning the eight cub scouts arrived at the corral half an hour before the appointed time and were left there by the mother who had driven them up from town. Seven of them immediately made a noisy rush for the nearest horses, while the eighth, a tall, shy boy of about nine, lingered behind.

"Easy, fellas." Rob deflected the blue-jeaned tornado to a safe place looking down on the corral. "Before we start riding we ought to get acquainted. Why, I don't even know all of your names, and you don't know what any of my horses are called or what each one is like."

"I'm Billy Spring and, boy, do I want to ride a horse like Silver!"

"Ah, he's no good. I'd like to ride Trigger."

"I'm Chuck."

"I'm Donald. And I think Gene Autry's Champion is the best of all."

The boys' own names and the names of television cowboys and cow ponies exploded like cap pistols, but somehow Rob managed to get seven of the children seated on the ground in front of him. "When you said that about what your horses are like, did you mean they're all different?" The shy boy still avoided the others and spoke directly to Rob. "Not just the way they look, but different inside, the way people are?"

"That's it," Rob said, and nodded encouragingly. "One sign of a good rider is how quickly he gets to understand any horse he's riding. And now what's your name and where have you ridden before?"

"I'm Jakey Weathers and I just moved here from the Bronx. I haven't ridden much but I read that about horses being different, only I didn't know until now it was true," the boy said.

"You bet it is." Rob stood up and led the way to the horses he had saddled. "But of course they have a lot of things in common. No horse likes to be scared or startled. They all do better in the long run if you handle them quietly at the beginning."

"So you want us to pipe down!" The boy called Chuck grinned at Rob. "No Indian yells until we get going."

"Right you are," Rob said, and lifted Chuck onto Pigeon's back and showed him how to hold his reins and grip with his knees. Janey helped Billy Spring up on Mike, and in a few minutes they had everyone but Jakey Weathers walking around the ring.

"No," he said when Janey tried to get him on Chesty. "I guess I'll wait."

"Sissy!" Billy Spring grinned down at him. Jakey Weathers winced, but he only shook his head until Rob took him off around the shed and a few minutes later they came back with Jakey riding Tote bareback.

"Oh, boy! Look at Jakey."

"On a burro. Yah."

The other boys started teasing but Rob cut them short. "Riding a burro bareback isn't so easy," he said. "But it's the way some of the best Indian riders learned. I let Jake ride Tote because he has longer legs than the rest of you, but maybe next week Chuck or Donald could have a chance."

From then on the class went smoothly, and by the time the boys were called for they were sputtering with enthusiasm.

Rob didn't have any other customers that morning, but since Mrs. Baker was delayed in Albuquerque they ate fairly late and Janey was hungry. "My, this omelet is good," she said, but Mrs. Baker brushed off the compliment with elaborate plans for supper.

"I think we'll have pato al horno and maiz Fernando. They're Twinks's favorite Spanish dishes and perhaps you'd like them too."

"I'm sure I will," Janey said, "and I'm positive I'm going to go home fat as a pig."

A little while after lunch Rob went back to the stable and Janey started for her own room to change her clothes. She was surprised to find Twinks waiting for her. "I came to ask you to be sure and be back on time," Twinks said after she had carefully closed the door. "Buck's likely to make you late."

"Are you thinking about the pato al horno and maiz Fernando?" Janey asked. "Your mother warned me they tasted best when they were piping hot."

"That's only part of it," Twinks said. "But they're a lot of work and Mom's tired already. Besides if you're out late with Buck, Rob'll start to worry because he and I really know what kind of a guy Buck is. And when Rob feels worried or responsible sort of he can get pretty cross."

"This time neither of you need feel worried or responsible!" Janey said. "I can take care of myself."

136

"I guess the others all thought so too. Dolores, and a girl called Martita Rand who used to live right down this road, and that Tina Ramirez. Tina and Buck were both at La Tavernita at my last Friday performance when he stood her up."

Janey turned, eager to hear more details but, as she saw Twinks's alert little face, decided against asking, and continued to dress herself with ostentatious care. "You're going to look very nice," Twinks said, and when Janey didn't answer she went on more slowly. "Look, Janey, I don't want you to think that Rob's jealous of Buck Hughes over you. Rob's not the jealous kind but he does feel awful responsible for people and sometimes that makes him ornery."

"You don't have to worry!" Janey said, and pushed Twinks gently but firmly toward the door. "And I promise I'll be back in time for supper if I have to walk, or hitchhike, or fly. So now let me get dressed in peace."

Twinks stepped sedately over the doorsill. As she turned to pull the door shut her dignity dropped away and she began to giggle. "Jeepers," she got out. "I'd like to see you or anybody else get out of that dream-boat car of Buck's and walk home. That would be something!"

"Shoo!" Janey said. "Scamper. Beat it."

The little girl shut the door and Janey went back to her dressing, glad to be finally left alone. Twinks is incredible, Janey thought. Unbelievably sophisticated one minute and a babe in arms the next. She's so dazzled by big brother Rob that she'd say anything, absolutely anything she thought was to Rob's credit or the discredit of someone he happens to dislike. If you listened to Twinks you'd think Buck was the Big Bad Wolf of all time.

Janey settled down to giving herself a home manicure, and now she was no longer thinking about Twinks's personality or even speculating as to what the little girl might have seen happen between Tina Ramirez and Buck Hughes. Of course Rob isn't jealous over me! Janey told herself. It would be too deadly if he was. We're perfectly good friends but it's simply on a business basis, tied up with the ranch and working with the horses. Janey shrugged and tried to think about something else. She was not very successful. No matter which way her mind turned Twinks's unexpected and uncomplimentary remark stayed uppermost in her thoughts.

A few minutes later Janey heard Buck's car and hurried out onto the porch to meet him. "You look marvelous!" Buck said as they rolled away from the front door. "I like your sun dress."

"It must be caviar to the admiral then," Janey said. "I had it all last summer and you're the first man who's ever mentioned it."

"That shows the men of Connecticut are slipping," Buck said, and slowed down at the stable where Rob was working over Beau's loose shoe. "So long, Rob. Don't get a sunstroke. It's a hot day for blacksmithing."

"Good-by, Rob." Janey leaned out to wave. "See you at supper."

"Have fun." Rob called back, but Janey noticed he didn't even glance away from his work as he spoke. "And please shut the cattle gate."

"The Lone Ranger's mighty conservative," Buck said when he climbed back into his car after fastening the gate. "You'd think he was running a thousand head of prize cattle."

"Rob's worried about the grass," Janey said, and Buck nodded cheerfully. "Oh, sure, I don't blame him," he said, and began talking about things that had happened that morning at the Sandia Air Base. Janey tried to listen, but it was hard to follow when she didn't know any of the people Buck mentioned, and, besides, her thoughts kept returning to what Twinks had just said.

"You're awfully silent," Buck said once, and reached out with his right hand toward Janey's knee. "Worried about something?"

Janey instinctively pulled her knee away and then, not wanting to seem too prudish, tried making a joke. "Oh, I'm not worried. I'm just the sweet, still type. Feminine equivalent of the strong, silent male."

Buck laughed and put both hands back on the steering wheel. "Janey, you're terrific," he said. "And I'm glad we're going to swim. The Hoguets couldn't make it, but Tom Pierce will be around and there's the regular crowd at the pool I'd like to have you meet."

"I can't wait to see that pool," Janey said, and pointed to the glistening mirage of water on the road ahead of them. "I'm so dry that if you hadn't taken pity on me I'd have gone berserk and tried to plunge into that. We don't have hallucinations about water where I hail from. Even when it's broiling hot there's always the Sound."

Once more Buck laughed, and by the time they reached the officers' club Janey was feeling on top of the world. The club was even more luxurious than Janey had expected, with a wading pool for small children and a larger oval pool surrounded by tables and striped umbrellas for adults. "Does it remind you of Warwick or Bayport or wherever it is you swim at home?" Buck asked when they had changed into their bathing suits and met at the edge of the water.

"Not a bit!" Janey waved at the neatly kept military buildings to the left and the mountains straight ahead. "The Community Beach hasn't even got a pool and the one at the Bayport Club is about the size of a bathtub. Everything out here is newer and handsomer and better-looking."

"Except the girls," Buck said, and ushered her past a group of mothers and small children, toward the table where Tom Pierce, Elsie Kohler, and several other bachelor officers and their dates were waiting. "Come on over here. This is where our crowd always meets. Away from overenergetic infants and ancients."

That's like Bayport, Janey thought, remembering how Maisie Taylor's cronies always met at the porch steps while the older people and small children played tennis or swam.

Buck's crowd was certainly friendlier and less cliquey than the Bayport set, and by the end of a half hour Janey felt completely at home. They all went in swimming, and when they came out and had dried off Buck took orders for drinks. Elsie and the girls Janey had just met ordered cocktails, and she hesitated for a fraction of a second before she asked for ginger ale. At Bayport everyone in the crowd that Larry had introduced her to drank and it had been hard to refuse, but here it was no problem. Mary Alice

Hughes ordered a Coke and so did a big blond ensign who reminded Janey a little of Hank.

In what seemed like no time at all it was six o'clock and Janey said good-by regretfully and went out with Buck to his car. "That was fun," she said as he drove off the base. "Terrific. My, what a nice gang."

Buck turned to glance at her, and once more his hand reached for her knee. "Janey, don't let's stop now. Let's go some place for dinner and I'll drive you out to the Bakers' afterwards. Or better still, call them up and spend the night at Sis's, and she'll drive you out in the morning. She'd love it, Janey."

"I'd love it too," Janey said. "But it's just no dice. Mrs. Baker's planned a special dinner and tomorrow morning early Rob and I are riding over to Fortune. Rob even hired a friend to run the stable for the day while we're gone. I can't back out from all of that now."

"Hang it!" Buck swore and looked annoyed, but a moment later he was as breezily cheerful as ever. "Still I guess I shouldn't be too surprised. As the old folks say, what's bred in the bone comes out in the flesh. From what I've heard your grandpa sure went out of his way to be kind to Mrs. B. years ago when she used to come out from Virginia to visit her father for the holidays."

"Buck, what do you mean?" Janey asked. "What are you talking about?"

"I'll talk about anything you like," Buck said, and stopped his car at the side of the road. "But I'd really like to talk about us, Janey. To begin with I think you're awfully cute."

"Stop it!" Janey pushed him away. "I want to know, I have to know what you meant about Gramps and Mrs. Baker."

Buck shrugged as he moved back behind the steering wheel. "Oh, she was just a young girl then, and according to my mother they were very good friends. Maybe what *Time* calls 'great and good friends,' but I doubt it and anyway it all happened ages ago. What possible diff can it make?"

"But it can!" Janey was suddenly uneasy. "Buck, please tell me everything you ever heard about Gramps."

Buck looked at her curiously and his eyebrows lifted. "Oh, relax, Janey," he said. "You and Rob Baker aren't some queer half brother, half what-will-you relationship, if that's what's worrying you. Figure it out for yourself. Rob's not quite twenty-two and your grandpa pulled out nearly thirty-five years ago and Mrs. Baker never saw him after he left here."

"I know that!" Janey was disgusted, embarrassed, and completely bewildered. "I wasn't even thinking so much about Mrs. Baker but about Gramps and my grandmother McGovern. Gramps always spoke as if she was the most wonderful thing in his life."

"Probably she was," Buck sounded bored as he started his car again. "I know my mother loved her and Mother'd have talked plenty if your grandpa had trotted off from what she thought was the straight and narrow path. Mother was a dear but she was the most strait-laced creature who ever lived. It made my old man's life decidedly complicated."

"Yes, it must have," Janey said vaguely, but now her mind was not on the late Mr. and Mrs. Hughes or even on the grandmother she had never seen.

"Dad managed very nicely." Buck smiled at his own reflection in the driver's mirror. "But for heaven's sake, Janey, think about something else. The only reason anybody ever heard of what was undoubtedly a harmless and deadly dull relationship between them was because your grandfather went to see the then Miss Marston the afternoon of the Placita smash. That's all there's to it."

"But it isn't," Janey insisted. "Unless Gramps's going there had something to do with the mine. Rob's too sensible to care about a silly flirtation that took place, if it happened at all, ages ago, but there is something about Gramps and the mine that nearly kills him."

"I'm distressed," Buck said, but his sarcasm was lost on Janey who was completely absorbed with her own thoughts. A moment later they reached the cattle gate where Twinks was waiting for them.

"You're just in time!" Twinks said when she had opened and shut the gate and jumped into the back of the car. "This is a nifty car, Buck. How long have you had it?"

"Six months," Buck said, and drove on up to the house. "Janey, how about going swimming on Thursday?" he asked when they reached the door. "Or going over to see the Isleta pueblo. I'm on early duty all week."

"I don't know," Janey began, but just at that moment Rob came out of the house and Buck called over to him: "Can you spare your hired hand for a swim or sight-seeing Thursday? Her conscience is holding her back."

"You better take Buck up on the swim." Rob opened the car door for Janey as he spoke. "It's been mighty hot around here this afternoon."

"I'd rather go to Isleta!" Janey said, and hurried toward the house. "Thanks a lot, Buck. I'll see you on Thursday."

CHAPTER TWELVE

The next morning Janey was up early, but as usual Rob had had breakfast ahead of her. When she went down to the corral she saw a tall, gangling young man standing by the stable, and a moment later Rob introduced Chuck Hemsted.

"Janey, I'm sure enough glad to meet you," Chuck said, and his engagingly homely face wrinkled with humor. "Anyone who's convinced old Rob that an easterner, and a girl at that, can really ride deserves a medal."

"I don't know if I've done much," Janey said. "Rob's given me the breaks on horses." They shook hands, and Janey remembered an old saying of Gramps's that the average westerner had forgotten more about spontaneous friendliness than his New England equivalent would ever know.

"Chuck's being able to come over today is a real break," Rob said, and fastened a saddle bag behind Beau's saddle. "This is his only day off."

"Hope your dudes think so," Chuck drawled as Janey mounted Blue Belle. "I've been poking around engines too long."

Rob and Janey rode off and when they were out of earshot Janey asked about Chuck. "Twinks said you'd been friends for ages," she said. "Is he going to teach too?"

"Nope, he's at law school. And he's earning his way through working at Platt's garage. We've always liked different things but we like 'em in the same way if you follow me."

"Yes, I do," Janey said, and gave herself up to the present enchantment of riding the springy footed mare across gloriously open countryside. "Rob, what a morning! It's the most perfect day we've had since I've been out here."

"Hope it stays that way," Rob said as he eased Beau into a loping canter. "But there's a good chance of a cloudburst."

"I don't see how it could rain today," Janey said later on when they had reined in their horses and were walking side by side in the direction of Elbow Crest. "Did you listen to a radio weather report?"

Rob shook his head. "I haven't put much stock in radio reports since last year when they forecast drought just before the flood that almost wiped out the Orionville development north of Albuquerque. That was a mess, Janey. Forty families left homeless, all because a contractor from Kansas built over the Jimenez arroyo. We've had much worse floods in the past, but they didn't do any harm because the water ran down the old Jimenez bed. Once that was filled in the flash flood went right through Orionville and knocked it flat. Any reasonably weather-wise kid who was raised out here could have seen what would happen."

"I didn't know you were an amateur weather prophet," Janey said. "Did you study meteorology at college or at school?"

"Neither." Rob looked amused. "And your eastern lingo makes it sound a heap more impressive than it is. My dad had the regular old-time rancher's savvy about the weather, and I reckon I picked up a little from him about the time he taught me to ride and to handle this rope."

"I noticed you were all dressed up today," Janey said, and nodded at Rob's chaps and his lariat. "You should have used those yesterday to dazzle the cub scouts."

"And a pair of pistols loaded with blanks!" Rob agreed. "The only one of the kids who wouldn't have been fooled is Jakey Weathers."

"But, Rob, he's a New York City boy! He told me himself his family only moved out here last spring when his father got admitted to the New Mexico bar. I should think he'd be the first of all the cubs to be taken in when he's so new out here."

"Except for Billy Spring the others are pretty new too," Rob said, "and most of their families have come out here to make a fast buck in uranium or real estate and then they'll move on. Jakey's family have come here to stay, and you can bet Jakey's read more about this state than all the other kids put together. Jakey's bright and he doesn't do anything until he knows what he's doing. Within a month he'll ride circles around the others."

"I thought he was hopeless," Janey confessed. "And I still don't see how you hit on the idea of his riding Tote and then got him to do it."

"I thought of it because I'd have acted exactly the same way at Jakey's age," Rob said. "I was more scared of not being able to do something I'd started out to do than of anything else on earth, and Jakey's the same way."

"I can see that when you spell it out to me," Janey said. "But what I still don't follow is how if you understood Jakey so quickly you also got on to all the other kids who acted entirely differently."

"It's genius," Rob said, but he sounded pleased. "As a matter of fact kids are so much more understandable than grownups that when I meet someone for the first time I try to guess what they really are by imagining what they were like as children."

"Did you do it with me?" Janey said, and for the first time in days she thought with distaste of the moment on the station platform when she had abandoned Gramps. "I think I must have been a little stinker."

"Well, I don't," Rob said, "or your brother Hank either. The only time I met him I wished I'd known him when we were both brats."

"Hank *was* nice," Janey said, but she had no desire to talk about her older brother. She hesitated for a moment and then told Rob the whole story about Gramps. "I've never told that to anyone," she finished up. "But I thought you ought to hear it if only to know that your guess about me at the small-fry stage was cockeyed."

"I don't think so," Rob said. "And from everything I've heard about your grandfather he'd be the last person to blame you. He was terribly generous about letting other people save face."

"Who told you that?" Janey asked, but Rob only shrugged. "Oh I sort of picked it up," he said vaguely. She might have persisted but they had reached the point below the crest where they had to go single file.

Rob rode in the lead, and as Janey followed she thought of what he had said of imagining grownups as small children. Rob may have felt the way Jakey does, Janey decided, but from his little boy photographs in Mrs. Baker's room they certainly didn't look alike. Rob had been short for his age but muscular, and neatly built, and compact-looking. Janey smiled, remembering a snapshot of Rob, aged about eight, mounted on a big, rough-looking piebald. Rob's small athletic body seemed glued to the saddle, while his face had the same look of absorbed concentration which often came over it now.

Janey's thoughts went on to Mrs. Baker and an image of a spoiled, coquettish little blonde instantly came into her mind. Big, kindly Sis Weaver was easy too. Then Janey thought of Larry Saunders, and a picture of a puny, undersized boy who always plotted and contrived to get what other boys took as a matter of course immediately presented itself. Larry's still scheming over every girl he meets, Janey decided, when for the first time it occurred to her that she herself had not been entirely guileless in her dealings with him. I wasn't ever really in love with him, she realized. I was just thrilled over the places he took me and the glamour world I thought he was offering. I was a sponge and a gold digger without even knowing it.

Janey's self-analysis was decidedly unpleasant, and as they rode on up the narrow trail she tried to imagine what Buck Hughes had been like when he was little. For the first time no credible image came to mind at all. Janey had seen one picture of Buck as a big blond three-year-old at Sis Weaver's house, but even so it was impossible to imagine what he had been like before he had developed into the handsome, virile young man he was now.

"Your stunt's fun," Janey told Rob when they finally reached the ridge near Elbow Crest. "But it doesn't always work. At least not for me."

"Oh, it isn't infallible," Rob said, and pointed to the view below them on the far side of the crest. "Janey, take a look at that. Cinder Cone's down there to the south and Fortune's straight ahead over that low range of hills."

Janey looked where he pointed, and the slumbering, endless majesty below left her speechless. She didn't say a word until they had ridden a fair distance down the far side and reached a place where the two horses could walk side by side. "I didn't really see that view the time I was up there with Betsy," she said. "Or at least I was too scared to feel it, if you know what I mean."

"Don't I? When I was a kid I used to think of fear as a cold, smothering blanket that cut you off from everything else in the world. Even hearing, or seeing, or smelling."

"That's it," Janey said, pleased at his simile. "Exactly!"

They rode on, and in a few minutes the trail led through sheltered groves of beeches and piñon pines. "But this is all perfectly lovely!" Janey said once. "I don't see how people could build in a place like this and then turn around and leave. I should think even after the mines ran out some people would have stayed on here and driven into Albuquerque to work."

"You'll see why they pulled out when we reach Fortune," Rob said. "Mining knocks the daylights out of any countryside. And besides Fortune was already a ghost town by the time the state began building the new big motor routes so they by-passed the whole area. There's never been any quick and easy way of getting in and out to Albuquerque. Now, how about a trot, Janey?"

"It's good with me," Janey said, and a few minutes later they left the woodland behind them and trotted onto a rutted, sun-baked road leading up to a cluster of dilapidated little buildings.

"This is it," Rob said, and pulled down to a walk again. "The one and only Fortune."

Janey looked around, too amazed at the contrast between the dingy reality and her vague but romantic expectations to speak. On either side of the road stood little wooden houses separated by ugly gaps of unfenced waste land. The small, boxlike buildings had never been painted, and now they sagged in gray neglected rows. One or two houses still had dirty curtains moldering at the front window, but in most places the glass had been broken and the hole crudely blocked off by a few flimsy boards. Almost every house sported a tall, narrow stovepipe and the stacks that had not been knocked askew by storms were still capped with overturned tin pails that might once have held lard or paint.

"Those tins are to keep out cloudbursts," Rob said, and looked up at the sky as he spoke. "Around here a nice useful squaw rain is the exception. It's usually flood or drought."

Janey was too interested in her surroundings to think about the weather. She saw a few battered windmills and beyond the first cluster of little houses a long empty stretch covered with sandy top soil blown there by the winds of many years. "There were houses there once," Rob said. "Wiped out by fire. That was the real threat in these towns."

"I know," Janey said. "Gramps's cabin burned down the same day as the trouble at the mine. Do you suppose that could have been over there?"

"It might have been," Rob said. "But there've been a good many fires."

"Rob, look!" Janey pointed to a low building slathered with wooden curlicues which still displayed an elaborately lettered sign reading, "Paradise Bar and Grille. Tables for Ladies." "Now that's something!"

"The store's pretty good too." Rob walked Beau up to a long dilapidated building with a covered porch that ran from one end to the other. "When I was a little kid there were still one or two families living around here, and an old lady with a complete set of gold teeth kept the store open. The first time she smiled at me I nearly died of fright."

They dismounted and Rob loosened their saddle girths. He carefully tested one of the wooden columns that supported the roof of the store porch and, finding it sound, tied the horses to it. "Let's walk up to the top of the hill and look at the cemetery first," he said. "You can see the layout of the whole place from there. Then we'll come back here and eat in the shade."

Janey followed him up the rutted main street past a dozen or more little houses. One had an old broom still standing by the front door and near another a battered kiddy car lay in a sandy waste that must once have been a play yard. At the next house a rusted Ford car had been abandoned under a sagging network of half rotted laundry lines. Janey saw a legless doll face down by the broken stoop and looked away, momentarily so depressed by the evidences of defeat and disorder all around her that the very idea of locating La Placita, let alone finding anything in it, seemed futile. "The bar and the store are gorgeous," she said out loud. "But the rest of the town isn't a bit what I expected. It's much too poor, and hopeless, and pathetic."

"The mines are why." Rob led the way to the side of the road where they could look down at great ugly scars in the tawny earth directly below them. In some places the mine heads were merely dark openings, but occasionally they were filled in with broken scaffoldings that looked like rotting teeth.

A little further off Janey saw the remains of a single cog railroad and one broken-down caboose. "Was there coal mining here?" Janey asked, and pointed to the acres of black grimy earth below them. "Gramps never mentioned anything but gold."

"People have mined for just about everything around here at one time or another," Rob said. "The Indians mined turquoise, silver, and gold, then the white men found more gold and later on coal. There are lots of towns like this in New Mexico, but of course now nobody's looking for anything but uranium."

For an instant Janey only looked down moodily at the scarred earth, and then an idea flared up like a rocket in her mind. "But,

Rob that's it!" She turned toward him. "The answer to everything. Gramps said in his last letter, 'before I'm through with it La Placita won't owe me a thing.' He must have been thinking of uranium."

"I don't think so," Rob said, but Janey was too excited to notice the change in his voice. "But I'm sure of it," she rushed on. "And he probably came up here that last time to arrange for a new claim and everything else."

Rob said nothing and she almost shook him in her impatience. "But it must be that. Nothing else makes sense. And your mother, Rob, I'm sure she'd agree with me. Why, the very first night I arrived I was absolutely certain she thought Gramps had told me something important about the mine. You ask her yourself."

"I don't have to," Rob said, and now Janey couldn't escape the bitterness in his voice. "The day after you arrived she had an old friend of hers, a mining engineer named Keith, go over every inch of this territory with a Geiger counter. There wasn't a sign of uranium but Keith sent in his bill anyway, including the time he'd spent walking in the last mile or so."

For a moment Janey only wanted to drop through the earth. "Rob, I'm sorry," she got out. "I—I was just dramatizing. Talking off the top of my head. I've been a fool."

Rob had already turned and was walking up the hill so fast that Janey had to run to catch up with him. She was hot and out of breath by the time she reached him, and the instant she saw his stony expression she knew she would only make matters worse if she said anything more about what had happened. It isn't my fault if he's ashamed of his mother, Janey told herself, but at the same instant she had an uncomfortable feeling that mention of Gramps and La Placita had been the direct cause of Rob's sudden change of mood, and not embarrassment over Mrs. Baker. I don't understand it, Janey thought, and now she was so keenly interested in Rob's reaction that she stopped inwardly justifying herself. I don't have an idea of what it is that upsets him about Gramps and the mine.

There was no hope of finding the answer now, and she walked

through the rusty gate Rob held open for her. "I reckon this cemetery isn't what an easterner would expect either," Rob said, and his voice was polite but perfectly impersonal. "Unless your brother wrote you and told you about it."

"Hank never mentioned it," Janey said, and as she looked around at the tawdry, neglected little graveyard her heart sank.

Rob led the way to the only new grave, in a far corner near the iron fence. Janey followed him without speaking. She looked down at the mound of raw red earth and then saw the plain granite marker on the grave beside it. "Jane Conant McGovern, b. June 24, 1893 d. Dec. 29, 1919."

"Your grandmother was about Sis Weaver's age when she died," Rob began, but Janey shook her head, not willing to listen. She was thinking about Gramps's stories in which Jane McGovern had invariably been the heroine, and trying to block out what Buck Hughes implied about his affair with Rob's mother. Gramps did love his wife, Janey told herself, I know he did. She stared down at the two graves, but there was no comfort there. If Gramps loved her and understood her the way he said he did how could he bury her in a place like this? He always said his Jane loved growing things and natural beauty more than anyone he ever knew.

Janey felt the prickle of tears in her eyes and moved off forcing herself to look at the other graves. A few, like her grandmother's, were marked with plain stone markers but more bore elaborate wooden crosses or slabs from which the gilt had long since pealed and even the carved letters were beginning to fade. "It's all pitiful," she said out loud. "Practically no one lived to be old, and the graves seem to be in two bunches, one around 1890 and the other over thirty years later."

"Eighteen-ninety and 1919 were the years the town had a boom," Rob said. "In between I imagine it was nearly deserted."

"And during the boom years life was rough, tough and terrible." Janey spoke with a briskness she didn't feel. "Sounds like all the gold-rush movies I've ever seen."

Rob walked over to the iron fence beyond Gramps's grave and

beckoned to Janey to follow him. She stood beside him and as she looked out over miles of open range and on and on to the purple mountains beyond she realized for the first time that from this hilltop cemetery the mine pits, the scarred earth, and even the crumbling ghost town itself were completely invisible. So that's the answer, this view, she thought. Gramps probably hated Fortune and everything connected with it, but what you see from here is the essence of what he and my grandmother loved most about New Mexico.

She turned to Rob, struggling for the right words to express what she felt, but before she could speak Rob began to recite.

"Under the wide and starry sky,
  Dig the grave and let me lie.
Glad did I live and gladly die,
  And I laid me down with a will.

This be the verse you grave for me.
  Here he lies where he long'd to be;
Home is the sailor, home from the sea,
  And the hunter home from the hill."

Janey flushed and her heart pounded but she didn't speak or stir as the sound of Rob's deep, quietly resonant voice floated off into the distance.

CHAPTER THIRTEEN

As Rob finished reciting, a horse whinnied loudly to the east of the cemetery. Janey jumped, and the rainbow spell of Rob's poetry was broken. "Was that Beau or Blue Belle?" she asked. "It sounded practically on top of us."

Rob shook his head. "Could have been miles away," he said. "Sound travels far around here. Further, maybe, than any place else in the country."

"That's what Gramps always said! Why, he even had a story about it," Janey began, and, suddenly feeling she was on dangerous ground, hurriedly went on with Gramps's anecdote. "There were two Yankee cavalrymen," she said, and avoided looking at Rob's face. "They were both New York City boys, rookies, who had never been west of the Hudson until they were sent out here. They were out on their first bivouac, and although they slept in different tents they both heard a coyote howl during the night. Each man was positive the coyote was sitting just outside his own tent, and crept out and fired at the sound. By good luck they missed hitting each other, but they woke up the sergeant, who told them the coyote was miles away and always had been. Probably laughing at them."

In the moment before Rob could answer Janey looked at the red soil at her feet, off into the distance, and everywhere but directly at Rob before she plunged on again. "I know it's a very corny little story," she apologized, "and I think if anyone had asked me about it a few weeks ago I'd probably have forgotten I'd even heard it, but since I've been out here all sorts of silly little things like that that Gramps told me ages ago keep popping into my mind. It's too absurd."

"I can see those rookies!" Rob said appreciatively, and Janey looked up, amazed at his enthusiasm. "And I don't call that story corn!" She took a step forward, trying to see the expression on his face. "You know I like——" Rob went on, but as Janey moved he apparently changed his mind about finishing his sentence and looked up instead at the sky. "Time we left," he said shortly. "Unless you don't want to eat, or want to get wet on the way home."

For an instant Janey was completely bewildered, but she knew now that it was useless to try and break down Rob's sudden waves of reserve and turned away for a last look at the view. "I'm coming," she said a moment later. "But first I just want to stare out there long enough so that I'll remember those mountains and not the peeling gilt monuments. I wish I could go through the cemetery blindfolded."

"You won't have to," Rob said, and beckoned to Janey to follow him through a break in the iron fence which led back to the road without going through the cemetery. "I didn't see that gap when we came up."

Neither of us was in any mood to notice it, Janey thought, but she didn't say so and hurried after Rob back to the horses where he unpacked the lunch he had brought along in a saddlebag. Janey was hungry and Mrs. Baker's homemade bread tasted even more delicious than usual. "I'm made over!" she said when they had finished, "and I'm glad we did the graveyard first and got that over with. Pretty soon let's explore around here and then I can hardly wait to see Cinder Cone. It sounds heavenly."

154

"Heavenly?" Rob's eyebrows lifted but he sounded amused. "That's a pretty fancy word and I wouldn't bet on your even liking the place. My folks and even an old friend like Chuck can't figure out what I see in it."

"I bet I will like it," Janey said, and stretched herself in the clear sunshine. "And I just can't believe it's going to rain, so we ought to have a marvelous ride. There's nothing I like better than riding through new country with a real destination ahead. I don't know how I'm going to stand being limited to Mr. Wentie's field and a few measly miles of trails when I go back home again."

Rob, who was busy fastening the saddlebag to the cantle of his saddle, said nothing, and a few minutes later Janey stood up and tried to look through the dusty windows of the general store. With the light behind her she made out a litter of yellowed newspapers, sheets of old flypaper, and in the back a long shelf still stocked with a few tin cans. She moved to the door and tried to open it but the lock held tight. "We can get in here," Rob called out, and she turned and saw that he had gone over to one of the small, one-room houses diagonally across the road. "This lock has been sprung for years."

Janey followed him across the road and they walked inside into a dark, low-ceilinged room littered with old rags and dirty papers. Behind the main room was an attached, windowless shed which was empty except for a rusty oil stove.

The gloom and the smell of stale oil, dust, and dry rot were indescribably depressing. Janey looked around trying to picture what daily life had been like when this place was inhabited. It was impossible to imagine anything glamorous or even bearable in such hopelessly sordid surroundings, and she was relieved when Rob led the way out of the back door.

All the houses had been built on a ridge facing the main road they had just left. As she stood on the back steps Janey saw that directly below them the land sloped to a narrow pathway where cart tracks and dry horse dung were still visible. "What was this used for?" she asked as she and Rob followed the path uphill behind the row of houses. "Did it lead to the mines?"

"This was used to get water. When there was any," Rob said, and pointed to the dry, cracked river bed at the bottom of the valley. "They didn't need paths to most of the mines. This whole place is honeycombed with tunnels and there may have been a dozen mineheads within yards of here. You'd never know it because the openings are all covered over by sand and dust. In the spring the sandstorms can be bad."

It must have been a nightmare for the women, Janey thought, but before she could say anything Rob nodded to a battered windmill just above them. "There were only a few of those," he said. "Most people depended on what water they could carry themselves or haul with a burro. I don't see how any woman lived through it."

A moment later they reached a crumbling adobe retaining wall and Rob climbed over it and, turning, helped Janey onto a flat, open space overlooking the valley. Janey looked around to where clumps of cholla cactus and wild zinnias made welcome splashes of color on the drab earth.

"Oh, this is nice," she said, and took a deep grateful breath of the dry aromatic air. "Blessings on whoever didn't build here."

"But there were houses here once." Rob pointed to charred logs that poked up through the sandy earth. "Maybe a half a dozen."

"I'm glad they aren't here now, then." Janey sat down with her back to the wall, feasting her eyes on the golden orange zinnias. "Golly, that shack we went through was grim. How could any human being live in a hole like that even for a week?"

"I think the people who built these houses had hopes and dreams we don't know anything about," Rob said. "And because we know few of them ever got what they wanted all we can see are the signs of failure they left behind."

"The whole place reeks of despair," Janey said, and for the first time it occurred to her how much of the defeat and disappointment in Gramps's life was connected with Fortune. "I wish I could imagine what it was like when the hopes and dreams still existed. Do you suppose it was all noise and excitement like a gold-rush movie?"

"Maybe a little," Rob said, and chewed meditatively on a long straw. "But without the Hollywood build-up. I've seen pictures of the main street during the last boom, and it was jammed with horses, mules, and model-T flivvers. I guess the store and the bar made money, but I don't believe there was much knifing and shooting. Of course everyone who came here came to line his own pocket, and the prospectors didn't pretend to be idealists. Still, from what the old-timers tell me I think most of them had a rough but real sense of justice, and I guess they managed to get along O.K. with each other."

"But, Rob, would you have liked it? If you'd been alive and the age you are now would you have come here to seek your fortune?"

"Not by a long shot," Rob said. "But that's because I've always been hipped on the idea that the end doesn't justify the means but the other way around. I aim to make a good life right along instead of just hoping to end up with a rich living. But maybe you don't go along with that or even understand what I mean. Probably you think the whole idea sounds as crazy as going loco over gold."

"No, it does not!" Janey said. "And I guess it's one reason why you've kept on with your livery stable. You'll stick to hard work that you like and respect rather than jump into a desk job you know you'd loathe and could only stand if you could kid yourself you were going to make a fortune out of it."

"Janey, that's it!" Rob said, and once more his voice, his face, and his whole personality grew more alive and vibrant as he spoke. "And you're the first person who's ever really understood what I'm driving at. I think everybody else I know, even Chuck and Miss 'Nita, think I'm playing ostrich. Just ducking reality."

"I don't believe either Miss 'Nita or Chuck ever thought you were ducking anything," Janey said. "I don't believe it for a minute and neither should you."

"You've helped me not to!" he said, reaching out impulsively. "Janey, you sure have helped me." She gave him her hand, but as their palms touched he drew back. "We'll have to get moving," he said abruptly, and stood up. "I've been jawing too long as it is."

"Don't be silly!" Janey began, but Rob moved off toward the road, and she realized that no matter what she said or did his expansive, confiding mood was over for the time being. She felt cramped from sitting in one place so long, and as she turned to push herself upward she felt a draft at her left side and looked around to see what it was. For a moment she could see nothing except the reddish rubble of baked earth and then, half hidden behind a thick clump of cactus, she saw a small, dark hole. She jumped up and, covering it with her hand, felt cold, damp air coming from the opening. "Rob!" she got out. "Look! Could this be a hole leading into a mine?"

Rob didn't answer, and as she started to speak to him again she heard the clanking of a shovel in the valley below them. At the same instant Rob hurried to the retaining wall and stared down in the direction of the sound. "Rob! Look at this!" Janey tried again. "I'm sure it goes down into a mine. Practically positive."

Rob reached her in two quick strides.

"Come on!" he said, and grabbed Janey's elbow. "We're clearing out."

"Rob, stop," she protested, but he only gripped her arm more firmly and led her onto the main road. They reached the horses in a matter of moments, but long before that Janey's temper had reached the boiling point.

"This is crazy!" she stormed. "I'd just found something really exciting and you bundle me off without looking at it. I won't go."

"Oh yes, you will." Rob untied the horses as he spoke. "There's a cloudburst practically on top of us. You better get on Belle in a hurry."

"I think you're making it up," Janey grumbled, but she did as she was told. "I don't see a sign of rain."

Rob said nothing, and swung himself into the saddle. A few moments later as Janey followed him around the curving end of the village street Blue Belle shied so suddenly that she almost lost her balance. "What was that all about?" she demanded, and at the same moment she saw the big, rangy piebald that had startled Belle. The horse was saddled and tied up behind the last of the little houses. "Rob, I bet that's the horse we heard whinny. Why didn't we see whoever rode him down here?"

"I did," Rob said. "It was Juan. I saw him down in the valley just before we left."

"Juan? I didn't know he owned a horse?"

"He doesn't," Rob said. "He probably borrowed it from a friend near Moriques where the car road was washed out."

"But how did he know where we were going? Do you suppose Twinks or Chuck told him?"

"I doubt it," Rob said, and looked anxiously over his shoulder. "But, Janey, we can't talk about Juan now. We've got to move!" He began to gallop, going faster and faster so that it was all Janey could do to keep up with him.

They tore on over the red clay road until suddenly the landscape ahead of them darkened and the rain fell. In a matter of seconds Janey's glasses were useless, and she shoved them into her shirt pocket.

"Janey, can you handle Belle?" Rob shouted to make himself heard above the pounding rain. "There's shelter a little way ahead."

"I'll manage!" Janey concentrated every nerve and muscle on riding her horse. Belle's ears were back. She fought for the bit, and the reins tore at the wet skin of Janey's fingers. "Easy girl. Easy!" Janey coaxed, but the rain beat the sound back on her lips. There was nothing she could do but grip with her knees and give and take on the hard, slippery reins.

"Janey!" Rob shouted again. "This way!" He turned sharply right and Belle, doubling like a cat, plunged after him up a steep woodland trail.

The wet branches slapped and stung on Janey's head and shoulders, pushing her off balance. She gripped harder than ever with her knees, but now her heart pumped madly and her breath grew short. I can't hold out much longer, she thought. I can't! I'll have to stop.

An instant later Rob pulled Beau to a standstill, dropped to the ground, and grabbed Belle's bridle. "Over there!" he shouted, and Janey saw a broken-down shack just beyond them. "Can you make it?"

Somehow Janey slid off and stumbled breathlessly through the gaping doorway. She turned and saw that Rob had let go of Beau and had both hands on Belle's bridle. The mare whinnied and tossed her head, but he managed to lead her into the broken-down building. "Janey! Are you all right?" he demanded. "I could kick myself for not starting sooner."

"I'm O.K.," Janey said, and found that she was shaking all over. "But that was some ride! Do storms always come as quickly as that around here?"

"Usually," Rob said, and fastened Blue Belle to one of the thick, half-fallen timbers at the side of the building and went out for Beau. "The horses'll be all right," he said as he finished. "I've used that beam as a hitching post before. It's you I'm worried about."

"I'm really fine." Janey tried to wipe her wet face on her drenched sleeve. "Just soaked and completely lost. Are we anywhere near Cinder Cone?"

"Behind it," Rob said, and pulled a windbreaker out of his saddle bag and forced it on Janey despite her protests. "I used to ride down here when I was a kid. That's why I knew about this place."

They went to the doorway and stood together, gazing in hypnotized silence at the pelting rain. "No chance of seeing Cinder Cone now," Rob said gloomily. "As soon as this lifts we'll have to take Roger's Cut through the bottom of the canyon and we'll be lucky if we don't have trouble at that. This is sure to cause flash floods. I was a fool not to leave Fortune as soon as we'd eaten."

"I wouldn't have missed the exploring for anything," Janey said. "And Rob, I'm almost positive I found a hole into a mine tunnel at that cleared place. That's why I nearly blew my top when you made me leave. Where do you suppose the hole leads to?"

"It leads to the mine entrance in the valley," Rob said. "I know because I saw Juan working there when I looked down just before we left."

"*Juan?* Was it his shovel we heard? What was he doing in the valley?"

"Covering up the mine entry because he knew this storm would finish the job for him. He's probably been waiting for a day just like this for weeks."

"So his going to Fortune didn't have anything to do with us after all," Janey said. Rob didn't answer, and as a new idea struck Janey she went on more quickly. "Rob, do you suppose that mine where Juan was working was La Placita? Juan must know where it was located."

Rob only shifted his feet uneasily, and as Janey turned to look at his face her sudden guess hardened into a certainty. "You think so too!" she burst out. "You were probably certain that mine was La Placita the second you saw Juan by the opening. I bet you were sure of it when you turned and hurried me back to the horses. You were sure, weren't you?"

For a moment Rob stood perfectly still. "Yes," he said finally, and his curt monosyllabic answer worked on Janey's temper like heat on a pressure cooker.

"I like that!" she sputtered. "You know perfectly that I want, that I absolutely have, to find that mine, and yet when we learn exactly where it is you haul me off without saying a word!"

"We had to go because of the storm," Rob said. "We should have gone sooner——"

"Indeed we should!" Janey interrupted angrily. "Then I'd never in this world have found La Placita. But even so you don't have to worry. You know I'm terribly nearsighted and a fool about directions and that it'll only be sheer luck if I can find anybody living who knew where it was and who can take me there. I don't know why you don't want me to go near it but I'm certain your precious Juan won't spoil your fun by taking me." She talked on and on, and as one bitter, sarcastic word bred another even more unpleasant Rob listened in silence.

When Janey was finally still he looked down at her, and his lean face was rigid with self-control. "Are you all through?" he asked. "Because if you are we ought to start for home. Storm's nearly over."

CHAPTER FOURTEEN

For an instant Janey glared at Rob without speaking. Gradually the tide of her temper ebbed and she looked down at her wet shoes, feeling thoroughly ashamed of herself. "Look," she began, "I didn't mean everything I said just now. I know you'd drop dead before you'd cheat anybody of anything."

"Thank you," Rob said coldly, and busied himself with the horses.

Janey said nothing until he had Beau ready and had turned and lengthened Blue Belle's stirrup leathers. "What are you doing that for?" she asked. "They're just the right length."

"I'd like you to ride Beau home," Rob said, and he sounded as though he were talking to Billy Spring. "There's sure to be water in the bottom of the canyon and I've never tried Blue Belle at fording a stream."

"I'm riding Belle!" Janey said, and swung herself into the saddle before Rob could stop her. "Riding's one thing I learned how to do at home, even if nobody ever taught me anything about mine claims, or queer old Indians, or—or cloudbursts in the desert."

"Janey. Listen," Rob protested, but Janey only wheeled Blue

Belle out of his reach, and a moment later he mounted Beau and led the way along a trail behind the shack which had given them shelter.

For the next ten minutes they rode single file and in silence. Janey shivered as the drenched branches sent icy trickles down her neck, and her legs ached from reaching for the overlong stirrups. "Are you all right?" Rob turned in his saddle as the trail leveled off at the bottom of the hill. "Do you think you can manage with those stirrups until we get to the river?"

"I'm fine," Janey said, and forced herself to sit erect. "But you look half frozen. Sure you don't want your jacket back?"

"Positive," Rob said, and guided Beau down the right-hand side of a fork in the trail. It widened almost immediately, and for the first time since the storm had broken Blue Belle moved along as calmly as old Chesty. After a few minutes Janey reached down with her right hand to shorten her stirrup. The wide, double-holed leather strap of the western saddle was still unfamiliar to her, and her hand was awkward with cold. She pulled Blue Belle to a stop but she wasn't any more successful and she knew she would either have to dismount or ask for help. She looked up to call to Rob, but when she saw he had disappeared around a bend in the road she dropped the saddle flap and urged Blue Belle forward. I'll ride like this if I'm stiff for a week, she fumed. Rob isn't the only one with a little pride.

She rode along for perhaps five minutes without seeing Rob. When she came to a place where a high wall of rock forced her to make a choice of which way to go she was suddenly frightened. The ground below was too stony to show hoofprints and there were no other signs. "Rob!" she shouted. "Rob, where are you?" She heard the eerie, twisted echo of her own voice and Blue Belle's shrill whinny. The mare's muscles tensed and she grabbed at the bit. Before Janey could stop her Belle wheeled to the right of the huge rock.

Belle's wrong. Rob didn't go this way! Janey sawed at Blue Belle's mouth but the mare kept on going. She clung to the pommel, ducking the pine branches, and a moment later Belle charged out of the woods onto the riverbank. As the mare slowed down Janey caught sight of Rob. He had dismounted and taken off his chaps. He stood at the edge of the river, looking relaxed and at ease as he contemplated the muddy water. You'd think he was fishing. Janey's spine still prickled with receding fear as she rode toward him. And he must have known I'd lose my way at that rock!

"We'll switch horses right here," Rob said when she was only a few yards away from him. "Beau's done plenty of fording, so he won't give you any trouble. The best place to go in is right there. I've cased the riverbank while I was waiting for you."

"Waiting? I didn't notice it!" Janey was much more conscious of answering Rob than she was of handling Belle, who began to fidget, with her ears pricked forward, as they neared the rushing water. "And do please remember I'm not one of your cub scouts."

Belle pawed at the ground. Rob reached for her bridle and Janey jerked the reins away from him. Blue Belle reared! Janey's feet flew out of the overlong stirrups. An instant later they clattered down hard against Blue Belle's flank. Blue Belle squealed and lunged forward into the water. Janey was knocked hard against the pommel. Then everything happened at once!

Janey felt the cold, roaring force of the water on her right. She heard Beau whinny. Over it all Rob's voice shouted, "Get clear of Belle's heels! Janey, for God's sake get clear. Let yourself go with the current!"

The next instant Janey was swept out of the saddle and rushed headlong down the muddy stream. She began to swim, struggling and floundering in her heavy clothes and expecting at any moment to feel the mare's shod hoofs in her side.

She went with the current and managed to keep her head above water. In a few moments she found she could touch, and pushed herself slantingly forward toward a promontory on the far bank. She caught at it breathlessly and for an instant hung suspended. She tried again and now, as the water whirled and sucked at her feet, pulled herself to safety. For a second she lay still, fighting for breath, with her ears ringing. A moment or two later as she crawled further up onto the bank she saw that Blue Belle was upstream near where they had first gone into the water. The mare was floundering through knee-deep mud with her head back and her eyes rolling with fear.

If it's quicksand she's gone! As the thought flashed through Janey's mind she saw that Rob had crossed the river on Beau, flung himself to the ground, and was moving toward Blue Belle.

An instant later the mare found a footing and plunged up the shallow bank. As she reached solid ground she snorted wildly and shook herself. Then she collected her legs under her belly to bolt, and Rob flung himself forward to stop her.

Rob'll be hurt! Janey's throat and chest ached with fear. If Belle gets him with her front hoofs she'll kill him!

Rob grasped at Belle's bridle with both hands. The mare squealed and reared, lifting him off his feet. Fifty yards away Janey crouched in silence, caught in the helpless immobility of a nightmare.

Belle threw back her head again and again, but her first frantic fear was lessening. Rob began to talk to her, his deep voice soothing and very calm. Blue Belle side-stepped and balked, trying to break Rob's grip, but he held on. A few moments later he was able to lead her further up the bank and tie her firmly with his lariat.

Thank God! Janey dropped her face on her arms, while her heart thundered and the blood drummed in her ears. Oh, thank God, Rob wasn't killed or hurt.

For a long moment Janey stayed still, her eyes tightly shut. The river roared on below her but she no longer heard it. Gradually as the dizzying impact of sudden fear and equally sudden relief receded she breathed more easily. How queer, she thought, I'm not in love with Rob. He's never once made me feel the way Buck did at the square dance, but for a second just now I felt if Rob'd been killed I'd be dead too. Perhaps it was seeing it all happen and not being able to do a thing to help. The way I was frightened about Betsy at Elbow Crest, only a thousand times more so. Probably if I'd had to watch Buck in danger like that I would have fainted.

A few moments later Janey pushed herself to her feet and for the first time realized that she was covered with clinging red mud. She tried shakily to brush it off and then she saw that Rob was running toward her. "Janey! Are you hurt? If Blue Belle kicked you I'll shoot her myself."

Janey shook her head, caught between laughter and tears. "I'm —all—right." The words sounded breathless and incoherent. She fumbled in her shirt pocket and pulled out her glasses, dirty but unbroken, and held them out as a symbol. "I'm perfectly all right. Just—just filthy and terribly ashamed."

"It was my fault." Rob's hands stretched out toward her. "It all happened because I've been such a stubborn fool."

"I was worse. About changing horses, about leaving Fortune, and about La Placita. Wh-what Gramps used to call a whim of iron."

Rob's hands dropped to his side and he stopped as suddenly as though she had slapped him. "We can go back to the mine whenever you want," he said. "It's the last thing on earth Juan meant to do, but he showed me where the entrance was so I couldn't forget it if I tried. I'll take you back to it as soon as we can arrange to go."

"I know you will!" Janey said, and now the location of the mine seemed insignificant compared to understanding Rob and explaining herself to him. "I think I really knew that all along, even when I lost my temper back in the shack. I was—was just letting off steam."

"Don't blame you." Rob stood perfectly still, but as Janey looked up at him she felt he was retreating from her as surely as though he had taken to his heels and run away.

"But, Rob, there's more to it than my having a tantrum. Don't you see that? Every time we move, every time anyone even mentions Gramps and the mine it's like a stone wall coming between us. I like working on your ranch, I have the feeling we're good friends, and then suddenly the mine comes up and we're absolute strangers. Don't you understand at all what I mean?"

Rob stared at the river for a long time before he answered. "I agree that you ought to see the mine," he said finally, and his voice was entirely matter-of-fact. "Before I knew where it was I thought you'd be better off if you forgot the whole thing, but now I see you can't. Will you wait until next week when I can get Chuck back so we can ride over to Fortune again?"

"Of course! But my seeing the mine isn't the whole point. It's getting to the bottom of the mystery, clearing away the block that comes up every time it's mentioned that really matters."

"I'm dead sure there isn't anything in that mine that's worth stealing," Rob went on. "If there had been Juan would have taken it for my grandfather years ago."

"That doesn't matter," Janey said, and choked over the realization that all Rob had understood was her interest in the mine and not its threat as a barrier between them. She started to say so, hesitated, and went on again, choosing her words with agonizing care. "I was a fool to think we'd find uranium," she began, "but I'm like that. Ready to ride off in all four directions at once. Before I left home I was sure it was crammed full of gold. But Rob, the point is that Gramps was the same way before me. Too quick and too hasty. Ever since I've been out here the feeling's grown inside of me that Gramps had to go back to that mine to save his own soul. I don't know why or for what reason, but perhaps it was some kind of expiation. And I've avoided that idea, turned my back on it by telling myself he was just a lovable old boy who never meant anybody any real harm."

Rob shook his head but she went on in spite of him. "You can do harm without meaning it," she said. "Especially if you're quick and impulsive. And Gramps knew that and tried his best to teach me."

"He did nothing wrong at La Placita," Rob said, and Janey was startled at the bitterness in his voice. "Except perhaps to leave people indebted to him in a way they'll never be able to repay."

168

Janey looked at him, wondering. "I don't understand," she said. "I don't know what you're talking about."

"You ought to," Rob said. "You still feel guilty because of a childish but perfectly natural thing you did when you avoided your grandfather on that station platform. Hasn't it ever occurred to you that my family, especially my grandfather and my mother, may have really hurt him?"

"But that shouldn't matter to us!" Janey burst out, but Rob had already turned and was leading the way back to the horses. She stood still, watching him, until he stopped and beckoned to her. "Please, Janey, come," he said. "It won't help if you catch pneumonia."

She followed after him, her cold feet squelching up and down in her soaked shoes. Her clothes clung to her clammily and the rough wet denim chafed at her knees. She was suddenly aware of being tired, and it seemed like a long walk along the twisted, uneven section of the riverbank which separated her from where Rob had tied the horses. "Take your time," Rob called back to her. "If you're all in when we get home Mom'll be terribly upset and I wouldn't blame her. She feels responsible to your family."

"I'm all right," Janey said, but as she moved forward a sudden sense of depression weighed down on her. Rob's earlier friendliness and all the interest and concern he had shown during their long day together stemmed more from his sense of responsibility than from any personal attraction or real understanding. He means to be nice to me, Janey thought, and the idea only added to her dejection. But exactly the same way he means to be nice to the cub scouts or Mrs. Appleton or anyone else.

CHAPTER FIFTEEN

When Janey caught up with Rob she saw that he
had shortened the stirrups on Blue Belle's saddle
and was holding the mare's head, waiting for her to mount. "Feel
like riding her?" he asked. "She's calmed down and it's a good
idea to——"

"Ride the horse that's just thrown you." Janey finished the sentence. "I was brought up on that too. In fact Gramps borrowed
money for my riding lessons because he thought learning to manage a horse was the one perfect discipline."

"I go along with that," Rob said, and held Belle's head while
Janey mounted. "So much so that I'm going to have horses at my
school, no matter what it costs. There's nothing like riding to teach
self-control."

"It didn't work with me," Janey said. "And today proves it.
Betsy Appleton would have done a better job of taking Belle across
that river than I did."

"Maybe she would." Rob chuckled as he swung himself into
the saddle. "But it was my fault for not following my pet theory.
The first time I saw you I guessed that you were a hot-headed

little spitfire when you were a kid. If I'd acted on that and *dared* you to ride Beau instead of asking you to because it was safer I couldn't have kept you off his back."

"I guess you're right," Janey admitted. "You probably are." They moved off, and Janey realized that although she was still cold and wet, now that she was actually in the saddle she was less miserably uncomfortable and depressed than she had been a short while ago.

"Belle's really amazing," Janey said a few minutes later. "Right now she's as gentle as can be and as bridle-wise as a polo pony. It's only when she gets frightened that she's hard to handle."

"Whoever broke her fouled things up at the beginning," Rob said. "The man I bought her from had only had her for a few weeks and didn't know who'd raised her, but whoever it was made a mess of it, probably by trying to teach her too much too fast."

"How would it be if we sort of started all over again," Janey suggested, "and used her in the ring every day at a walk, trot, and canter? Or is that treating her too much like an eastern saddle horse?"

"Sounds like a good idea to me," Rob said, "but it's going to take time. I wish I could afford to keep her over the winter."

"I do too," Janey said, and didn't add that she wished even more that winter wouldn't come for a long, long time. The summer, and especially her visit West, which had seemed such a solid block of time only a short while ago, was melting away. It was startling to realize how soon she would be going home.

Rob led the way along a dark, stony trail beneath cliff-like walls that glistened from the recent rain. "That's called Sabre Cleft," he said once, and pointed to where heavily fissured rocks jutted out in an incomplete arch overhead. "From a place like that two men could keep off an army."

Or keep people in, Janey thought, looking at the prisonlike walls on either side. This place would give me the creeps if I went to school near here.

"The land in back of us opens up wide," Rob went on, and Janey felt that he had read her mind. "This isn't a trap like the dead-end canyon where Kit Carson bottled up the Navajos. Cinder Cone spreads out into a regular plateau at the top, and there are two good trails coming in from east and west on the way up."

"Good," Janey said. "I'd hate to think your dream school was going to be built in a natural prison."

"No, ma'am!" Rob grinned at her and began to talk about Kit Carson and the Navajo exile to Fort Sumter. Rob told his story so well that Janey felt as though she were listening to an eyewitness account. She forgot her surroundings, and in what seemed like no time at all they came out on the familiar range below the Bakers'.

From there on the footing was excellent, and they rode at an easy canter until they were within a few hundred yards of home. Janey was thoroughly warmed up by the exercise, and when they reached the corral she began to jump off as though nothing had happened. The minute her feet touched the ground she knew she had made a mistake. Every nerve in her body twanged like an aching tooth, and her knees felt rubbed raw. She grimaced as she pulled the muddy levis away from her chafed legs. It was bad enough to feel filthy dirty, but it was even more depressing to realize she must look worse than she felt. As she straightened up, pushing the hair out of her eyes, she saw Rob was looking over at her. "I'm a mess and I know it!" she said. "All the charm of a half-drowned rat."

Rob shook his head. "I was thinking how curly your hair——" he began, but before he could finish Twinks popped out from the stable where she had been waiting for them.

"Boy, are you two ever wet and muddy!" she said, and wrinkled her straight little nose disdainfully. "You both smell something awful."

"We know all about that," Rob said. "So suppose you go and run a good hot bath for Janey? Otherwise she'll be stiff as a board tomorrow."

"That saddle and Blue Belle's canter may save me," Janey said as she took a few gingerly steps forward. "If I'd had to trot home on an English pancake I'd be dead now."

"Rob! Janey!" Mrs. Baker's voice shrilled down to them from the kitchen porch. "Whatever happened? I declare when that storm came and Chuck left I almost went out of my mind worrying about you. Do come up here right away. Both of you!"

"Janey's on her way," Rob called back. "And I'll be up as soon as I've taken care of the horses."

"Rob, you hop it! Mom means business!" Twinks spoke out of the side of her mouth. "I'll put the horses away and you can finish later."

"Look who's taking over. The new stable sergeant." Rob smiled and riffled his hand through Twinks's straight hair. She threw her arms around his neck and, pulling his head down, whispered furiously. As he straightened up his expression changed and he no longer looked amused. "I know I promised," he told Twinks, and to Janey's surprise he left the horses and walked up toward the house so quickly that she had trouble keeping up with him.

The moment they reached the kitchen door Mrs. Baker hurried Janey toward the hall. "I have a nice tub with bath salts in it waiting for you," she said, and flicked on each light switch as they passed. "And you'll have time for a nap before supper. You must be worn out."

"Oh, I'm fine," Janey said, and saw that Mrs. Baker motioned behind her back for Rob to wait in the kitchen. "But the tub sounds heavenly, especially the bath salts. I reek of wet horse and mud!"

"I brought your bathrobe and slippers in here." Mrs. Baker sounded as fluttery as she had on the evening of Janey's arrival. "So just leave your clothes in a pile by the kitchen and I'll wash them later. You must have had a dreadful day. These western storms are too horrible, and Fortune is so unattractive even in broad sunlight." Janey started to speak, but before she could say a word Mrs. Baker hurried on: "Oh, Janey, there are some letters for you on your bureau that came while you were gone. And now if you are sure you have everything you need I must go and speak to Rob."

She shut the door and Janey heard her quick, nervous footsteps pattering down the rugless hall. What's that all about, Janey wondered, as she undressed and eased herself cautiously into the tub. Is Mrs. Baker really just upset over the storm, or didn't she like our going to Fortune in the first place?

There was no way of knowing, so Janey lay back in the tub and gave herself up to enjoying the warm, fragrant water. Soon her thoughts floated back effortlessly over the high spots of the long day she and Rob had spent together. She saw Rob as he had looked trotting into Fortune, reciting poetry, leading Belle from the river, and during a dozen other clearly defined incidents. Rob's looks changed with his mood the way the New Mexico countryside changed with the shifting light, Janey realized, and smiled to herself. But, like the mountains and the plains which only appeared to change, Rob's courage and self-discipline, which were the essential part of his character, stayed constant. He's about the strongest personality I've ever met, Janey decided, and for a fleeting, unself-conscious second imagined herself held close in Rob's arms the way she had been in Buck's arms at the Weavers' party.

The next second Janey's self-awareness returned and she sat bolt upright and began to scrub furiously. I'm being a fool, she scolded herself. Rob's simply a friend. He's never even thought of me as a girl, and I'd probably hate it and be bored stiff if he did. I've only been going on this way because so much has happened while we were together and I haven't seen Buck for ages. Not since Saturday night.

As Janey went on washing herself she tried to conjure up a picture of Buck as he had looked and seemed when they had been together. She could see the crisp, starched press of his uniform when he strode into the airport and the rich, dark red of the shirt he had worn square dancing. She even remembered a dozen luxurious details of his car, but her image of Buck himself stayed as static and incomplete as when she had tried to guess what he had been like as a small boy.

She consciously tried to picture Buck during the electric moment at the end of the round dance. Her own surprised—thrilled

174

—and eventually embarrassed reaction was much clearer than any image of Buck. Finally she found herself again mentally dueling with Hank, whose letter she still had not answered. Hank doesn't understand a thing about Buck Hughes or about the real me for that matter! Janey stepped out of the tub and dried herself off. He means well but he's the perennial older brother and he can't or won't accept the fact that I'm grown up.

She slipped on her bathrobe and, picking up the dirty clothes, carried them into the hall. The kitchen door was shut for the first time since Janey had been at the ranch. As she came up to it she heard Mrs. Baker's high angry voice through the thin wooden panel. "Robert, I no longer expect you to consider me," Mrs. Baker was saying, "but I must ask you not to interfere with Twinks's future. After all, one of the reasons why the poor little thing——"

Janey dropped her bundle of muddy clothes and fled to her own room. She reached for her letters and lay down on the bed. Why is Mrs. Baker always picking on Rob, she fumed, and now the urge to stand up for him drove every other thought out of her mind. She loves him but she can't see how she hurts him by trying to make him into something he isn't.

There was nothing Janey could do about it so she began to read letters. Uncle John's began with enthusiastic thanks for the letter Janey had written to him and went on to describe places in London he knew she had read about. Mum wrote of Linda's excitement at seeing the crown jewels in the Tower and Pete's thrill in double-decker bus rides. "Your letter and the darling picture that Miss Murphy took have really made my summer," she continued. "I am so proud of you and so happy that you are getting so much out of the Southwest. It's going to be marvelous when you, and Hank, and the four of us here are together again in September. So many experiences and six different points of view. It'll be thrilling."

Janey turned to the postcards. Linda's was neat, tidy, and conventional. Pete's was a smudgy scrawl of exclamation points and stars, ending with a row of sprawling X marks. They're different all right, Janey smiled, as she put down the cards. And maybe that's why they're both such wonderful kids. The twins have had breaks Twinks doesn't know anything about. Nobody has ever tried to change them or mold them into a stiff set pattern.

She lay back and pulled up a light blanket. Mum never tried to change Hank or me either, she realized, and neither did Uncle John when he came into the family. They've both always encouraged us to be our best selves, and I never appreciated it until I came out here. She closed her eyes, still thinking about her family, and fell fast asleep. She didn't stir until there was a knock on her door. "Supper's almost ready!" Twinks called out. "And it's steak and fried potatoes and we're starving."

"I'll be there in two secs!" Janey hurried into clean clothes and went out to find that Rob and Twinks were already seated at the table. "I'm sorry I'm late," she said as Rob, looking supernaturally clean and brushed, pulled out her chair.

"You're not." Mrs. Baker brought the steak in from the kitchen as she spoke. "You're exactly on time and I do hope you're rested."

"Perfectly," Janey said. "I don't even think I'm going to be stiff."

"I'm so glad. I always think bath salts help." Mrs. Baker chatted to Janey as she served the food, while Twinks peppered Rob with questions about the flash flood.

"Oh, Janey," Mrs. Baker went on. "I mustn't forget to tell you that Buck Hughes telephoned while you were out to say that he's been able to arrange his hours on Thursday so that he'll be off duty much earlier than he expected to be. He wants to call for you at one and run you down to Hayesville before you visit Isleta."

"Hayesville?" Janey looked up to find that Twinks had stopped in the middle of a sentence and was staring at her across the table. "What sort of a place is that?"

"It's the new uranium center of the state."

"You don't want to miss it."

"It's really one of the things you ought to see out here."

Mrs. Baker and Twinks seemed to vie with one another urging Janey to accept. "Buck has taken so much trouble to get off duty that I do hope you won't disappoint him, Janey," Mrs. Baker said. "It seems he has to start work at six every morning this week in order to be free on Thursday."

"Just think of that car of his. Wow!" Twinks waved her arms in a pantomime of flight as she spoke. "You'll sure enough zoom down to Hayesville!"

Janey looked from Mrs. Baker to Twinks and back again, puzzled by the unexpected pressure, and then Rob spoke. "We've a light afternoon at the stable, if that's worrying you," he said. "And the country on the way to Hayesville is worth seeing. I'd go if I were you."

"Why, yes. I think I'd love it," Janey began, and Mrs. Baker nodded approvingly.

"Good! I told Buck you'd accept if he didn't hear from you. And by the way, Jancy dear, Buck also left word that your square set performance at La Tavernita was moved up to this Saturday."

"But we need more practice!" Janey looked over at Rob for support but now he was busily eating and once more Mrs. Baker and Twinks launched into a chorus of persuasions and encouragements.

"I still think it's too soon," Janey said when they paused for breath. "I've only done 'Butterfly Whirl' that one evening, and Tom Pierce said he wasn't very sure of it either."

"I felt the same way when Mom first told me about it after we came home," Rob said, and it occurred to Janey that this had something to do with the angry words she had heard through the kitchen door. "But the Weavers are sure that if we practice at their house just before the show——"

"Everything'll work out just swell!" Twinks interrupted, but Mrs. Baker frowned at her to be still and took over the conversation herself.

"The Weavers and Buck have arranged things beautifully," she said. "You're to have light refreshments at their house and a good hour for practice before you go to La Tavernita. And of course they expect you to stay on there, as their guests, for a really delicious meal after your performance. Rob didn't risk taking my word for it and so he telephoned and checked on every detail for himself."

"Yes. I spoke to Herb Weaver," Rob said. "And Janey, I called Chuck Hemsted and he can come here a week from today."

"Oh, that's fine," Janey said, but for the moment her mind was more on the coming square dance performance than a future trip to Fortune and the mine. Before Janey could say anything more Mrs. Baker spoke up again, and it was perfectly clear that as far as she was concerned the matter was settled.

"Everything's turned out very well," Mrs. Baker said, "as things usually do if we don't waste our time borrowing trouble. And now, Twinks, do tell Janey and Rob the story you told me when you brought in the mail."

Nothing loathe to be the center of attention, Twinks launched into a graphic account of Chuck's troubles with a fat, elderly and very timid customer who had turned up at the corral just when Twinks had gone for the mail.

Janey tried to pay attention but she was still too absorbed with the coming square dance to take in much of what Twinks was saying. She was glad when supper and tidying up were over and she could go back to her own room to read. She picked up the worn copy of *The Land of Poco Tempo* which Rob had loaned her a few days ago, saying it was one of the earliest and best collections of Indian folk tales in English. She had enjoyed the first few chapters enormously. Now, while her eyes followed the printed letters, most of the meaning escaped her as her thoughts spiraled off to wondering about Buck and Rob and her relationship to both of them.

At quarter-past nine she gave up the pretense of reading and undressed herself and turned out the light. For a long time she lay on her back, looking up into the darkness, trying to sort out and evaluate everything that had happened to her since she had left her bed early in the morning. Evaluating, or even chronologically remembering, exactly what had occurred seemed to be utterly impossible. The day had been such a kaleidoscopic jumble of sunshine and storm, excitement and fear, understanding and bewilderment that in thinking it over Janey felt as though she were trying to jump back onto a madly plunging seesaw. Tomorrow, she told herself, tomorrow I'll be able to make more sense.

She sighed and turned over and stretched herself out more comfortably. She closed her eyes, and gradually her healthily tired body took over. Janey fell asleep and didn't wake up until the morning sunshine slanted across her bed and the oom-pa-pa of Twinks's record player wafted in through the open window.

She dressed and breakfasted quickly and started for the stable. From the porch she saw that Rob had most of the horses already saddled and tied to the corral and that he himself, hatless and bare to the waist, was busy brushing Blue Belle. "How's Belle?" Janey called out. "Did yesterday do her any harm?"

"Not a bit!" Rob waved his brush exuberantly. "She's fine but the big point is, how are you? Stiff? Saddle sore? You had a workout."

"I feel fine," Janey answered, and was surprised to realize that what she had said was true. "Simply wonderful."

She had slept deeply and had woken refreshed and confident. Now as she walked toward the stable she felt that she had exaggerated and overdramatized the confusion and concern which had beset her last evening. I was probably more exhausted than I realized, she thought, and when I couldn't concentrate I started inventing troubles. Right now everything's cleared up. Rob's a fine person, we work well together, and I'm glad he's decided to help me see La Placita, but Buck Hughes is the important man in my life. Why, Buck's so attractive Maisie Taylor and her crowd would swoon if he ever came to Bayport. And Buck went to all the trouble of changing his duty hours just so that he can come over on Thursday to take me out.

A few moments later when Janey reached the corral a sudden little gust of dusty wind made her sneeze. "Why, the earth's just as dry as ever," she said as she put away her handkerchief. "The corral, and the ring beyond, for as far as I can see look parched. If there wasn't some river mud caked on my shoes I'd think I'd dreamed or imagined both the storm and the flash flood. Everything looks just the way it did before."

"It is!" Rob said disgustedly. "A flash flood carries top soil down the nearest arroyo but it doesn't water or irrigate or do any good. Nothing round here's changed a bit."

Rob finished brushing Blue Belle, put on her saddle and bridle, and suggested that Janey might begin schooling in the dirt ring. "Take it easy and let Belle limber up slowly," he said. "We've plenty of time. The cub scouts aren't coming until ten-thirty."

"Good." Janey patted the mare's pretty dark head, collected her reins, and mounted.

"Let's take a look at that cinch." Rob moved beside Blue Belle as he spoke and reached under the saddle flap. "Sometimes the canvas gives or a buckle gets rusty after a wetting. No point taking a chance on having the saddle roll if we don't have to. Let your foot swing free, Janey, so I can see what I'm doing."

Janey did as Rob said in silence. Now that he was so very close to her she was suddenly much less certain that all the thoughts and feelings which had come to her last night were exaggerated. As Rob pulled on the cinch his brown, muscular shoulders and his close-cropped, light brown hair pressed against Janey's side and sent a sudden electric spark of awareness through her whole body.

"Brother, but this thing's stiff," Rob grunted. "I should have oiled it last night when I cleaned the rest of the saddle. Stupid thing is I never thought of it until just now."

Rob was completely absorbed in his work and didn't look up as a hot, embarrassed blush spread up from Janey's neck. This is crazy, it's—it's disgusting, Janey thought, and shifted around so that she was almost sitting sidesaddle away from Rob. Rob didn't even know he'd touched me and I practically turned inside out. But it doesn't mean anything. It can't. It's just some stupid reflex that hasn't anything to do with how I really think or feel.

Rob pulled upward again and then stepped back. "That does it," he said. "You better ride over to that post and back so I can see if it's going to hold."

Janey rode off, still arguing within herself. It was a reflex. Mere reflex. One half of Janey's mind repeated the pleasantly ambiguous word over and over. An equally persistent half made it clear that here was a direct proof that Janey had been quite wrong when she had told herself positively that she would be bored or irritated by any demonstration of affection from Rob.

"Saddle looks all right," Rob called out. "So how about bringing Belle back? I only meant for you to go as far as the hitching post."

Janey turned and rode back, and when she reached Rob he looked at her curiously. "Sure you want to school Belle this early?" he said. "Belle's going fine but if you want to start training her over again in the ring you'll have to watch out every second. You looked as though you were daydreaming when you rode her past the post."

"I've just woken up!" Janey shook herself hard, hoping to get rid of the inwardly arguing voice. "So let's see what I can do to make Blue Belle into a model show horse." She touched the mare lightly with her heel, and as Blue Belle sprang forward Janey concentrated her mind, and nerves, and muscles on the job of schooling.

She walked, trotted, walked again, and then, urging and restraining equally eased the mare into a slow controlled canter. Belle responded perfectly and moved on at a gentle, flowing gait that was nearly flawless. Janey went through the whole cycle over and over again until Rob told her that it was nearly ten o'clock, when she trotted Belle slowly toward the corral.

"Not half bad," Rob said, and, as he dropped down from the high fence where he had been watching, Janey saw that he had on his hat and shirt and looked ready for business. "You really had an idea yesterday. Belle looks like a natural for the show ring. Maybe we got something out of that flash flood after all."

"I hope so." Janey said, but as she watched Rob deftly unsaddling Blue Belle she wasn't thinking of the mare's education or future but of the indescribably frightening moment by the river when Belle's steel-shod hoofs had been perilously close to Rob's head.

What does it mean? What does it mean when you're so afraid for someone else you're paralyzed? Janey asked herself, and now her own answer of yesterday seemed hopelessly unconvincing. For a moment the question churned through her mind, and then for the second time that morning she forced herself into action. "I'll get Sponge and Chesty ready!" she told Rob, and hurried off to the wooden bar where the saddles were kept. "I'd bet anything you like those cubs'll be here before ten-thirty."

CHAPTER SIXTEEN

Janey was entirely right about the cub scouts. Fifteen minutes before the appointed time a dusty green station wagon drove up the hill and the excited little boys tumbled out as it stopped moving.

"I'm going to ride the burro!" Billy Spring shouted. "If Jakey can ride him so can I. Jake'll ride my horse and I'll ride old Tote like a N'indian."

"I want to ride Tote too."

"So do I."

"Me too."

As the cub scouts capered around the corral Janey wondered how Rob could possibly handle such a tidal wave of enthusiasm without using force. She saw him speak to Jakey Weathers and saw Jakey nod enthusiastically. "All set, fellas," Rob sang out. "Jake's going to ride Sponge today. The rest of you can each have a turn riding Tote bareback until we start in trotting and cantering, when we'll just use the horses. Let's go."

In a surprisingly short time Rob and Janey had all the boys mounted and walking slowly around the ring while they stood on a clump of dry gamma grass in the middle and watched them file by. "Rob, your spade work of last time's begun to show," Janey said when the cubs had gone twice around the big circle. "They're behaving beautifully."

She had hardly finished speaking when Billy Spring, who was on Tote, yelled out: "Tote's so bony I'm splitting in two. And he wants to go into the middle. Let me swap with Chuck!"

"Ride him once more around," Rob said, and hurried over beside the burro. "Tote's just sociable. He'll mosey along first-rate if I go with him."

From then on Rob walked beside whoever was on the burro, and after three turns around the circle brought him into the center to change with one of the other cubs. Chuck was the next to last to ride Tote, and as Rob moved off with him Janey saw that Rob was beginning to limp. "Rob, let me take Chuck!" she said impulsively, and hurried forward. "Your foot must be killing you."

"We'll be using the horses in five minutes." Rob nodded to Chesty who was all saddled and ready for use. "And I'll ride Beau when we start trotting——"

The sudden toot of a car horn interrupted him. Janey turned and saw that the Appletons' car had just drawn up to the corral. Betsy got out and immediately afterwards Mrs. Appleton drove off with the dust billowing up behind her. "Good Lord, Rob! Look at who's turned up. Betsy didn't have a ride booked today, did she?"

"Nope." Rob never took his eyes from the small boys circling before him. "Maybe if you could get her to go up and play with Twinks for a while we can give her a ride later on."

Janey nodded and hurried off to the corral. Betsy had climbed onto the high fence and was staring disconsolately over toward the ring. "So it's Brussels sprouts day," Betsy said, and didn't even turn as Janey came up to her. "I told Mum she ought to phone for a horse ahead of time, but she was in such a rush to go to a dopey old flower show in Lope she wouldn't listen. Guess she meant to park me here until 11:30, whether I could ride or not.

The mean thing is Mum said I had to be right here waiting at 'xactly half-past eleven!"

Janey hesitated as she realized that Rob's suggestion wouldn't work. "Come on down, Betsy," she said finally, "and we'll go over and watch. The cubs have had a high old time riding Tote."

"Dumb boys!" Betsy said fiercely, but as she clambered down from the fence her broad, usually cheerful face was so forlorn and tearstained that Janey couldn't help feeling sorry for her. "Mum just wanted to get rid of me!" Betsy burst out, and it was clear she was struggling not to cry. "But I don't mind. I can take care of myself."

"Of course you can," Janey said, remembering how abandoned she had sometimes felt at about Betsy's age, shortly after Mum had married Uncle John. I'd have died those first weeks they were married if it hadn't been for Gramps, she thought, and spoke more quickly. "Come on, Betsy, Rob's just through with Tote, so perhaps you could ride him. Tote moves quite fast if somebody goes along beside him."

"Rob wouldn't let me." Betsy kicked at a small mound of clay as she spoke. "I'm too heavy. And even if Rob said 'yes' Tote would just fold his legs and lie down like a burro I tried to ride at a fair last week. I wish I was skinny; then Mum would like me better."

As they reached the edge of the ring Janey saw Tote was tied near Belle and Beau, that all the cubs were on horseback, and Rob had gone back to the mound of gamma grass to watch them. Betsy could ride Blue Belle! Janey darted forward the instant the thought had flashed through her mind. "Stay here, Betsy," she said out loud. "I'll be back in a second."

As Janey walked toward Rob it occurred to her that he would probably be as sternly disapproving of her idea as he had been when she and Betsy had ridden to Elbow Crest. Still, there was nothing to lose, so she plunged in, lowering her voice so no one but Rob could hear. "Do you suppose Betsy could ride Blue Belle? Mrs. Appleton's coming for her at 11:30 so she won't be able to ride later on. Betsy's really pretty pathetic, Rob, and it'd give her a big boost to ride Blue Belle along with the cubs."

Rob kept on slowly pivoting so that he could watch all of his pupils. "Even if we were ready to try it Betsy wouldn't be," he said. "She's scared stiff of Belle and says so."

"I've heard her but I think she'd try it now. I'm sure of it. Besides Belle's an absolute lamb in the ring and she's just had a good workout."

"You're right about Blue Belle," Rob said, and Janey pressed home what seemed to be an advantage.

"I'd walk beside Belle's head while we see how it works out," she offered. "You could stay right here until you're ready to use Beau and keep an eye on things without having to do any more walking on your bad foot."

"My foot hasn't anything to do with it!" Rob reddened and strode off to the edge of the ring. "All right, boys, keep on just the way you're going," he called out. "I'm going to put Betsy Appleton up on Blue Belle, and then in twenty shakes you can start trotting."

"Ride Blue Belle? Me?" Betsy's face looked like a round red balloon when she saw Rob lead the mare toward her. "Jeepers, Janey, I couldn't! I'd die of fright."

"Rob said you'd be too scared." Janey was consciously challenging. "But I said I thought you'd do it. Belle's been out in the ring before today and she behaved beautifully."

"I—I'll try," Betsy got out and let Rob help her up without saying another word.

"Let me lead her." Janey tried again when Rob had adjusted Betsy's stirrup leathers. "I'd like to, honestly."

"No, thanks," Rob said, and started talking to Betsy. "O.K. Betsy girl, sit up straight, take a deep breath, and you'll feel fine. Then you can show these cub scouts how much you've learned this summer."

As Janey watched Rob move away she realized that he was forcing himself not to limp. That's his lookout, Janey shrugged to herself. I told him I wanted to walk beside Betsy and I meant it.

At that moment Tote brayed noisily, and as Janey turned to look at him she saw he was yanking back on his short halter shank while Beau side-stepped nervously beside him. It was clear the burro was ready to cause trouble, so Janey untied him and led him uphill toward the far side of the corral between the stable and the house where he was usually staked out. It took Janey several minutes to find the stake and the long rope attached to it. As soon as Tote was securely tied she started back to the ring by way of a short cut behind the adobe stable. When she went down the slope she saw the oval, dusty track from a new angle and stopped short. The cub scouts and Betsy Appleton were actually trotting, Rob no longer held Belle's head but he ran close beside her. If Rob overtires his foot it'll be all his own fault, Janey thought, but as she moved forward she was suddenly filled with misgivings. The cub scouts looked so small and insecure as they joggled along, struggling valiantly to obey Rob's orders.

If anything went wrong Rob would feel responsible, Janey realized, and for the first time she wished she had never suggested Betsy's riding Belle. If Belle got out of hand it might panic the whole class. Rob thought of that right away, and that's why he wouldn't let me lead Betsy. Janey went on the rest of the way to the ring, and by the time she reached it Rob had called the class to a halt and formed the cubs into a long line away from the ring. "You've all done so well we can start cantering," he said, and swung himself onto Beau. "We'll begin with each of you cantering along with my horse one at a time. If you keep on the way you've been going we'll be able to canter together in no time flat. Like to begin, Jakey? Sponge canters much easier than he trots."

Jakey nodded, and followed Rob into the ring, his small face as rapt and absorbed-looking as a young poet's. Janey walked over to where the other children were waiting and patted Belle's neck. "How did you like her, Betsy?" she asked. "It wasn't as hard as you thought it would be, was it?"

"Glory! No!" Betsy never took her eyes away from her horse's head as she spoke. "Belle's super, Janey. And Rob says if I copy you I'll be able to ride her on trails and everything. He says you've got the trick of riding Belle light an' easy but keeping watch every second so you'll be ready to make her behave. Rob says you've got Belle's number!"

"I didn't yesterday," Janey began when she saw Chesty put back his ears and hurried to him just in time to keep Pigeon away from his heels. A moment later Rob rode over, with Jakey riding breathless but triumphant beside him, and took Billy Spring into the ring for a canter.

The rest of the morning was an unqualified success. Rob cantered with each of the boys and with Betsy separately. After that he spaced the children, on the same horses, at careful distances around the ring so that they could all canter at the same time. As Billy Spring pounded past Janey on Pigeon she saw he was crowding dangerously close to Chesty, who was just in front of him. Before Janey could open her mouth to speak Rob flashed across the ring on Beau, showed Billy how to hold Pigeon back, and trouble was avoided before it actually happened.

They cantered twice around the track without incident, and then Rob made them all walk their horses to cool off. At that the children were still panting and rosy from exercise and excitement when Mrs. Appleton, followed by the green station wagon, drove up to the corral. "Mummy! I've ridden Belle!" Betsy shouted, and raced toward her mother's car. "I've had the best, super best time ever!"

Even Jakey was too thrilled to be shy and stopped on his way to the station wagon to praise Sponge to anyone who would listen. "Cantering Sponge is special!" he told Janey. "It must feel like that when you ride Pegasus, the poetry horse, in heaven."

Finally the cub scouts left and Janey who had gone over to see them off went back to the stable where Rob was already at work sponging down the horses. "I've lost my heart to Jakey Weathers," she said. "Betsy's happy again, and Mrs. Appleton wants to pay for a private lesson because she didn't let you know ahead. Unless your foot's kicked up from all the walking you've done I'd say this morning was a knockout."

"I'm O.K.," Rob said, and went on sponging. "And thanks for your help. Putting Betsy on Blue Belle was a brain wave."

"I thought so until I saw the way you had to run when you let her trot," Janey said. "I still don't see how you managed that or how you caught on to what was happening when Billy's horse began crowding Chesty while you were all cantering. You must have eyes in the back of your head."

"To make up for my gammy leg?" Rob sounded annoyed.

"Rob, don't take it that way. I didn't mean to be interfering or —or oversolicitous."

"You haven't been," Rob said loftily. "I just want to convince you I'm not a hopeless cripple. My foot's getting better all the time, and if I exercise it enough the doctor swears I'll be as sound as any man living."

"I'm glad," Janey said. "Truly I am. Twinks told me that but I wasn't sure she knew."

"You can ask Mom." Rob started on the next horse. "Or if you don't trust Mom you might try 'Nita Murphy. She's come back for a couple of days to do some developing and she's taking this afternoon off to go out riding. I think you'd believe her."

"I believe you and your mother," Janey said, and felt her temper rising. "If you say your foot's fine I'll take your word for it."

"Then that's that," Rob said, and went on sponging with ostentatious care.

Janey walked back toward the house feeling angry at herself and at Rob in unpleasantly equal parts. Still the thought of seeing Miss 'Nita Murphy again was vaguely encouraging. She'll help me, Janey told herself. She understands Rob better than anybody else in the world. I wonder if she knows Buck Hughes and the Weavers.

Rob had only one party that afternoon so that he and Janey, Miss 'Nita and the Sydney family all left the corral together. Rob rode in the lead with Miss Murphy beside him, the two Sydney children were next, and Mrs. Sydney and Janey brought up the rear.

Mrs. Sydney, who was a friendly, soft-spoken New Mexican,

was an amateur camera fan, and she talked about her hobby as they rode along. "I'm glad I didn't bring my camera today," she said once and nodded ahead of them. "Miss Murphy's so absolutely amazing I'd be embarrassed to have her see the way I flutter and fumble."

"Her pictures of people are uncanny," Janey said, and as she remembered the brilliant, nakedly revealing portraits she had seen in the drugstore at Lope she was not quite so sure that she wanted to discuss either Rob or Buck, much less talk about herself to Juanita Murphy.

"'Nita Murphy isn't simply artistic but she's technically so clever. Except for Laura Gilpin in Arizona I don't think there's a photographer in the whole Southwest who can compare with her," Mrs. Sydney said, and went on talking about the fine points of photography until they reached a place on the ride home where they had to go single file. Janey reined in behind Mrs. Sydney. Later on when the narrow trail opened onto the rolling range land surrounding the ranch she didn't hurry to catch up. Finally when Belle rounded one of the small bare hills east of the cattle gate Janey saw Rob and all three Sydneys cantering off into the distance while Miss Murphy sat still on Spot's back directly ahead of her.

"I waited for you because I wanted to hear how you were coming along with your search," Miss Murphy said, and once more Janey felt that Miss 'Nita's big dark eyes could see right down to the soul. "And also to congratulate you because Rob's just told me what wonders you're doing with Belle."

"Rob's only being nice," Janey said, and was suddenly determined not to talk about Gramps again to Miss Murphy. "He's giving me a build-up."

"I don't believe it," Miss Murphy said pleasantly. "If Rob says anything he means it. It's one of the most satisfactory things about him. That and the way he's always known what he wants and gone slowly and steadily after it. But now tell me how you've been getting on. Rob told me you've both been very busy, and I scolded him for overworking you. You look tired, Janey."

"I'm not. Not a bit." Janey protested. "I've never felt better in my life." She saw that they were still some distance from the corral and rushed on quickly, volubly, determined to shield her inner self behind a wall of words. She talked about the things she had seen and done, touching on facts and avoiding everything she had felt or thought. "Oh, and I went over to the officers' club at Sandia," she said as they reached the corral. "It's fabulous. Makes the beach club near where I live positively crumby."

"Twinks told me you'd been there when I first came over this afternoon," Miss Murphy said, and she looked amused. "Twinks has never seen the club but she certainly described Ensign Hughes's car in glowing detail."

"Do you know Buck Hughes?" The question came out involuntarily and Janey was oddly relieved when Miss Murphy shook her head.

"I've only met his brother-in-law, Mr. Weaver," she said. "He wanted me to take some progress pictures of the family's mines but I couldn't do it. I'm very poor at industrial work."

"But Herb Weaver's a lawyer. And Hank said he wrote on the side. I didn't know he was interested in mining too."

"I guess he'd have to be if he married into the Hughes family," Miss Murphy said. "And I know he told me his law firm did very little work except in connection with the family holdings. You see the Hugheses not only own one of the biggest and best general mining companies in the state, but they've been at it for several generations, and they're very naturally proud of a tradition of continued success. It's really a small empire, and in a way I don't blame Ida Baker for being disappointed when she'd carefully arranged it so that they offered Rob a job and he wouldn't even consider it." At that moment Rob came toward them to lift Miss Murphy out of the saddle and the conversation was over. That was the offer Buck told me about when we drove in from the airport, Janey thought as she dismounted and turned to help put the horses into the corral.

Twinks had a performance that evening, so Janey and the Bakers had supper early. They had barely finished when a man and a woman drove up to the stable in an unfamiliar car and Rob hurried out to see what was wanted. A few minutes later he came back just long enough to say that the couple were tourists driving on to California early next day. They had heard about the ranch when they had stopped at Chuck Hemsted's for gas and wanted to go out riding right away. "I'm taking the horses we didn't use this afternoon, and we'll ride while it's still daylight," Rob said as he started out again. "These people don't want to be gone long and they're ready to pay cash on the barrelhead."

"All right dear, I only hope you don't get indigestion," Mrs. Baker said, and then as she glanced at her watch jumped up from the table. "Twinks, darling, hurry! It's much later than I thought. Janey, please leave the dishes and I'll do them just as soon as I come back."

Mrs. Baker rushed Twinks into the car, and when they were down the driveway Janey began to do the dishes by herself. She had just carried everything to the kitchen sink when she remembered what Miss Murphy had said about the Hughes's empire, and grinned as she scraped plates and dropped scraps into a battered garbage can. I could use some of the empire's minions right now, she thought, especially if they were perfectly sweet like the maid who works for Sis Weaver.

CHAPTER SEVENTEEN

Buck called for Janey the next day at one o'clock and they drove off immediately. "Boy, it's a relief that you're actually here sitting beside me," Buck said when they had left Lope behind and swept on into a valley Janey had not seen before. "Until I picked you up just now I was worried silly you wouldn't be able to go."

"But Buck, Mrs. Baker told me that if I didn't telephone back to you that you'd understand I was going. Did she give me the message wrong?"

"Oh Mrs. B.'s much too efficient for that," Buck said, but he sounded vaguely scornful. "No, I was scared the old Lone Ranger would decide at the last minute he wanted help with his gee-gees and work on you not to go off with me. I thought he might even invent a crisis if he didn't have one handy."

"Rob wouldn't do a thing like that," Janey said. "In fact he and Mrs. Baker and Twinks all urged me to go the minute I had your message. They practically made me go!" Janey paused for breath and, deciding that she had sounded rude, went on more quickly.

"Besides I wanted to go with you, Buck. Why, I've been counting on it."

"Then we'll have ourselves a time!" Buck began to grope toward Janey, but just then a big car roared toward them and he had to put both hands back on the wheel. "Because I've been counting on it plenty much."

Buck settled down to his driving and Janey looked out of the window on her side of the car. They had not been gone long, but already the scenery was totally different from anything she had seen near the Baker's ranch. Here the plains looked perfectly level, stretching out in barren, silent dignity to wall-like mesas that framed the horizon. Except for the road they were on and the telephone wires strung alongside it there was no sign of human life or even of anything man-made. Janey found the vast, impersonal landscape unexpectedly restful and sat back gazing at it, her mind free of the questions and self-doubts which had intermittently haunted her since the day of the flash flood.

"This is a godforsaken section," Buck said. "But we're almost through it and near Hayesville and the best uranium prospects on earth."

"Tell me more about uranium," Janey said. "Practically all I know about it is that Rob told me that half the people in New Mexico own a Geiger counter."

"I don't blame them. Janey, there's millions to be made in uranium mining. I've a few shares tucked away, but as soon as I'm through the Navy I'm going to see that Multiple Minerals, that's my folks' firm, really get in on the ground floor. All the way!"

"I heard about your family's business," Janey said, and, remembering Miss Murphy's remark about the Hughes "empire," wondered what it was like to be the heir apparent. "But I didn't know until just now you were so interested in it. Did you want to be a miner even when you were a little boy?"

"Not by a long shot and I'm not starry eyed over ye olde family traditional stuff right now. I went to Colorado School of Mines to please my old man, but I was bored stiff by practically everything except the skiing. No, it wasn't until I woke up to what there was in uranium for yours truly that I gave a darn about Multiple Minerals. You'll see what I mean in a few minutes, Janey. We're only a couple of miles from the Mexiana plant."

Janey saw that once more the landscape had changed and that they were passing craggy black masses of rock and acres of earth as grim and desolate as the land just below Fortune. "Does the Mexiana plant do coal mining too?" she asked, and nodded at the side of the road. "This looks like coal."

"Lord, no. That rocky stuff's just old lava and not worth a thing. No, the beauty of the Mexiana is that it's uranium and nothing but! And that's what I'm going to do with Multiple Minerals. Right now old Herb and the directors run the show as though it were some kind of benevolent association for small shareholders and old employees. They've stuck to diversified mining because that's what my great-grandfather did and so they're letting companies like Mexiana clean up!"

"Is the Mexiana plant where they process uranium?" Janey was beginning to get confused. "Separate the valuable stuff from the earth or rock or whatever it's found in?"

"That's it. And let me tell you the Mexiana board knows what it's doing," Buck said, and launched into an account of mine techniques and financing Janey found difficult to follow. She tried to help herself by thinking up anything and everything she'd learned about mining during her day in Fortune. She could still picture rotting scaffolds and the yawning mineheads, but when she tried to remember specific details her mind drifted back to the pitiful little houses and to the talk she and Rob had had about lives of the people who had built them. Then Janey thought of the cemetery and her grandmother's grave, and Rob's fine voice reciting the "Requiem" rang in her memory as clearly as though she were hearing it for the first time.

"Ninety-eight thousand! And believe me Janey when I can take over my controlling interest it's going to be ten times that. Or else!" Buck stopped on an emphatic note, and Janey realized with a start that she hadn't taken in a word of what he had just been saying and that he expected her to comment.

"It—it sounds fascinating." Janey decided flattery would be safe. "And, Buck, you certainly know your stuff. You're terrific!"

He grinned delightedly and drove on faster than ever. "You're pretty terrific yourself. It isn't everybody that has the vision to see that uranium is just about the only way you can make a killing no matter how taxes skyrocket. Janey, if I'd known you were so interested I'd have arranged for us to go through the Mexiana today. A friend of mine's the manager, and as a matter of fact if I called him now it'd probably be a breeze for him to fix it. The plant's just a couple of miles from here and there's a phone box at the gate. They won't let in strangers but Bill Grieves'd be glad to give us the complete tour."

"Oh, I'd hate to bother him," Janey said quickly. "If I can see it from the road that would be perfect."

"Well, we don't have to decide now," Buck said. "We'll have something to eat and drink in Hayesville and then see how we feel about it."

Buck drove on so fast that Janey could hardly focus on the country beside them before it was left behind. Once he overtook a sedan and an oil truck and passed them as though they stood still. "We're practically flying," Janey said, reveling in the smooth, effortless speed. "It's super."

A moment later Buck slowed down and skillfully stopped the car by a tall barbed-wire fence that stretched out for miles ahead of them along the side of the road. "This is all Mexiana property!" he said. "And there's the factory. Oh, Janey, isn't she a honey?"

Janey stared across acres of raw, scraped-looking earth to where a battery of chimneys on a vast drab building spewed up sulphurous smoke into the blue summer sky. It's hideous, she thought, and her heart sank. Unbelievable. "It looks enormous," she said out loud. "If we walked all over that you'd end up by having to carry me."

"Don't think I wouldn't go for that!" Buck exulted. He turned in his seat to look at Janey, and there was an expression on his face she had never seen before. He put one arm around her shoulder, and as he pulled her slowly toward him his eyes and lips seemed magnified out of all proportion.

He's going to kiss me, Janey realized, and a shiver starting at the top of her head shot down her backbone. And then he did. Janey closed her eyes. An instant later she thought of the cars whizzing by on the road and pushed Buck away. Her eyes were wide open again, and her face and neck were a hot, embarrassed red.

"Say, what's the big idea?" Buck demanded, and suddenly his voice, his whole personality were so changed by anger that Janey felt as though she were looking at a total—and unappealing—stranger. A moment later Buck shrugged and the coarse, hard set of his mouth gave way to his usual exuberant grin. "Am I rushing things, honey?" he asked. "Don't tell me you didn't know that I've fallen for you like——"

"It's not that, Buck," Janey interrupted, and wished that she could stop blushing. "It's just this place is so—so public." As soon as she had spoken she was sure she had sounded like a silly, unsophisticated child and flushed harder than ever. I'm jittery because Buck picked such a poor place, she told herself. I've known from the first time I ever laid eyes on him that he was the most fascinating man I've ever met. Even if he didn't own this car or wasn't an officer in the Navy he's so attractive himself that everyone at Bayport would rave over him.

Buck switched on the ignition. "Is there anybody else?" he asked as he drove back onto the road. "A guy back in Connecticut or has Rob Baker made you fall——"

"Rob doesn't know I'm alive!" Janey was stung into passionate honesty. "And there isn't anyone at home. I tell you I just don't want to get involved——"

"Then everything's all right!" Buck stepped on the gas as he spoke. "Because from now on I'll do anything you say. You'll never have a reason to be afraid of me again. I swear you won't."

Janey didn't answer, completely absorbed in the sudden realization that while Rob's attitude toward her had not changed ever since the flash flood she had been more and more vividly aware of him. The thought was depressing, and Janey pushed it away and looked out just as they passed a straggling line of motels, gas stations, and diners on the edge of town.

"We'll go to the Big Strike Grill," Buck said. "They have the best bar in town." Janey didn't answer and he went on. "Their martinis aren't half bad, but, Janey, you can order a Coke or coffee or anything you like. You know I honestly like your not drinking. It's one of the things that makes you so special, like your cute little Yankee accent and the way you're interested in things around here most people take for granted."

"It pays to be a visiting fireman." Janey forced herself to sound jauntier than she felt. Buck laughed, and she was encouraged to ask questions about Hayesville. "What are the people who live here like?" she asked. "And what do most of them do? Rob told me once that in some places you can tell exactly what the men work at by looking at the kind of boots or shoes they're wearing."

"Maybe." Buck sounded puzzled. "But why would anyone want to know what a lot of dumb bunnies are working at? The only thing that matters in Hayesville is uranium. Of course most of the big shots live out of town and drive to the plant, and one or two have their own planes and fly down from Albuquerque. Except for uranium Hayesville's just a dump of a string town like dozens of others along the main motor routes."

"But what happened here long ago?" Janey asked, thinking of the way Rob and Miss Murphy had made the past and present of Lope alive and significant. "The town didn't just start with uranium did it?"

"No, I guess not." Buck parked the car by a glaringly new café of glass and chromium, and helped Janey out. "I've never thought about it." He piloted Janey off the highway to a corner where they could look down a side street of ugly and completely shadeless houses. "That's Hayesville as is!" he said. "And I always say it pays to live in the present."

"Oh, you're so right." Janey used the vaguely acquiescent technique of Maisie Taylor and her Bayport crowd, and didn't add that so far neither the past, present, nor future of Hayesville seemed alluring.

"I knew we saw eye to eye," Buck said as he led the way back to the Big Strike Grill. "Why, the very first time when I met you at the airport I guessed you lived in the present. I was sure you'd be bored stiff with the way Rob moons over the dim and dusty past with all his Indian stuff."

"He really doesn't say much about it," Janey protested. "And Mrs. Baker can't stand anything to do with Indians, so the subject hardly ever comes up."

"Thanks be to Pete for small favors," Buck said. "And I guess it was a break that Herb bought the best of Rob's arrowheads and what all just a couple of weeks before you came out here. Before that the Bakers' place must have been littered with ancient junk."

"You mean to tell me that Herb bought Rob's collection?" Janey stopped short as her mind flashed back to Rob's going off with Herb before the square dance and his unexpected defense of Herb after they had come home. "I couldn't be more surprised. Herb!"

"It does sound out of character," Buck said. "Herb seems too much the up-and-coming lawyer to bother with anything so dull. But he uses his head about it. All the museum boards and committees he gets involved in are good business contacts. As a matter of fact he bought Rob's junk and handed it over to the Tepique Museum. There's some legal rigmarole so Rob couldn't have sold it otherwise. And of course Rob was desperate for the cash to buy nags for the summer. He can't keep 'em through the winter and Herb found he'd sunk his last nickel into taking care of that Indian who used to work for his grandfather. You know, that old buck Juan what's-his-name that Mrs. Baker can't stand. So I guess Herb felt sorry for Rob."

Rob spent his savings to take care of Juan! For an instant Janey was speechless, as things that Twinks and Mrs. Baker had said and Rob had avoided saying suddenly fitted together and made sense. "I think it's wonderful," she said finally. "The most generous thing I've ever known."

"Very decent," Buck said as he pulled open the door of the Big Strike Grill. "But of course with income tax deductions and all Herb didn't lose out on it."

"I meant Rob!" Janey said as she walked in, but her words were lost in a blare of juke-box music. The brassy tune roared to a deafening crescendo and came to an end a few moments after they were seated. There were only a few other customers in the restaurant, and as none of them moved toward the juke box to put in another coin Janey gave a sigh of relief.

"You look all in." Buck's voice seemed supernaturally loud in the sudden silence. "Sure you won't change your mind and have a highball?"

"An orangeade would be just right. I'm practically parched," Janey said. "The air conditioning's marvelous in here, but it really was broiling outside."

"Fierce," Buck agreed. "Hayesville's apt to be hotter than either Albuquerque or Lope." The waiter brought in their order and as Buck drank his dry martini he began to talk about the Mexiana plant again. "How about something to eat?" he said a few minutes later. "A sandwich'll give you quick energy for the rest of the afternoon."

"The orangeade was just what I wanted," Janey said and, suddenly afraid that Buck meant to go through the plant after all, she went on more quickly: "You know I can hardly wait to see Isleta. A pueblo sounds terribly exciting to a hick from Connecticut."

"This one isn't much," Buck said, and studied the olive in his glass. "But later on, Janey, if you like this afternoon, and if you'd be sweet enough to go with me for a weekend, we could drive down to Gallop for the ceremonials and go on to the Zuni pueblo. That's supposed to be worth seeing."

"I'd adore it!" Janey said, so relieved he had forgotten about Mexiana she missed the implications behind what he was saying. "It'd be marvelous."

"Janey, you're an angel," Buck said, and finished off his drink.

"And I can give you a good time. I know I can." He stood up and paid for their drinks and they walked back to the car.

The glare of the cement highway was blinding after the dark café. Janey groped her way to the steps but there was no handrail and when Buck held out his arm she gripped it gratefully.

"It's hot around here and getting hotter," Buck said as he drove off. "But there's a grove of cottonwoods below Isleta where there might be a breeze, and it's sure to be shady."

"Sounds heavenly," Janey said, and leaned back against the leather seat. Her head ached from the glare and not wearing her glasses, but when she looked for them in her straw handbag she realized she must have left them at the Bakers'. As she pictured her room, wondering where she had left the glasses, her mind went on to what would be going on at the ranch while she was away. Four o'clock. Rob was probably bringing in his last party, and in another hour he would take the horses off to graze.

Janey shut her eyes, conjuring up the evenings when she and Rob had taken the horses out together. She remembered the racket of hoofbeats, the hot smell of horse sweat, and the feel on her face of the sand and bits of clay the horses kicked up behind them. Moments later, as soon as the horses reached the grass, there was always a welcome lull, a quietness one could almost feel, and time to watch the evening miracle of changing light on the distant mountains.

Rob loves it, too, Janey thought. She smiled to herself as she remembered how more than once he had summed up in a single soft-spoken sentence of simple, homely words everything she had been struggling to formulate in more elaborate terms about the view in front of them. He felt exactly the way I did about the light, and the cool air, and the horses enjoying themselves. We were both perfectly happy.

But what difference does that make? Janey opened her eyes again. Even if Rob and I do like a good many of the same things it doesn't mean I have to swoon over the thought of it. Buck and I both like driving in a good car and—and—swimming, and probably lots of other things.

She forced herself to sit up straight, and Buck glanced toward her as she stirred. "Guess you had a little snooze for yourself," he said. "But we've been moving right along while you did. I've averaged around seventy since we left the Big Strike so we're nearly at Isleta."

A few minutes later Buck turned off the main highway and drove over a red dirt road to where a group of adobe houses and a whitewashed church lay ahead of them. "This is it." Buck slowed way down so that Janey could see the bare, flat-roofed little houses and the dusty yards crisscrossed by clotheslines and punctuated by round adobe ovens. "All one-story shacks and filthy," he said. "Not my idea of a pueblo at all, but don't say I didn't warn you."

"The beehive adobe ovens look just the way I thought they would," Janey said. "My grandfather used to tell me about buying coarse-ground corn-meal bread when it was still hot from an Indian oven, and it sounded marvelous. Have you ever tried it?"

"I've never had the nerve," Buck said. "And after you've looked around I bet you wouldn't either. My guess is these people are even filthier and lazier than they were in your grandfather's day."

He parked the car in an open space behind the church where two sad-looking horses were tied to a broken-down wall. A scrawny chicken ran squawking between two rain tubs, and a mongrel dog, who was sunning himself nearby, barked once in a bored way and settled back to sleep. "Is this what you expected, Janey?" Buck asked.

"I don't know." Janey looked around, marveling that the white perfection of Twinks's feather stole had been achieved in the dust and poverty that she saw around her. "I guess I thought everything would be bigger and more prosperous and that there'd be a lot of Indians around. Do you suppose this is a second siesta?"

"No such luck." Buck pointed to a crowd of little girls in factory-made cotton dresses who were running toward them. Each child held out a card of tiny beaded moccasins mounted on safety pins and, smiling or shy, speaking in fluent Spanish or broken English, they urged Buck and Janey to buy.

Janey fumbled uncertainly for her change purse, wondering how she could keep from two of the children without upsetting the others. "I'd like to get a pair for my kid brother and my kid sister," she told Buck. "But it's sort of——"

He moved off before she finished, beckoned to a tall, good-looking child to show Janey her card, and waved away the others. "You choose," he said good-naturedly. "They're all alike. Probably made for Woolworth's."

"Oh, these are fine." Janey pointed to a red and a blue pair. "But that isn't what I meant."

"For you." Buck pushed a dollar bill at the tall child, indicated that he didn't want change, and handed the moccasins to Janey. "Here are your trinkets. Give 'em to the kids with my compliments."

"Thanks, Buck. They'll be thrilled." Janey watched the crowd of children run after the girl with the bill like so many little bantams chasing a hen with a prize worm. "I hope they divide up the money," she said, and, remembering what Rob had told her about the Pueblo Indian's genius for communal ownership, added more cheerfully: "And I think they will. But I was absolutely stymied, trying to decide which kid to buy from."

"That was easy," Buck said as the girls disappeared around the last of the little houses. "I just picked out the best-looking one. But let's go take a quick squint at the church. This place is even hotter than Hayesville."

The stony, reddish earth of the crude square was blistering, and Janey moved after him eagerly. The squat, curiously proportioned little church looked interesting and, besides, the thick walls and narrow window slits promised refuge from the sun. "Are you sure we'll be able to get in?" she asked. "Rob or Miss Murphy told me something about having to ask the governor of a pueblo."

"Don't worry about that," Buck said, and Janey saw that six small boys had materialized from nowhere and were waiting to show them around. "No tour." Buck pressed a coin into the hand of the boy nearest him. "We just want to look in, savvy?"

The boy nodded and opened the heavy wooden door. He let Buck and Janey in and followed after them with his five blue-jeaned companions close at his heels. The building was very dark, and after the brilliant sunlight Janey blinked owlishly. She was aware of the close, musty smell and of the gleam of tinsel near the altar. She hesitated, and, catching a glimpse of a wooden crucifix, dark with age, on the wall at her right, moved over to look at it more closely. She had barely reached it when Buck caught her arm and swept her back toward the door. The boys were taken by surprise and scattered out through the narrow entry ahead of them, except for one stocky child of nine or ten who waited politely to let them go first. As Janey passed him their eyes met and she smiled, murmuring her thanks. The boy nodded, still looking at her intently, and Janey walked on, suddenly certain she had seen him before. She turned as they recrossed the square and looked back. The other boys had run off but he stood alone, a small infinitely dignified figure in blue jeans and no shirt, still looking after her. "I've seen that boy before," she told Buck as they got into the car. "The one who waited to let us pass. Or someone exactly like him."

"Could be," Buck said, and swung his big car onto a road that was meant for a single horse and wagon. "But kids of that age all look alike to me and I don't just mean Indians either. It drives most parents crazy."

"Can you blame them?" Janey said, but her mind was not on whether Buck was or was not interested in children but on the boy they had just left. I must have seen him in Lope or Albuquerque, she decided. There was no way of telling, and a moment later when Buck stopped the car by a stand of cottonwood surrounding a small pool the boy faded from her mind.

Buck led the way down a narrow footpath, and as Janey followed him through the shade she sniffed cooler air delightedly. "Buck, you're right," she said, and held out her arms away from her hot sides. "There really is a breeze."

"I'm glad," he said, and spread out a jacket he had brought

from the car for Janey to sit on. "If I could I'd turn this old mud hole into a crystal pool for you to sit beside."

"I like it as it is." Janey looked up at the tall narrow-leaved trees as she spoke. "Buck, did you ever notice how coolness and quiet and shade always seem to go together, and so do heat and glare and noise?"

"Janey, you're so right," Buck said, and dropped down beside her on the ground. "I was a fool not to think of it sooner. How crazy can a guy get—trying to make time with the cutest girl in the world right near a hot, noisy highway? I was just cracked, screwball!"

Buck edged so close to Janey as he spoke that his voice boomed like a loud-speaker in her ear and she felt more bewildered and upset with every word. Was this all Buck had grasped from what she had tried to tell him earlier along the highway? Did he simply think she wanted to be brought to a more secluded spot and carry on from there? How could she explain how she really felt without sounding like an unsophisticated prig? "You d-don't understand," she stammered, and unconsciously leaned away from him. "I only meant just now that I think this place is lovely. Even m-more unspoiled and cool than you said it would be."

But Buck wasn't listening. The queer look that had puzzled Janey before had come back into his eyes as he took her hands in both of his and held them tight. "Janey, honey, I'm crazy about you," he said. "When you told me that there wasn't anybody else and that you'd go to Gallop with me it was better than striking uranium. I've never felt like this about anyone before."

Janey's heart pounded in her throat. She couldn't speak or move as Buck pulled her against him. "Janey, you don't know what you're doing to me. I want you so terribly——"

At that instant a twig snapped somewhere to the left. Buck jumped up, swearing under his breath, and stamped off into the underbrush in the direction of the sound. Janey breathed more slowly and found she could move again. She stood up and a moment later she saw Buck looking hot, disheveled, and furious, forcing his way through the briars back to the edge of the pool. "Must have been a gopher," he got out as he reached her. "Anything bigger would have gone down the path. I'd like to wring its dirty little neck."

Janey peered nearsightedly around her. "I don't see anyone," she said, and found that although her heart was still thumping she once more could speak without stammering from nervousness. "But I suppose the children from the pueblo come down here to play."

"They better hadn't while I'm here!" Buck said. "But anyway that noise couldn't have been an Indian kid or I'd have seen him. There isn't enough cover for a good-sized dog. But let's clear out, Janey. I'm sick of this place."

They went back to the car, and as Buck turned it to drive away the cluster of trees around the pond was on Janey's right. She looked out vaguely until her eyes focused on something moving. Then she leaned out, straining her eyes to the utmost, and for an instant she thought she saw the boy who had waited for them by the church door. "Buck, stop. I thought I saw that boy. The one who let us go by." The instant the words were out of Janey's mouth she regretted them but it was too late. Buck jammed on his brakes. "Where?" he demanded, and reached for the door handle. "If he's anywhere near here it must have been him we heard down at the pool, and he's sure going to catch it! No Indian brat's going to spy on me or any other self-respecting white man and get away with it."

Janey turned, fearful for the boy, but now she couldn't see anything move except the peeling bark of the cottonwoods. She sank back in her seat, giggling with nervous relief. "I'm nuts," she said. "Cuckoo. Guess it comes from seeing mirages for the first time. There isn't anything there at all."

Buck stood on the running board and looked around him. Finally he shrugged and climbed back into the car and drove off. "I don't blame you for being jumpy," he said when they had passed Isleta and were back on the main road. "That twig snapping threw me and I don't throw easy. But Janey, honey, I know just how you feel and it's all my fault. I should never have taken you down to that pool to begin with, but I thought it would be cool and quiet and maybe you'd like it. Now I wouldn't go back there for anything. The damned place might just as well be haunted. I was a fool."

"And it all seemed so perfect when we first saw it." Janey was totally unaware that she was talking more to herself than to Buck. "The shade and the breeze and the reflection of those tall, strange trees."

"You're an angel to take it that way," Buck said huskily, and now he kept both hands on the steering wheel and stared straight ahead as he spoke. "But from here on I'll know better if only you'll give me another chance and go out with me again."

Janey looked at him, wondering at the change in his voice, and he went on pleading. "I love you so, Janey. I want you—need you, so terribly. You're probably furious with me now and I don't blame you, but Janey, if you'll go out with me again things'll be different. Really they will."

At that moment they reached the cattle gate below the ranch, and as Buck jumped out to let them through Janey looked after him, touched and softened by what he had just said. Buck means it, she thought, and now what 'Nita Murphy had told her about need being an essential part of love flowed through her mind, underlining and enhancing Buck's words.

Buck drove on up to the house without speaking, and Twinks ran off the porch to meet them. "Hi, Janey!" she shouted, and hurried toward Janey's side of the car just as Buck brought it to a standstill. "Jeepers, I'm glad to see you. I thought you'd never come back."

"I'm glad to see——" Janey began, but before she could finish her sentence or move out of the seat Buck had jumped out, run around the front of the car, and opened Janey's door with wildly exaggerated gestures. "Ah has to keep steppin'," he said, and looked over his shoulder to make sure Twinks was listening. "Pretty Connecticut Yankee ladies lak Janey is used to service. An ole southwesterner lak me has to hump himself or she won't forgive him for a cheap treat, two-bit visit to a dusty ole Indian reservation. Lovely Yankees who is used to real stylish seashore resorts just naturally don't favor ole Bucko at a mud-hole pond like the one we done visit." He let Janey out, winked at Twinks, and stepped back, bowing and shagging in a grotesque pantomime, to the driver's side of the car.

Twinks laughed as he slid into his seat, and he winked at her again as he began to move off. "See you day after tomorrow, Janey," he called out. "We'll be expecting you and Rob at six-thirty, and then you and I can make plans for another date on our own. I'm counting on it! So long, Twinks. Be seeing you!"

"So long." Twinks waved after him and Janey stood perfectly still, too surprised and irritated to speak. He didn't understand a thing, she fumed. He thought I was playing hard to get because I didn't like the pond. I think he really meant what he said just before we got here, but how can he turn around and make a cheap laugh out of it all three seconds later?

"There. Buck shut the cattle gate!" Twinks said, and turned back to Janey. "Didn't you like the Isleta pool? I've never been there but Juan says it's neat. He says that Indian kids have been playing there probably since the Earth Twins—you know, the sort of Pueblo gods—were young."

Then I did see that boy, Janey realized, and at the same moment another thought struck her and she looked down at Twinks. "Is the pool part of the reservation?" she asked. "Does it belong to the Indians or to some white people?"

"To the Indians," Twinks said, but a moment later her forehead wrinkled with uncertainty. "At least I guess so, but Juan says lots of land has been taken away from them so maybe this has too. But why do you want to know? Was Buck right about you not liking him because you didn't like the pool?"

"I thought it was very pretty!" Janey said, uncomfortably aware of Twinks's sudden curiosity. "I—I just wouldn't like to trespass on land that was so important to the Indians."

"Oh, they wouldn't mind," Twinks said. "If you ask the governor of a pueblo for permission he'll let you go anywhere you like. But if you really want to know who owns the pool Rob could tell you for sure."

"Where is he, down at the corral?" Janey asked. Twinks shook her head and, picking up her skip rope, began to twirl it expertly.

"Nope," she said, "he had some late dudes the Bylers sent over and he won't be back until dark. He had his supper before he left, and Mom wants the three of us to eat as soon as you're ready."

"I'll hurry up and wash," Janey said, and went into her own room, feeling as though she had been away from it for a lifetime. Buck undoubtedly knew that the pond was off the reservation, she told herself. And besides it doesn't really matter. I just wish he hadn't been so angry about that Indian boy or acted the way he did to the little girls up by the pueblo. She tried to put the whole afternoon out of her mind and to concentrate on getting ready for supper quickly. She brushed her hair so hard her scalp tingled, but even so the impression of the last few hours stayed with her. Buck was less attractive and congenial than she had thought he would be when they had first met. This afternoon he had been boring, frightening, and coarse, and yet when he had spoken of his love just before they had reached the ranch he had been unexpectedly moving.

If he were only more like Rob! The idea insinuated itself into Janey's mind, and the instant she was aware of it she dropped her brush in sudden anger at herself. Why should Buck be like Rob? Why should he? Buck's rich and good-looking and—and gay. Janey scolded herself. He loves me, he needs me! That's the thing about him I ought to remember.

CHAPTER EIGHTEEN

All during supper Janey was so absorbed by her own thoughts that she found it hard to concentrate on what Mrs. Baker and Twinks were saying. Once when the telephone rang she jumped up to answer it as it flashed through her mind that it might be Buck to explain and apologize for his badly timed clowning. He was probably just so startled and surprised by seeing Twinks he couldn't think of anything else to do, Janey thought as she lifted up the receiver.

The call was for Mrs. Baker, and as Janey went back to the table she stopped to look out of the window to see if Rob had come back to the corral. Rob makes sense about people, Janey thought. If I told him about this afternoon and made it sound as though it had all happened ages ago with someone Rob's never seen, like Larry or somebody else back home, perhaps he could help me understand Buck.

There was no one at the corral, and Janey sat down again and tried to eat the light, fluffy lemon meringue Mrs. Baker put on her plate. Later on when she and Twinks had just finished tidying up the dishes she thought she heard hoofbeats by the stable and rushed to the kitchen window. The sound was only Chesty and Sponge moving around inside the corral, and when Janey looked up the road and over the plains as far as she could in either direction there was no sign of Rob or his party. She sighed, and as she turned away suddenly realized that Twinks was watching her with a shrewd, observant look in her eyes.

"You still waiting to ask Rob who owns the pond?" Twinks teased. "I thought you said it didn't matter."

"It doesn't," Janey said, and brought up the first idea that came to her. "It's going to be a spectacular sunset, and I thought maybe you'd like to take me up to that crow's-nest of yours back of the house."

"It's O.K. with me if you can tear yourself away from listening for the telephone *and* waiting for Rob," Twinks teased, and skipped out of the back door. "Must be awful to be all in a dither over two boy friends at the same time. 'Specially when they're as different as Rob and Buck. Should think you'd get dizzy."

"Don't be so silly!" Janey said, and controlled an impulse to take Twinks by the shoulders and shake her. "I'm not in a dither over anybody and I'm not dizzy."

"Sez you?" Twinks said, and danced out of reach like a small, graceful, and utterly infuriating pixie. "Anyway now you'd better mosey. *If* you really want to see the sun set."

Janey followed her without saying another word. They reached the wide, clay ledge in the steep side of the old river bed, which Twinks called the crow's-nest, in plenty of time for the luridly beautiful fireworks of the sunset. Janey looked steadily westward, but she might just as well have stared at a blank wall for all the aesthetic pleasure the sky gave her. Still she forced herself to stay where she was until Twinks started for home. "Come on, Janey," she called over her shoulder. "It's getting dark and Robbie's sure to be back at the stable."

"I don't doubt it," Janey said, and yawned elaborately. "He won't take parties out at night unless there's a moon and he doesn't like to do it then. Too much of a risk for the horses. Mr.

Wentie, the man who taught me to ride in Warwick, felt the same way."

When they reached the house Twinks asked her mother about Rob and found he had come up to the house a few minutes ago and then gone back to the stable. "Now you can go," Twinks told Janey, and giggled. "Waiting time's over."

"Go where?" Janey picked up a magazine she had read from cover to cover and stared at it until Mrs. Baker took Twinks off to bed. A moment later Janey jumped up, picked up a flashlight, and hurried outside. I will ask Rob who owns the Isleta Pond, she decided. It's a good impersonal question, and if I knew the answer it might tell me something about what Buck's really like.

It was dark when she reached the corral and, except for the soft sound of the horses stomping or swishing at flies, very quiet. She moved on to the stable and saw the yellow light of a lamp in the loft window. I'm too late, she thought, but she went inside anyway hoping that Rob might still be cleaning tack. The ground floor was empty and Janey turned away, feeling frustrated and let down. It doesn't matter, she told herself, as she moved slowly back past Rob's neatly stacked bales. It wouldn't have done me any good if I had seen him.

The air by the bales was thick with dry hay dust and Janey sneezed violently. Instantly there were footsteps overhead and Rob called out, "Who's there? That you, Twinks?"

"No. It's me, Janey." She moved to the foot of the ladder and Rob, still dressed in his blue jeans and work shirt, looked down at her. "I didn't know it was so late," she said. "I just wondered how everything went this afternoon with those people the Bylers sent over."

"Why, fine," Rob looked surprised. "Just a man and his wife, and they'd ridden a good deal so there was nothing to it. Twinks make it sound like a bad headache?"

"No, not a bit. As a matter of fact I really wanted to ask you about that little water hole near Isleta. Twinks thought it belonged to the reservation but she wasn't sure but she said you'd know."

"Belongs to the Indians," Rob said, looking back over his shoulder. "There was a big fight about four years ago when an out-of-state mining company wanted to go in there, but that time the government looked out for the Isletans and it's never been touched. Say, Janey, my room's a mess, but if you give me half a sec to tidy it up I'd like to have you come up and see it."

"Good," Janey said, and then sneezed again and again. "But I'll wait by the door away from these hay bales. You shout when you're ready."

She heard Rob's footsteps overhead and the squeak of a drawer opening and shutting. A few moments later he let himself down the ladder and gestured for Janey to go back up ahead of him. "You go first," he said, smiling. "That's the least I can do if you're ready to climb up to see my summer quarters."

"I've been wild with curiosity to see it for ages, and you know it," Janey said as she started upward. "But you and Twinks made it awfully plain I wasn't wanted."

"Oh, you know Twinks," Rob said. "She's at the age for clubs and secret passwords, but there aren't any kids her own age near here so she clamps onto anything she can."

Janey nodded and looked around her. The room was meagerly furnished but well aired by two louvers that didn't show from outside. The floors were bare and the walls were unpainted, but the steeply sloping eaves gave the room a tentlike coziness that was oddly attractive. Janey turned slowly and saw a Navajo blanket carefully folded over the cot, an old but very orderly bookshelf, and on the wall behind Rob what looked like some of Miss Murphy's pictures carefully thumbtacked into place. "Why, it's terrific," Janey said. "Neat as a pin and so much cooler and airier than I expected. I don't feel nearly so badly about——!" She clamped her hand to her mouth and Rob laughed.

"At turning me out? That's why I wanted you to see it for yourself so you'd know I was living in clover. Miss 'Nita told me yesterday she was sure you knew you were in my old room, even if Mom never mentioned it."

"Twinks told me," Janey said, and as she realized that Rob was really amused she laughed too. "But how Miss 'Nita knew I knew defeats me. She sees right through people, with or without her camera." She glanced toward the pictures, but Rob edged her away from them.

"Oh, these are like the ones she gave you," he said, and pulled out a homemade wooden chest onto the middle of the floor. "But you haven't seen any of my Indian things, and maybe after going to Isleta this afternoon you'd be interested." He laid aside a few arrowheads and a small chipped tomahawk and held out a badly cracked pot of reddish clay. "This isn't anything much, but it's the kind they used in one of those beehive adobe ovens you must have seen."

"Oh yes, I did." Janey said. "Do they still use pots like that?"

"Nowadays most of them use metal pots and pans for cooking," Rob said, and lifted a gourd-shaped jar from his chest. "But quite a few of them still use water jugs like this one. Too bad you and Buck only had time to glance in at the church. The houses are really much more interesting."

Janey turned and stared. "How do you know we only glanced at the church?" she asked. "Or are you guessing?"

"Oh no. Juan told me." Rob began carefully repacking his chest. "The old boy was waiting down at the cattle gate to see me when I rode home just a little while ago. It seems his great-nephew, young Pablo Villa, saw you and was duly impressed. He thought la Señorita McGovern was *muy bonita.*"

"Pablo! Juan's great-nephew!" Janey gasped. "That's why that boy looked familiar. But how on earth did he know me?"

Rob shrugged. "I don't know, but my guess is that Juan told him you were coming and to look out for you and report back to Uncle. And Pablo did. He thought you were very *simpático* and that you didn't like being rushed out of the church to go down to the cottonwood grove. Juan says Pablo was worried about you."

Janey sprang to her feet, flushing so the blood pounded in her ears. "I think that's disgusting!" she choked out. "Do you mean to tell me I can't have a date with Buck Hughes without your paid spies trailing after me? I call that rotten!"

Rob straightened up, staring at her. "Janey, what are you talking about?"

"You. You and your precious Juan! When I heard you'd sold off most of your collection to pay his medical expenses I thought it was the finest thing I'd ever heard, but now I don't. There's nothing fine or even decent about it when you bribe Juan to spy——"

"Janey! Stop!" For the first time since Janey had known Rob he interrupted her. "I had nothing to do with Pablo seeing you and telling Juan about it. And as for my bribing Juan it's the other way around. Juan worked for my grandfather for years, practically without pay, and just before Grandfather died he made me promise to look out for Juan until he either died or went back to his pueblo to live."

Janey felt sick as she realized her mistake. "Rob! Please——" she began, but he went right on with what he had to say.

"As for Juan's always being around, his trailing and spying as you call it, I don't enjoy that either. I thought I made that clear the very first day we went riding. I tried to spell out to you then that I hate any kind of spying so much that it irks me even to have a harmless old man act as watchdog to the family of a man he adored."

"You did spell it out!" Janey was nearly in tears. "Rob, I'm ashamed of myself. I knew, if I'd only stopped to think, that you wouldn't have anything to do with that boy or Juan watching me."

"Thanks for the vote of confidence," Rob said, and pushed back the hatchway door over his ladder. "Better late than never."

Janey climbed down the ladder and Rob escorted her to the door. "Here's the flashlight," he said, and handed it over. "You'll need it going up to the house."

In the instant that their hands touched Janey's hope bubbled upward. "Rob, don't be angry with me," she pleaded. "I know I behaved terribly but it doesn't mean anything. It's just—just that this whole afternoon was so long, and hot, and confusing. I'm too mixed up to make sense."

"I'm sorry." Rob's voice sounded honestly concerned. "Why don't you knock off work tomorrow and get rested up?"

"It isn't that!" Janey turned toward him with her arms out-stretched. "If only you're not angry with me? If you're really satisfied I misunderstood?"

"I'm not angry." Rob moved away, avoiding Janey's arms, and walked back to the ladder. He stopped at the foot of it, one hand on an upper rung, and spoke without turning around. "As long as you understand that I know and always have known that what you do or see with Buck Hughes is none of my business I'm perfectly satisfied," he said coolly. "Good night, Janey."

Janey didn't answer. She stood still by the door, staring numbly out into the darkness as he climbed up to the loft. A moment later Rob's hatchway door thudded shut. Janey shivered and walked away from the stable.

Tote brayed as she passed the corral, but Janey didn't hear him or notice the bright lights or the sound of the radio at the ranch house above her. She started up the little hill, unaware of any-thing except the wave of self-revelation which had just swept over her. She knew now she loved Rob Baker with all her heart and had loved him since the day of the flash flood. Everything she had thought and tried to feel about Buck in the past few days was merely an unconscious attempt to keep face, to bolster her pride, so that she would not have to admit even to herself that she had fallen in love with Rob when he did not love her in return.

But maybe Rob does love me! Janey walked up and down just outside the house, ransacking her memory for every possible sign of hope. Perhaps he just can't say so, or maybe he still hasn't realized what's happened and doesn't know what he really wants. No matter how Janey twisted and turned her thoughts the en-couragement she was groping after eluded her like a will-o'-the-wisp. Finally she went into her own room and flung herself face downward on the bed.

"Rob says what he means—Rob knows what he wants." The words Juanita Murphy had said only a few days ago rang over and over in Janey's mind like the wild discordant pealing of bells. "Rob says what he means. Rob knows what he wants."

CHAPTER NINETEEN

Janey slept badly and woke up early, feeling washed out and depressed. As she dressed she realized that the nervous indecision she had felt after Buck had brought her back to the ranch was all gone. In its place was a dull, leaden certainty that stayed with her like a nagging pain.

Rob knows how I feel about him already, Janey thought, and winced at the recollection of how he had purposely avoided her arms down at the stable the evening before. And Twinks will guess if I'm not terribly careful. I'll simply have to bluff and keep my chin up and act as though I felt exactly the way I did when I first came out here. I couldn't stand going out alone with Buck again, but now that I know how it feels not to be wanted I can understand better why he acted the way he did. He probably sensed that I don't love him when he told me how he felt, and his clowning and calling back that he was counting on another date were just his way of keeping his chin up. I'll have to be cleverer than he was and do a better job of acting from now until I go home, but it won't be easy.

The fact that the next two days were very busy helped, and

so did the bustle and excitement that surrounded the arrival of Gramps's saddle and a box of papers which were unexpectedly delivered by Railway Express truck on Saturday morning.

"I've never seen anything quite like it," Rob said when he had opened the crate for Janey and carried the saddle down to the stable. "The leather's like old velvet, and the tooling is an Indian design, not Mexican. See this little line that goes right around the cantle? That's the Indian symbol for the rainbow."

"The saddle's a lot plainer and homelier than I expected." Janey was determined to stay brisk and casual. "But Gramps always did exaggerate."

"Try it," Rob urged. "Right now on Belle."

"Not a chance," Janey said, and nodded toward two cars that were just pulling up to the corral. "You've got a crowd of customers including Mr. and Mrs. Appleton, who probably want to see their precious darling ride Belle. Besides I'm going to do my homework on Gramps's papers until it's time to go to the party. What do you bet they're all as dull as ditchwater?"

Even as Janey spoke she knew she was bluffing, putting on an act of hard-boiled disinterestedness for Rob's benefit. A few minutes later when she opened up the box in her own room her hands trembled with excitement. Here, as safely hidden from the eyes of any stranger as though it had been written in code, would be the message for which she had waited. She picked up the top paper eagerly. It was a cancelled IOU from a man she did not know who had borrowed $25 from Gramps three years ago and had apparently never returned the money. On the back of it was a note in Gramps's handwriting which read: "W. Jones died April 2, 1955, leaving a widow in very poor shape financially. C.J.McG." And so Gramps never asked her for the money, Janey realized, and picked up another paper. It was only a receipted bill, and she dropped it immediately and chose more deliberately, selecting a stiffer paper that looked older, more yellowed by time than the others. It was the menu for a testimonial dinner Gramps's cavalry regiment had given its commanding officer in 1919. She went on and glanced at a few more receipted bills and several newspaper clippings that had no significance whatsoever.

It isn't possible. It can't all be as dull as this, Janey told herself, and started to read the entries that Gramps had written in a ruled brown notebook. There must be something that's important.

The notebook had been begun six months earlier. Gramps wrote on the first page that he had decided to write his memoirs for publication. "I have lived through stirring times that are already of interest to a wide public," he wrote, "and experiences far less dramatic than my own have been the background for dozens of best sellers."

This is what Gramps was hinting at in the letter to Uncle John, Janey thought, and read on more eagerly. This is how he was finally going to make a fortune!

She started off with an enthusiasm that flagged more and more with each page. Finally she reached the end and put down the notebook with a sigh of relief. The whole thing was hopeless and useless. Gramps's "book" was a lifeless skeleton of dull and often self-contradictory facts and figures awkwardly draped in hackneyed clichés and wordy, unconvincing descriptions. The only mention of La Placita were two ponderous, contrived sentences that told Janey nothing she did not already know.

And his stories were so wonderful, Janey thought sadly. He must have been tired and sick when he wrote this. She went through the other papers one by one. By five-thirty she had looked at them all and there was not one that could possibly be construed as more than a pathetic souvenir. Most of them were not even pitiful but only completely insignificant. Janey pushed them back into the box feeling uncomfortably disloyal and began to dress for the evening.

Rob was ready and waiting for her by the time she had finished, and they left the ranch on the dot of six. He talked about his afternoon's work as they drove toward Albuquerque, but when he turned onto the Weavers' street he asked her what she had found in Gramps's papers. "Don't tell me anything you don't want to," he ended up. "I probably shouldn't have butted in and asked you about it in the first place."

Janey laughed, a forced, cackling titter, to cover her own disappointment. "Junk. Plain tripe," she said, and, determined to sound casual at any cost, went on. "They just might be useful to light a fire if we don't have any old newspaper hanging around. I might have known it."

Rob looked uncomfortable, and as Janey walked up the Weavers' steps she realized that he had been as shocked by her answer as she had been by Buck's clowning when he had left her at the Bakers'. Buck couldn't help it either, Janey thought, remembering his face by the pool. When you want something terribly and you can't have it the only thing left is to act like a clown. At that moment Herb Weaver opened the door, and from then on Janey was sucked into the whirlpool pattern of a party with no time for introspection or regret.

From the very beginning the evening was hurried and hectic and entirely different from Janey's earlier visits to the Weavers'. Both Sis and Herb kept reminding everyone that they had to reach La Tavernita by nine o'clock. And over and above the Weavers' emphasis on time Janey sensed a restlessness, a feeling of disenchantment which seemed to touch everyone in the room. It's probably just my imagination, she decided, but as she glanced at Rob and turned to see Buck looking over at her she knew that the crisscross pattern of their hopes was both real and unsatisfactory.

She was definitely relieved when the clock struck half-past eight and it was time to leave for La Tavernita. Janey knew the Weavers were going with them, Herb to act as caller and Sis to watch, so she was surprised when Herb beckoned her into his study. "Rob told me you received the things from your grandfather's estate today," he said, and fingered his necktie. "Did you have time to read the proposed book, and if so what did you think of it?"

"I read every word," Janey said, and looked at him curiously. "And I thought it was terribly dull. Why do you want to know?"

"Because your grandfather sent it to me to read a month before he died," Herb said, and now he didn't sound patronizing or stiff but only honestly distressed. "I thought it was hopeless but I didn't have the heart to say so and I just mailed it back with a vague letter. Whenever you mentioned him I felt embarrassed and sort of guilty, but I didn't want to say anything about the book until you'd seen it for yourself. I thought maybe there was something in that which might mean something or at least be of interest to his family."

"I couldn't find anything," Janey said. "But thank you——" At that moment Sis called out to her from upstairs and she hurried off to get her coat.

The hall was empty, but as Janey passed the living-room doorway she saw a man's massive figure and a girl's slighter one locked in a tight embrace. Janey moved faster, averting her eyes, and tripped on the third step of the stairway. She caught herself, but in the instant before she could run on again she looked down and recognized Elsie Kohler.

Elsie and Tom. But they didn't see me. Janey raced breathlessly upward. And I hope, hope, hope this is what they both want. Even if I'm unhappy and Buck's unhappy I'd like them to be happy.

When she came down again everyone but Rob and the Weavers had left. Rob hurried her off to his family's car. He didn't say anything during the short drive over, but as they walked up under La Tavernita's gaily striped awning to where the manager, a slight, dark man in fancy dress, was waiting for them he suddenly took her arm. "Don't worry about the performance," he said, and they followed the manager to a curtained hallway outside of the main dining room. "You know the steps perfectly."

The rest of their eight were in the hallway ahead of them, listening to the sounds of music, voices, and the tinkle of crockery that floated out through the curtain. "I'm not exactly scared," Janey said, and smiled up at Rob, "but plenty excited."

"Good!" Rob said. "I'm glad because——"

Before he could finish Buck Hughes came up, with the manager only a few steps behind him. "Rob, you're dancing with Mary Alice," Buck said, and motioned Rob aside. For a second Janey gasped, not fully aware of what had happened. Then Buck took her arm and led her toward the door just as the music broke into "Butterfly Whirl."

"Buck! Rob! This is crazy. I won't do it." Janey turned in time to see Rob, his face as impassive as an Indian's, walk back and offer his arm to Mary Alice.

"I can't!" she began again, but now the manager held back the curtain. Buck swept her forward and she found herself circling after the Hoguets past small, closely packed tables in the dining room.

"Ladies fair and gentlemen tall, honor your partners one and all!" Herb's voice, enlarged and exaggerated by the microphone, boomed into Janey's ear, and she curtsied instinctively and moved back into position for the square set. I've got to go on with it, she realized, and followed Sylvia Hoguet as the call came for "Ladies to circle light as air, circle and honor the corner pair." There's nothing else I can do.

"Back to your partner, swing your own!" Herb chanted. "Then chassé——!"

"Janey! I had to dance with you!" Buck spoke directly in Janey's ear so she missed the end of Herb's order. "I've got to explain——"

"Not now!" Janey shook her head, struggling to follow the call. She turned, flurried and uncertain, and stepped out in the wrong direction. She moved back, but now she was behind the beat and so she stood alone as the others chasséd to the right. Janey saw Tom Pierce laugh, heard a tittering gasp from the audience and the metallic boom of Herb's call. She was hopelessly bewildered, and for an instant the big room seemed to rock around her.

"Janey, turn right," Rob whispered, and moved so quickly that only Janey and the other dancers saw him steer her into place. "This way! Then follow Sylvia."

Janey felt herself floundering clumsily but she managed to do as Rob said, and finally she was swept back into the pattern of the dance.

222

A few minutes later as they broke into the final promenade Janey was beside Buck again. "It's your fault!" she told him, knowing that the jigging music kept her words from reaching anyone else. "All of it."

"Because you take it that way! There's no harm in my kissing Elsie. I've known her all my life and she's a cute girl. But I don't feel about her the way I do about you. That's what I had to tell you right away."

They reached the doorway as Buck finished. Janey turned with the others and curtsied mechanically while her mind blazed with sudden understanding. Buck and Tom are the same size and their hair's the same color. I only saw the man from the back, going up the Weavers' stairs. I didn't have on my glasses so I thought it was Tom who was kissing Elsie, and it was Buck.

Janey straightened up as the audience applauded. The four couples danced out and the manager dropped the curtain behind them. The music switched to a rumba and the square set was over.

"That was great." "We weren't half bad."

"Janey, I'm sorry I laughed, but you covered yourself like a pro." Tom Pierce hurried over to Janey, but Buck shouldered him aside and pinned Janey against the white stucco wall with his long arms.

"You've got to listen!" he said, and leaned toward her. "I'm sorry you saw Elsie and me, but you're old enough to understand. I've never kidded you into thinking I was a monk. And while you enjoy yourself playing hard to get I've a perfect right——"

"Buck, be quiet!" Janey ducked under his arms and darted across the hall just as Rob came toward her. "I want to go home," she blurted out. "I couldn't stand staying for supper."

"You don't have to," Rob said, and she saw he held out her coat. "I've told Sis we were leaving. Come this way and the others won't notice us."

She followed him out by a side door and they hurried to the car. Rob had just maneuvered it free from the narrow parking space when Herb Weaver ran down the restaurant steps and hurried over to him. "Rob, I just want to tell you I'm sorry about the switch in partners," Herb said. "I would have stopped it, but Buck waited until I'd gone to the mike and there was nothing I could do unless I made a public scene. You know how Buck is."

"Yes, I do," Rob said, and drove off. "Thanks anyway, Herb."

"Buck Hughes is impossible!" Janey burst out, and told Rob in short, staccato sentences what had happened. "And I missed out on that step because Buck started explaining himself in my ear as Herb was calling. As though I gave a hoot what Buck does or doesn't do. I can't stand him."

"I knew he'd bothered you," Rob said. "So that's why I told Sis we were leaving without asking you first. I was sure enough glad to go myself."

Rob drove on out into the country, and Janey sat back, unpleasantly absorbed by her own thoughts. That she had caught Buck kissing Elsie didn't matter at all, unless it mattered to Elsie. The fact that his explanation was crass and unfeeling simply released her from ever worrying about him again. But what did concern Janey was the insight into her own actions and motives which this evening had revealed to her. From the very first she had been too impressed by Buck's looks and his fine car to really think of him as a person. Later when he had driven her back to the Bakers' ranch from Isleta she had misinterpreted his declaration of love and need mainly to bolster her own pride.

I knew what Buck was like long before he took me back to the ranch, Janey realized, but I wouldn't admit it to myself. As she remembered what had happened on the way to Hayesville and later by the pond her face flamed in the darkness. I knew what he really meant by wanting and needing but I wouldn't face it. I kidded myself into thinking I'd broken his heart, because that made me feel better.

A few minutes later Janey and Rob reached the ranch. As they walked into the spotless familiar kitchen Janey was so glad to get there she could have cried with relief. "What a perfectly gruesome evening," she said. "And I was the worst thing in it. You were right about my needing my glasses!"

"Practically no one noticed your mistake," Rob said. "And anyone who did probably thought it was cute. You got back on the beam mighty fast."

"Thanks to you," Janey said shakily. "But Rob, why did you let Buck get away with switching partners? He's a great big disgusting oaf, everything that Twinks said and then some. I tried not to dance with him but when you moved off there was nothing I could do."

"There was nothing I could do either," Rob said, and as he turned away Janey saw the muscle in the side of his cheek stiffen and grow rigid. "I wanted to knock him down but I couldn't. Not when he and the Weavers own the place lock, stock, and barrel where Twinks works. Mom needs the money Twinks earns dancing at La Tavernita."

"Did Twinks and your mother make you promise not to tell until after the performance?" Janey asked. "Were they afraid I'd either get stage fright or wouldn't do it at all?"

"Yes," Rob said. "And Mom thought the Weavers and Buck would be offended and she wouldn't risk that. She felt things were bad enough already because I wouldn't take a job with Multiple Minerals after she'd talked them into offering it to me, and of course she still hopes they'll offer it again and I'll take it. Anyway, I decided the square dance performance wouldn't really bother you so I went along with doing it. That first evening when I asked Herb to let me be your partner he made a bargain with me. You and I could dance together if I kept my mouth shut about who owned La Tavernita. The place is profitable but I guess doesn't add to the prestige of Herb's law practice or the Hugheses' mining concerns. They've always kept mum about owning it."

"The stupid snobs," Janey began, but Rob was still talking, looking down at his own hands.

"I didn't think it mattered," he said. "And besides I've tried to tell myself that with everything Buck Hughes could offer you that no matter how much I love you I ought to keep out of the way."

Janey moved toward him, her lips parted, her eyes soft with

love. This time her outstretched arms met his and he held her close. "Oh, Janey," Rob whispered. "Oh, Janey, I love you so."

"I love you too. I guess it began the day of the flash flood. I knew if Belle hurt you I'd want to die."

"I loved you long before that," he said. "The minute Tote brayed and I saw you spotlighted by the lamp, looking so small and straight and plucky the night you got here. I knew then you were the girl I'd always dreamed about and never expected to find."

"You didn't let me know it," Janey said. "Not then or later."

"I wouldn't accept it at first or admit to myself what had happened. But 'Nita Murphy knew the first time she met you and saw us together. You know that wrapped picture she gave me? I took it down from the wall just before you came up to the hayloft on Thursday. That was an enlargement of you with Blue Belle."

"Oh, Rob, if I'd only known then," Janey said, and once more he held her close. "The last two days have been a nightmare."

"For me too," he said, and brushed the top of her hair with his lips. "I love you! I want to marry you more than I want anything in the world, but there are so many things to stop us."

"We'll defeat them all!" Janey said, and in Rob's arms anything seemed easy. "We'll wait if we have to, but as soon as we can we'll get married. Perhaps I could go to college out here while you're getting your Master's. We'll both work on the side and, Rob, you'll have your school sooner than you ever expected."

"Janey darling, I know that," he said. "With the two of us together anything is possible. It isn't that. Or Mother or Twinks. They'd be a thousand times better off if you were my wife, and they'd be the first to say so. They love you, Janey."

He let her go, and as he paced around the room her eyes followed him, wondering. "It's the past," he said finally. "Everything that ought to be dead and buried and isn't. If I try and avoid it now it'll come back and haunt me so that the rest of my life will be more blind, and bitter, and useless than my grandfather's. And I'd drag you down with me."

Janey stood rooted. "Rob, you can't mean La Placita?" she said. "Even if when we go into the mine we find the absolute proof, the murdered bodies, if you like, of everyone Gramps loved, and knew your grandfather had done it, it wouldn't make any difference to us."

"Not to us," he said. "But to me. Ever since I was a child I've been led to believe that that mine was in back of all my family's troubles. It cost Grandfather his sight, to Mother it meant loss of money. And Juan made me feel from the time I was a little boy that there was secret guilt, a terrible, nameless tragedy attached to all of it. At first it was just a vague horror, but gradually as I grew up Juan made me think, and I can't tell you how he did it, that the tragedy wasn't completed and I might be a part of it.

"After Grandfather died I tried to find out about the mine for myself, but you know about that. Then this summer after you came out here I felt sure for the first time that the vague guilt, the thing Juan had made into a nightmare, was what my family had done to yours. And now I have to know what happened, even if I can't rectify anything. I still have to know before I'm free, or whole, or able to accept your love. That's the thing I learned the day of the flash flood."

Janey stood still and her heart pounded furiously. If we never went to La Placita? If we put it off until gradually the evil spell of it has faded away? As each thought flashed through Janey's mind she knew any hope of evasion would be useless. Rob had walked over to the telephone, and now he turned with the familiar battered telephone pad in his hands. "It'll only make it worse if we put off going," he said, "so maybe this message from Chuck is good news. His boss needs him on Tuesday but he's free tomorrow. He'll be here at eight-thirty unless I tell him not to come."

Janey glanced at Twinks's scrawl, which was an unsuccessful imitation of Mrs. Baker's old-fashioned handwriting, without being able to read a word. "And here's something else," Rob said, and held out another yellow page. "Mr. Appleton, Betsy's father, wants Blue Belle on a rental basis. He's ready to pay for her board and keep the year round as long as Betsy can ride her whenever she comes out here. The rest of the time we can use Belle any way we like."

"Rob, how wonderful! And you've certainly earned it."

"You earned it for me. If you hadn't thought of letting Betsy ride Blue Belle that day with the cub scouts none of this would have happened."

"I only thought of it because I guessed how Betsy felt," Janey said, and smiled at Rob. "And I guessed right because of what I'd learned watching you cope with Jakey and Billy Spring and all the other children who ride here."

"We did it together then," Rob said, and once more he put his arms around her.

"Yes," Janey said. "And tomorrow no matter what's in store for us at La Placita we'll handle that together too!"

CHAPTER TWENTY

The next morning when Janey reached the stable Rob acted as businesslike and matter-of-fact as though nothing had happened the evening before. He had put Gramps's saddle on Belle and fastened a small trench shovel and a pick behind his own saddle on Beau. As soon as Chuck Hemsted arrived and Rob had told him about the parties who were expected during the day he mounted and they rode off.

"Hope you strike it rich!" Chuck shouted after them. "But you should have borrowed a Geiger counter."

"We'll manage without one," Rob called back, and Janey saw that he was smiling as he let Beau into a canter. "Don't worry about that!"

She rode after him, wishing that she felt as calm and relaxed as he seemed. Her glowing confidence of the night before was gone, and in its place was a vague apprehension which grew stronger and stronger as they left the ranch and the familiar countryside around it behind them. "I wish there were some chance we could go to Fortune without Juan's being there," she said, but Rob only shook his head.

"He'll be there," he said. "He stopped in at Chuck's garage last night and so he knows just what we're doing. And I'm glad, Janey. He's a part of all of this. It can't ever be settled, for me anyway, unless he's there."

Janey said nothing, and they rode on in silence until Rob asked her about the saddle. "It's marvelously comfortable," she said. "I don't know why I was disappointed yesterday, except that to hear Gramps talk about it you'd think it was inlaid in gold or something absolutely special."

"It is special," Rob said. "Leather that's been kept like that is practically unique. He must have worked over it a lot even in the years he didn't use it."

"I guess he did," Janey said, but she couldn't keep her mind on the saddle, or the view, or anything except her growing fear of what was ahead of them. She didn't know what to expect or what it was that she dreaded, except that Juan was somehow at the center of it. She remembered his eyes, cold and unrevealing, staring at her in the airport. The Useful Evil Eye! She shivered in the warm sunshine, and with each mile her fear grew greater as her imagination turned Juan into a fantastic, superhuman creature whose sole purpose was to keep Rob and herself apart.

An hour later they cantered into Fortune. It was actually a relief when she saw that the same homely piebald Juan had borrowed before was tied to the deserted store and that Juan himself, looking old and anxious, was moving slowly down the steps to meet them. They dismounted, and as Rob tied up the horses Juan spoke to him in soft, sibilant Spanish, his old voice obviously pleading and concerned.

As Janey watched him her frightening fantasy disappeared like mist in strong sunlight. Why, Juan's pathetic, she thought, as the Indian shook his head and moved off toward the small derelict houses. And he adores Rob. He'd die before he'd hurt him.

Rob collected his tools and a big flashlight, and then he and Janey started down to the valley behind the main street.

"Juan did see your grandfather the last night he was alive."

Rob translated to Janey what he had just heard. "Juan didn't want to do it but he drove Mr. McGovern out here in the truck. The other road was passable then, and they reached the mine without too much trouble. Your grandfather started to open it and after a very few minutes he had an attack. He came out of it and Juan got him back to the hotel. He seemed in pretty good shape when Juan left him but as you know he didn't live through the night. Juan's certain that it's the mine itself that killed him."

"But, Rob, Gramps had a bad heart. He knew himself he didn't have long to live. Does Juan understand that?"

"No," Rob said, and now his blue eyes began searching over the crusty, uneven ground in the valley below them. "He's so convinced of the evil that he feels is part and parcel of the mine that he can't take in anything else. It's why he's tried to keep us away from it. It's why even now when he knows we're determined to go there he won't come with us. He's still hoping against hope that I won't be able to find the old opening without him."

Rob put down his tools and began circling the ground in front of them. Once he looked back, taking his sights from one of the stark little buildings behind him, and moved forward more certainly. He stooped, scraped back the earth with his hands, and straightened up quickly. "It's here," he said, and reached for the small pickax. "Could you bring over the lamp and the shovel?"

He began chipping with his pickax, and as Janey moved after him she saw Juan walk slowly toward them his head bowed, his whole figure a symbol of defeat.

Rob worked furiously for about five minutes. When he stopped for breath Janey saw the rough planking in the rubble of clay and dirt he had knocked loose. He shoveled it aside and, prying upward with his pick, pulled away a crude door in the side of the hill.

"That's it," he said quietly, and Janey stared in hypnotized silence into the dark opening ahead of them. "If you'll give me the light, Janey—we'll get to the end of this."

She held it out to him, but before Rob could take it Juan reached out and tore it out of her hands. She grabbed desperately, expecting Juan to run with it or hurl it away, but he stood still, his eyes on Rob. "I, Juan, must go then," he said in slow halting English. "But el Señor McGovern wished no harm to me, or my people, or the people of my foster brother."

"Juan, stop. Don't go in!" Janey reached forward. "I've told Rob I never wanted the mine reopened!"

She was too late. Juan moved forward into the tunnel slowly, inexorably, and when Rob followed she went with him, clinging to his hand.

They moved along through a dark narrow passageway for perhaps twenty feet. It widened, and by the round arc of the flashlight Janey saw a cheap tin box on a glistening stone ledge. Juan opened it and took out a little leather book. "This is all el Señor wanted," he said, and gave it to Janey. "Nothing else. He tell me that himself."

She took the book and started to turn, eager to be out of the mine. "Rob, please." She pulled at his arm. "Now we can go."

He only held her close and looked straight at Juan. "There is more," he said, and his voice was commanding. "The grandson of your foster brother is not blind. Give me your flashlight."

Juan's hand shook as he gave up the flashlight, and his face was a mask of despair. As Rob turned the light from one wall to the other even Juan's shadow seemed to look more shrunken and stooped.

Rob walked forward through the widest part of the mine with Janey beside him. When the mine narrowed again he pressed her arm. "Stay here, darling," he said, and moved on more slowly.

For a moment Janey hesitated, straining her eyes to see where Rob was going. For an instant she could only make out the dark walls narrowing ahead of him. Then as he lifted the light she saw the cascade of rubble just beyond. It was the place where the mine had caved in and the two workmen had been killed! "Rob, don't," she cried out, and moved after him. "Please. The walls— anything might happen."

"Stay where you are!" he got out. "There isn't room for two people." Rob crouched nearly double and picked his way cautiously between rocks and debris. A moment later Janey was left in darkness. At first she heard the sound of his boots, the clatter of small pebbles, and then there was silence. She stood rigid, one hand gripping onto the cold, stone wall. She heard Juan's shuffled steps behind her and the labored sound of his breathing.

She smelled the dead, lifeless air, and her heart pounded faster and faster until the blood roared in her eardrums. "Rob, come back," she pleaded, and her mouth was so dry with fear that each word was mumbled and indistinct. "I can't stand it much longer."

An instant later she heard the clatter of stones again and the sound of his footsteps. "Janey! Juan! I've found it," Rob shouted, and even the echo of his voice was triumphant. "It's great. Incredible. *Muy bueno.*"

He reached Janey, put his arm around her waist, and swept her back toward the opening. "Juan, come on. *Vamos!*" he shouted. *"Está magnífico!"*

Janey listened, too dazed by relief and the brilliant sunlight to follow what Rob was saying. Juan stood motionless, his eyes on Rob. *"Usted esta segura?"* he said, and Janey sensed the question in his voice, saw Rob nod his head, and heard the ring of affirmation as he answered.

Rob began carefully covering the opening and as he worked spoke to Juan in fluent Spanish. Janey heard the rise and fall of questions and answers passing between them, but it wasn't until Juan helped Rob pull the last boards back in place that either of them spoke in English. "Is good," Juan said, and the two words sounded like a benediction. "Very good." He straightened up and without saying anything more walked back toward the village street.

"Rob, I don't understand!" Janey looked after Juan's once more erect figure and then turned to Rob. "I don't understand what's happened."

"How could you?" Rob's voice was jubilant as he put his arm around Janey and led her back toward the store. "I don't begin to get all of it myself. But at the right-hand side of the mine, beyond where it was badly damaged by the explosion, there's what looks

to be a sealed room, possibly a kiva, crammed with Indian artifacts. There's only a small opening and I couldn't see too well
but I'm almost positive the pottery in there is very old. It may pre-
date the coming of the white man to this country."

"But why was Juan so relieved? Did he know it was there? Was
he afraid somebody other than you would discover it?"

"No, what happened was this: on the day of the accident Juan
and two other Indian workmen were digging up at the front of
the mine with my grandfather working with a detonator a little
way behind them getting ready to blast later on. I don't think
the Indians saw into the sealed room because the little opening I
found probably was made by the explosion. But Juan found a
human skeleton and some weapons which had undoubtedly been
left outside the room to guard it. Juan panicked, and as he rushed
out of the mine he knocked against the detonator; that's what set
off the blast that blinded my grandfather and caused the cave-in
that killed the two Indian workmen.

"After that Juan lived in an absolute hell of his own. At the
beginning he felt his panic had caused the accident. What was
worse, he was soon convinced that the whole thing was a matter
of tribal guilt and responsibility, and that only someone who
was an Indian by blood or adoption was in danger in the mine.
You see, your grandfather was away when the accident happened. Then when he went back to inspect it he not only wasn't
hurt, but he didn't find a sign of human bones or spears. Of course
that was because they'd been blown to powder by the explosion,
but Juan didn't see it that way. From the minute Mr. McGovern
went back into the mine the evening after the accident and came
out unhurt Juan was positive that the disaster was a purely tribal
matter. He was convinced that my grandfather's blindness and
the death of the two Indians was the vengeance of the gods and
that he himself had been spared, probably in part to take care of
Grandpa and more especially to make certain that no other Indian defied the spirits of this place again by going into it."

"But couldn't your grandfather have explained to Juan that it really was an accident and that everything he was afraid of was only superstition?" Janey asked.

Rob shook his head. "I'm pretty sure Juan never spoke of it. You see he felt Grandpa, who was after all only an adopted Indian, had paid in full with his eyesight and that from then on Juan himself, a full-blooded Isletan, was responsible for seeing no one went back to the mine. When I began digging in old abandoned mines Juan probably worried for fear supernatural forces, which wouldn't hurt an ordinary white man, might harm me as the grandson of his foster brother. Then when I hurt my foot when I was actually looking for this mine he felt his fears were more than justified and tried his best to keep watch over me. Until just now Juan would never tell me what happened at the mine the day of the accident. He was too frightened to talk about La Placita clearly at all, and the only thing I got out of his warnings was the fact that he was certain that your grandfather, Major McGovern, was the only person who wasn't in any way responsible for all the trouble the mine disaster had caused. And I misinterpreted that as meaning that maybe Grandpa Marston and possibly even Mother had in some way cheated or hurt your grandfather."

"And now you know they didn't!" Janey exulted. "And Juan isn't afraid any more, all because you went in and out of the mine just now and found those Indian things and there wasn't any trouble. So La Placita is a bonanza after all. Rob, it's priceless."

"In everything but money," he said, and smiled down at her. "The laws are complicated about selling anything like this, but even if we don't get a cent out of it, Janey, there's so much more. This will give me a thesis for my doctorate, professional standing with scholars, and, what's a thousand times more important than anything else, it gets rid of the obstacle between us."

A little later when Rob turned to speak to Juan, Janey sat down on the steps of the store and for the first time looked at the little book Juan had handed her in the mine. There were only a few pages covered in Gramps's familiar handwriting. She leafed

235

through it quickly and saw that there were dates, statistics, brief comments dealing with the operation of the mine. Gramps wanted this for the book he was trying to write, she realized. He was so sure that was going to be a best seller that he believed that when he found this it would be worth more than all the gold he'd ever hoped to find in La Placita.

She turned quickly to the last two pages. "As far as I've been able to reconstruct the accident," Gramps wrote, "it happened because one of the Indians knocked against Marston, who was working at the detonator, and set off the charge. I was not there when it happened, as I had gone over to see Ida, Jim Marston's daughter, that afternoon to try and persuade her to put the small capital she had inherited from her mother into La Placita. Marston and I had used everything else we could lay our hands on to buy out Alfred Hughes the week before, but Marston wouldn't even ask Ida for a cent of that money. I was so stubbornly sure we would make a killing that I went to see her without telling Jim I was going. Ida believed me and, God forgive me, I believed myself when I told her we were within sight of a fortune. She gave me a check for everything she had and I deposited it to our company's account on my way through Albuquerque. Two hours later I heard about the accident. I went out to the mine at once. They'd taken Jim Marston to the hospital and removed the bodies of the two Indians who had been killed. The place was a shambles, with men still putting out fires in the street behind the mine. I had to fight my way into the mine, but as soon as I got there the last blasting showed that Hughes had been right after all and we had reached dead end. Everything was a nightmare of confusion and uncertainty but one thing was clear—I had to get Ida's money back to her at once. I don't know what I would have done if Jane, my wife, had not made me pawn her engagement ring and a necklace she had inherited from her mother, and use the money to pay back Ida. I took it over to Ida at their Cinder Cone Canyon ranch the next day. Poor Jim was still unconscious and I told Ida never to tell him I had asked her for the money. She was very young and inexperienced and I had

236

no trouble in persuading her that the money had never been a part of La Placita's capital and that I had simply changed my mind about using it. I made a good story of the whole thing and told Ida the future wasn't as hopeless as it looked and that I was sure that someday we'd reopen La Placita and find our bonanza after all. Ida needed cheering up, so I went back to see her pretty often and kept on telling her hopeful yarns about the mine until I almost convinced myself they were true. My Jane knew what I was doing and encouraged my visiting Ida as often as I could. I went over pretty frequently until one day, about a month after the accident, I met Al Hughes's son and daughter-in-law in Main Street. After a lot of polite talk they insinuated that I was having an affair with Ida, and I never went near her again. Jane, bless her heart, laughed when I told her what the Hugheses had said, and thought I was a fool to listen to gossip and ought to go right on seeing Ida. I am glad now I didn't do it because every extra hour, every minute I had to spend with Jane herself, during my darling's last months in this world, have added to the blessed memories which I will live on for the rest of my life. C. J. Mc-Govern—1 February 1920."

Janey looked at the date and suddenly realized that Gramps had written this message only a few weeks after his wife, the first Jane McGovern, had died, and just before he had left New Mexico for good. She put her face in her hands and a moment later Rob was beside her. "Janey, Janey darling. What's happened? Are you all right?"

She nodded and handed him the little book. "It's all there," she said huskily. "About the accident, and why your mother thought right up to this summer that La Placita would bring in a fortune. She'd listened to Gramps, Rob. He'd told her one of his stories. No one could hear him without believing every word."

Rob began to read, and Janey sat beside him looking straight ahead of her. She could almost see Gramps now, and hear his voice, and for the first time she began to understand the difference between his miraculous storytelling and his unsuccessful writing. When he talked about anything he loved, whether it was

237

his old saddle, New Mexico, or people, every word was so illuminated and made radiant by his own loving enthusiasm that his hearer not only saw but believed in everything he said. But when Gramps tried to write without a listener beside him his gift disappeared, perhaps because he needed an affectionate audience to convince himself.

Rob finished reading and handed the little book back to Janey. "I wish I'd known your grandfather," he said quietly. "I wish I could have thanked him. He must have been a very great gentleman."

Janey nodded, not trusting herself to speak, and a few moments later she followed Rob over to the horses. Juan left before them on the road to Moriques to return his borrowed piebald. "He's happier than he's been for years," Rob said as Juan's thickset figure disappeared over a hill. "While you were reading I told him what I thought would happen to whatever is taken out of the mine. I told him it would go to a museum so the people of all races could see how his forefathers had lived generations before the coming of the white man."

"And he liked that?" Janey mounted Belle and followed Rob onto the road for Cinder Cone Canyon. "He didn't want anything left where it was?"

"No," Rob said. "I think he was pleased that it would be carefully dug up and preserved, but what really mattered to him was finally understanding that the accident was just that and nothing more."

They rode on for a mile or so, and then Rob led the way uphill along a wide woodland trail. "I wanted to go this way last week," Rob said, "but as soon as it started to rain I knew we wouldn't be able to get down on the other side. This leads up to the range behind the canyon. You'll be able to look down at the old ranch and see if you think it'll be the right place to build our school. But you may not like any of it, Janey, and if you don't we'll just have to find another site. No matter how many lucky breaks we get we're going to have plenty of time, too much I guess, for just looking and planning."

"I'm not worried," Janey said. "After today I've stopped believing in obstacles."

The two horses moved steadily forward, and Rob and Janey talked over everything that had happened. "Juan's at peace with himself for the first time in years," Rob said. "I think he'll be able to go back to his pueblo and feel he is a part of it. He'll always be interested in all of us but he won't feel any longer he's got to protect us from a doom he feared and felt he had partly caused. It'll make things easier for everybody."

A few minutes later they left the trail and came out on the range land that spread broad and tablelike before them. Rob led the way forward for a few hundred yards before he dismounted. "We'll have to leave the horses here," he said, and hobbled them with quick, expert turns of his rope. "The best place to see the view is almost like Twinks's crow's-nest, so we'll walk there."

They walked slowly toward the canyon, and as Janey looked around her she had the feeling she had been there before. "It's the strangest thing," she said, and told Rob what she had been thinking. "But I've had the same feeling over and over this summer of being at home, of belonging to a place I've never even seen before. Do you suppose it all comes from the things Gramps told me?"

"I'm sure of it," Rob said. "And that's another reason why I feel so grateful to him. I started to tell you that the first day we were in Fortune but I didn't dare go on."

"I wish you had," Janey said, and walked more carefully as Rob led the way into a narrow footpath that shot steeply downward. Janey half walked, half slid behind him until he stopped and helped her onto a ledge behind a natural parapet of reddish clay. "There it is," he said quietly, and motioned for her to look eastward. "Over there, Janey."

She turned and looked across the wide, sparsely wooded ravine. On the far side she saw what was left of a cluster of small buildings. The roof of the stable was caved in and the ranch house itself had been badly hurt by fire, but Janey hardly noticed the damage. She was too enchanted by the way the buildings nestled between two guardian aspen trees and the lovely slanting sunlight which turned the adobe walls into a rich, warm gold. "That's Cinder Cone," Rob said quietly. "What do you think of it, Janey?"

For a moment she couldn't speak as it came to her that she was looking at the unknown goal, the final enchantment toward which she had ridden so many times in the recurring daydream of her childhood. "Rob! This is the House of Gold!" she said. "The perfect place I rode toward in a story I told myself over and over when I was little. Gramps must have seen Cinder Cone in the sunlight just like this and described it without telling me where it was or who owned it, and I went on from there. I've been trying to remember the end of my daydream for months and now I've found it. It's walking into the Golden House and living there happily forever after."

Rob took her in his arms and it was a long while before he let her go. "There's only the shell of the old ranch left," he said finally. "And the walls aren't gold, but broken-down adobe. Do you suppose after all the waiting and the work we'll have to go through before we can live there that it'll still be the Golden House of your daydream?"

"I know it will," Janey said, "because love and hope make the only gold that matters. I think that Gramps sent me out here because he wanted me to learn that."